H.B. Pattskyn

BOUND
Forget Me Knot

Dreamspinner Press

Published by
Dreamspinner Press
5032 Capital Circle SW
Ste 2, PMB# 279
Tallahassee, FL 32305-7886
USA
http://www.dreamspinnerpress.com/

Bound: Forget Me Not

Cover Art by Shobana Appavu
bob@bob-artist.com

ISBN: 978-1-61372-765-2

Printed in the United States of America
First Edition
September 2012

eBook edition available
eBook ISBN: 978-1-61372-766-9

As always, I am grateful to my wonderful husband for his incredible support and endless patience (not to mention the occasional bottle of wine and not-so-occasional pot of coffee). His mom's pretty awesome too. And so is my ever-expanding circle of friends, the people who are there when I need them, back off when I need space, and generally help me stay something that vaguely resembles sane.

I owe a huge thank you to my main beta readers, cheerleading squad, and friends—Kitsa, Shira, and Tia—for kicking me in the pants when I needed it and helping me polish this one up enough to submit it. I'm darned grateful to the editing team at Dreamspinner, too, who polished it further, making it fit for publication.

I will always be grateful to my fan fiction readers, who gave me the courage to take my writing to the next level. Not sure how many of y'all will pick this one up, but I totally love you guys.

Chapter One

THE gray leather was so soft it felt like silk in Jason's hands. It was a good solid piece, though, about two inches wide, with four heavy D rings attached. It was the kind of collar that would tell a man he belonged to somebody—not that there was someone Jason wanted to belong to. *Not that I want to belong to anyone.* He swallowed back his discomfort. A little light bondage with his sometime-boyfriend Terry was one thing, but—

"Nice choice."

Jason jumped at the sound of the rich baritone voice behind him and not-so-silently cursed himself for getting caught window shopping. The dealers' room wasn't open yet; he was only allowed in because he was working off his convention membership by helping with setup. Setting up *didn't* include pestering the merchants.

Normally Jason didn't even pay attention to anything in the dealers' room at a con. He'd been going to science fiction conventions for eight years—since he was fourteen—and the dealers' room always looked the same: displays overflowing with novels and comic books, tables piled high with CDs and DVDs. There were movie posters and action figures. Plush Lovecraftian monsters. The sword dealer was set up next to the guy who sold replicas of *Star Trek* phasers and *Stargate* zat guns. Across the aisle was a woman who did custom corsetry work—for both women *and* men. Next to her was the guy who sold uniforms: Starfleet, Stormtrooper, Colonial (as in the Twelve Colonies of Kobol). If it was on TV or in the movies, he could get his hands on it.

The last few years Jason had noticed more brass and leather making its way in the dealers' room, thanks to the rising popularity of steampunk literature and the Victorian culture it came from. He didn't mind. There was nothing hotter than a good-looking guy decked out in Victorian-era garb, and all the better if he was wearing leather.

Jason wasn't wearing leather, but what he did have on was almost as good: a black fishnet shirt that showed off the silver hoops in his nipples, and a pair of ass-hugging jeans with a couple of gray bandanas tied into the belt loops at his right hip. Those were more for show than anything else. Nobody around the science fiction community knew the "hanky code" supposedly used in the leather community. Jason wasn't even sure anybody actually used it in real life; it was just one of those things he'd read about online. Different-colored hankies signified different kinks. Gray was for bondage.

He turned to face the shop owner to apologize for getting in his way (and hope the guy didn't complain about him being where he didn't belong)—but his mouth went dry and his throat refused to work. He found himself staring at a brawny chest. He looked up. The shop owner smirked down at him. The guy was at least a foot taller than Jason, and while he wasn't exactly Incredible Hulk muscular, Jason didn't think he lost too many arm-wrestling contests, either. He certainly made Jason feel small simply by standing there smiling.

The epitome of "classically handsome," the merchant had a strong jaw, cleft chin, and dimples. Jason loved drawing faces with dimples. His gaze flickered further up and he noticed the full mustache, baby-blue eyes, and short-cropped blond hair. He'd never liked mustaches much, but he was suddenly ready to make an exception.

"See something *else* you like?" the guy asked him with a lopsided grin.

Heat rushed to Jason's cheeks. "Yes. I mean, no! I mean…." He floundered, certain the tips of his ears were as red as the ballroom carpet. "Sorry, I know you're still setting up. I saw this"—he held up the gray leather collar—"and I guess I couldn't resist."

"I know *exactly* what you mean."

Jason's heart hammered in his chest. The guy couldn't possibly mean that the way it sounded. Could he?

"C'mon." He took Jason by the shoulders and turned him around so Jason's back was to him once more before lifting the collar out of his hands. "Let's try this on for size."

"I…." Jason licked his lips. Even without seeing a price tag on it, he knew he couldn't afford a collar like that. "I really don't think—"

But the merchant didn't give him the chance to finish his sentence. "Jesus, boy, you got enough hair? Lift that mop outta my way."

"I… huh? Sorry, I…," he stammered. Why was he apologizing to a total stranger about the length of his hair? Didn't he get enough of that shit at home? If it wasn't his father, it was Dad's girlfriend, Alicia, ragging on him about his hair, his clothes. His attitude. According to them, no one would ever hire someone like him. He usually didn't remind them that he had a job. After all, waiting tables wasn't "real work," it was what college kids and unskilled adults did to pay the bills.

"I should get back to work," Jason told the merchant. "I'm supposed to be helping with setup." He started to pull away, but the big man leaned in close and put his hands on Jason's shoulders, stopping him in his tracks.

"I'm sure you can play hooky for a few more minutes," he whispered into Jason's ear, his tone lilting. Seductive.

"Huh?" was the wittiest comeback Jason could come up with.

"Let's see what this looks like on you."

"I… yeah… okay." God, could he sound any more like a clod?

The merchant cleared his throat. "Hair, boy."

"Right. Sorry." Jason lifted the long, curly black hair off his shoulders, exposing his slender neck. He closed his eyes as the merchant slipped the gray collar around his throat. It was heavy. It felt good. The only collar he'd ever worn before was the one he'd bought for himself a few months ago, from the pet aisle at Walmart. It was *so* much more satisfying when someone else buckled the soft, sturdy leather into place, even if it was only someone trying to make a sale.

"There." The merchant laid his hands on Jason's shoulders once more. "How's the fit?"

"Perfect, sir." Jason faltered. But *sir* was a generic enough courtesy, and the shop owner looked a few years older than him. Well. Maybe closer to ten years older, not that Jason minded. Older guys knew what they were doing in bed. *Not* that he thought the merchant was flirting with him, he was just trying to make a sale. He wasn't going to succeed. "I'm sorry, sir, but I really can't afford something like this. I didn't mean to waste your time."

"Who says you're wasting my time? 'Sides, last time I checked, looking was free."

Jason glanced over his shoulder. "I can't actually see anything, you know."

The merchant rolled his eyes at Jason's petulant tone. "I think I've got a solution for that." He reached to the table behind him and passed Jason an antique brass hand mirror. "There you go. What d'you think?"

Jason gaped at his own reflection in the oval glass. The charcoal-gray leather was the perfect complement to his pale skin and almost the same color as his eyes. How was he ever going to go back to wearing a cheap dog collar after seeing the way he looked in a real collar?

He gave himself a good mental shake. Why would he *want* a real collar? Real collars were for submissives. Slaves. Jason wasn't either of those things, he just dabbled with bondage once in a while. He licked his lips nervously and cast another glance up at the merchant, because looking at the other man was easier than looking at his own reflection.

"Kinda makes you look like you belong to somebody, eh, boy?" the big man observed.

"Yeah. I was just thinking…. I, erm… just out of curiosity, how much is it?" He had to ask.

"The hardware on there is all hand forged. I can't go any lower than two hundred."

Jason's heart sank. "I really wish I could afford that, but I'm not even sure I'm going to be able to afford school next semester." God, he sounded pathetic. He wasn't trying for sympathy, the words had just come out.

"Gotta have priorities, boy."

Jason gave him a questioning look.

"School first," he elaborated. "You'll have time for stuff like this later."

"Yeah. I guess."

Jason took a last look at himself in the mirror before the merchant undid the collar's clasp. He felt an immediate loss when it came off his neck. He smiled anyway. "Thanks for letting me try it on...." He sought out the man's name badge, but the only thing printed on it was "Sir."

"Henry Durand." He held out his hand.

Jason accepted. "Jason Kennly."

"Good to meet you, Jason." Henry's hand swallowed Jason's up whole, but his grip was light. Friendly.

"You too. Well, I guess I should get back before somebody realizes how long I've been gone. See you around the con, *Sir*," he added, despite the fact that they'd exchanged proper names.

Henry quirked an eyebrow, then laughed. "I'll be right here, boy," he shot back with a wink. "I might even let you model a few other things, if you like. Got a set of cuffs you'd look good in."

With heat burning in his cheeks, Jason beat a hasty retreat. He told himself that Henry Durand was probably an accountant or something, that selling collars and leather BDSM gear was only a weekend gig, but even the thought of Mr. Tall, Blond, and Handsome sitting in front of a pile of income tax returns wasn't enough to make his dick go soft.

THE only advantage to showing up before 10:00 a.m. on the first day of a weekend-long convention to work setup was that as soon as his shift ended at six, Jason was free for the rest of the weekend. He had his own hotel room, a rare luxury and one he knew he was going to end up regretting at the end of the month, when his Visa bill came. The interest rate on his card was insane, but he was sick of sharing a room with ten other people, which was why he wasn't telling anybody he had his own room this weekend. He didn't want ten or more people suddenly deciding he was their very best friend in the hopes of getting crash space.

Jason took a long hot shower and used two towels to dry off, *just* because he could. He wrapped a third towel around his narrow waist and enjoyed taking as much time as he wanted to dry and style his hair. He shaved carefully—the only thing less attractive than stubble were the little nicks he got when he rushed—and applied smoky black kohl to his eyelids, and then got dressed. Instead of putting the fishnet shirt back on, he opted for a plain black turtleneck. He wanted to feel something around his neck, and after having a real collar on, if only for a few minutes, the Walmart collar in his suitcase wasn't going to cut it anymore.

Finally, he shimmied into his best ass-hugging jeans and tied a single gray bandana into the belt loop on his right hip. Wearing it on the right meant that he liked to be the one getting tied up—assuming anyone had any idea what it was supposed to mean at all. All that really mattered to Jason was that *he* knew what it meant.

After a last quick once-over in the full-length mirror to be sure he looked perfect, Jason headed down to the main lobby to see who was hanging out. He wasn't the best-looking guy in any room, but his mother had always said it wasn't what you had, it was what you did with it that mattered. He doubted she'd approve of his life choices, but it didn't matter. She wasn't around to see them.

As soon as he stepped off the elevator, Jason spotted his best friend, Kendra Lewis, across the sea of costumes and faces. Kendra was in full Colonial Warrior garb—original *Battlestar Galactica*, not the one from a few years ago. She was a purist. They'd grown up together in Troy, two kids from the same trailer park. Now she was a student way, *way* up north at Michigan Tech. He was living in the middle of nowhere with the father he hadn't even met until a few years ago, and going to community college.

"You coming or going, boy?"

Jason jumped at the sound of the rich baritone voice behind him and whirled around to find Henry Durand standing there, grinning down at him. Jason's brain seized up and his dick swelled painfully inside his tight jeans. Henry had changed into a black leather tank top and tight black leather pants. He carried a large duffel bag and had several lengths of nylon rope slung over one shoulder.

"'Course if that's not just for show"—Henry nodded toward the gray bandana on Jason's hip—"I'll expect to see you in the demo I got 'roped' into giving. Pun intended." He winked.

Jason opened his mouth. Then he shut it again. Henry knew…? *Shit.* Not that there was any way a guy like Henry Durand was ever going to be interested in him. Unless maybe Jason could tempt him into a casual fuck…? Hell, Jason would settle for blowing him in the men's room and having something good to think about later, when he jerked off in his room all alone.

"Well?" said Henry. "That just for show, or are you for real?"

Before Jason could make a second attempt at intelligent speech, he felt a pair of arms wrapping themselves around his waist. He didn't have to turn his head to know it was Terry, his on-again-off-again boyfriend. At the moment, they were off again, even though Terry didn't seem to realize it.

"I've been looking all over the con for you!" He landed a sloppy kiss on Jason's cheek. "You avoiding me or something?" His tone was playful and he smelled like cheap vodka and Juicy Fruit gum, a sure sign that he was already drunk.

Jason pulled out of the unwanted embrace and turned to face Terry. "I was working setup. Sorry you couldn't find me."

"Well, I found you now." He tried to grab onto Jason again, but Jason pushed him back. Terry pouted at him. "You're not still pissed at me about the other week, are you?" he wanted to know.

"No," he lied. Jason turned around to find that Henry was already halfway down the hall. He considered running after him, but how pathetic would that look?

"I'm headed up to the con suite," said Terry.

Jason shrugged.

"You *coming*?"

"I'll meet you up there in a minute."

"Where are you going? There's nothing happening for a few hours—"

"I said I'd be up in a minute!"

"I could give you a hand getting *up*," Terry offered lasciviously, brows raised.

"No. Thank you. I'll see you in a few." Jason turned on his heel and walked away as quickly as he could, hoping to get lost in the crowd.

It worked—either that, or Terry wasn't in the mood to chase after him. Jason didn't care which; he ducked into the first empty conference room he came to, to collect his thoughts. He didn't even know for sure why he'd bolted. The other week wasn't the first time Terry had stood him up. It probably wouldn't be the last. It didn't matter. All he wanted to do now was figure out what kind of demo Henry was doing and find it.

Feeling like an idiot, he peered out the conference room door to make sure the coast was clear before heading for the registration table to grab a program book.

TWENTY minutes later, Jason stood outside one of the smaller ballrooms. The door was closed, and he had a swarm of butterflies flapping around his stomach. He considered forgetting the whole thing—the demo had already started—but it was either go in late or meet up with Terry up in the con suite. Or wander around on his own, looking pathetic.

He didn't want to see Terry and he didn't feel like wandering around aimlessly.

The other option was to hang around outside the ballroom door, wait for the demo to end, and catch Henry coming out. But that would be even more pathetic than running after the guy.

Taking a breath to calm his nerves, Jason opened the door and stepped inside. Thirty or forty people sat up near the front of the room, listening to Henry talk about safe, sane, and consensual play.

Suddenly, Henry stopped speaking and fixed Jason with dark glare. "You're *late*," he snapped.

Jason's eyes widened—he was sure people in the hallway must have heard Henry's voice. Certainly everyone in the ballroom turned to stare at the intruder.

"I was starting to think I was gonna have to find me another volunteer," Henry continued in the same angry tone. Jason's stomach lurched and his dick snapped to attention—he had no idea why. He was *not* into humiliation, public or otherwise. Was he?

"Well, don't just stand there, boy. Get your ass down here! These nice people don't got all night, you know."

Jason swallowed hard. He had to be kidding!

"You want to get tied up or not?" Henry demanded.

God, yes!

Only there was no way he was going to let a total stranger tie him up in front of a room full of people he didn't know. Then again, what could be safer? Nobody would ever try anything underhanded in front of witnesses—not that he seriously expected Henry to do anything bad.

Trying very hard not to look at anyone—and knowing that everyone was staring at him—Jason walked the fifty or so feet to the front of the room. It was both the longest and shortest walk he'd ever taken.

"Have a seat." Henry nodded to the floor at his feet.

Jason hesitated—but then dropped passively to his knees determined to play along. It would probably be fun. He'd read the description in the program, and it definitely sounded enticing:

Tied up in Knots

Presented by bondage expert Henry Durand

Safe, sane, consensual, and FUN play begins with learning the ropes! Bring a partner and come for a two-hour bondage demonstration that will leave some of you tied up in knots. 18 and over only.

Trying to remember what he'd read online about the way a submissive was supposed to act, because he was pretty sure that was what Henry expected, Jason dropped his chin a little, squared his shoulders, and kept his eyes focused on the red carpet in front of him. He'd rather not have to look anybody directly in the eye, anyway. Instead, he glanced surreptitiously around the room and felt a wave of relief when he realized he didn't know a single person there. He settled his gaze back on the carpet and listened to Henry talk. When Henry reached out and started stroking his hair, Jason smiled and leaned into his touch. He could definitely think of worse ways to spend a Friday night.

Henry sounded like he knew what he was talking about, and he made a big deal out of safe play. He even harped about always using condoms as if people didn't know better—it was the twenty-first century, for crying out loud. Then again, looking at the number of people still contracting HIV and other shit… yeah, maybe it *was* important to keep talking about safe sex, even though Jason had no idea why anyone would choose not to wear a condom.

Suddenly Henry fisted his hand into Jason's hair and gave a sharp tug, forcing Jason to look up at him. "You done daydreaming, boy?"

"I… sorry… I…," he stammered, blushing. "Could you please repeat that please, sir?"

"I asked you if there were any medical conditions I need to know about." Henry sounded pissed.

"N-no, sir."

Henry paused, then gave a curt nod. He eased up his grip but didn't let go of Jason's hair. He knelt down so they were eye to eye with one another. "You gonna be okay tied up for an hour or so?"

"I should be." He wished he sounded more confident.

"Need a piss break before we start?"

Jason blinked and he stared at the other man, too startled to answer.

Henry smirked. "Guess I'll take that as a no." He let go of Jason's hair and stood up—and Jason saw that he wasn't the only one with a bulge between his legs. God, did he actually have a chance with this guy? He doubted it would be more than a casual fuck, but he'd take whatever he could get.

And Henry was glaring at him, seeming to realize his mind had started to wander again.

Jason dropped his gaze. "Sorry, sir."

Henry didn't acknowledge his apology. "Up on the table, on your knees, back to the audience."

Jason did as he was told. The table was hard under his knees; he wasn't sure he could really kneel on it for an hour. But he'd already committed to the demo, so he tried to relax and enjoy himself. His dick certainly seemed to think they were having fun—it was straining painfully against his jeans.

Henry leaned in. "How do you feel about taking off your shirt?" he asked, his voice pitched so only Jason could hear.

Jason gave him an apprehensive look. He didn't want to refuse, but he wasn't real sure about stripping in front of a room full of strangers either.

Instead of pushing him like Jason expected him to, Henry returned his gaze. His expression was calm, steady. Reassuring. "I'll be right here the whole time," he promised.

Jason licked his lips. Nodded. He removed his turtleneck and set it down next to him.

"Good boy." Henry smoothed his fingers through Jason's hair. "Hands behind your back," he said, loud enough for everyone to hear.

Jason obeyed. He closed his eyes, trying to relax as Henry wound and knotted the soft nylon rope over his arms. He worked slowly, explaining everything he did as he went. Jason let his whole world becoming the sound of Henry's voice, the steady, sure touch of his hands. The scent of well-cared-for leather. He didn't have to concentrate very hard on blocking out the rest of the people in the room; Henry was the only one who mattered. The only one who existed besides him.

Before long, Jason's arms were encased in rope. It felt... incredible. Sensual. He gave an experimental wriggle but couldn't move at all. He'd never felt so helpless. So horny.

Strong fingers brushed against his hands. Without thinking, Jason curled his fingers around Henry's. Henry leaned in close, speaking softly so no one else could hear him. "You doing okay?"

"Yes, Sir." *Sir* with a capital S.

Henry shot him a quizzical look—then he nodded. He gave Jason's fingers a gentle squeeze. "No pins and needles anywhere?" he asked. "No pinching?"

"No, Sir. I feel... I'm doing fine." He felt his cheeks growing warm again. He was doing better than fine, and if Henry took one look at the front of his jeans, he'd know it. One touch was all it would take to make him come on the spot. "I'm good, Sir."

Henry smirked, blue eyes twinkling with humor. "That you are, boy. But things are about to get a little more interesting." He winked, flashing that lopsided smile. "Hope you don't mind." Without waiting for an answer, he straightened and turned back to the audience. "Of course, if you've got a lippy little cuss for a partner, you can always fix that with more rope," he said, eliciting snickers from everyone but Jason.

Jason started to protest. He wasn't lippy!

But Henry cut him off. "Open up, boy," he ordered. He was holding a length of rope in front of Jason's mouth.

Jason hesitated. It was no longer a matter of pride, it was a matter of whether or not he was willing to give up what little control he had left to a total stranger. But he'd come this far—what was the harm in going a little further?

As if reading his thoughts, Henry leaned in close again. "It's brand-new rope. I took it out of the package a couple of hours ago," he whispered in Jason's ear. "It's never been used before tonight. Besides, do you honestly think I'm gonna try anything weird in front of all these witnesses?"

Jason almost laughed. "This isn't weird?"

Henry rolled his eyes. He seemed to be having a hard time not laughing, too. "I think gagging you was the right idea, boy. Now open up. You're making me look bad, here."

Jason smirked. "You could always spank me later if you want to, Sir," he teased.

"Watch it." Henry's tone was one of warning. "I might take you up on that. *Boy.*"

Fuck. Henry sounded serious. Jason's cock and balls ached. The only option seemed to be to play along, but.... "What if... I mean...." Only he didn't know how to ask what he really wanted to ask. What if there was a problem and he got a charley horse or needed Henry to untie him or something?

Henry just smiled. "You mean how're you gonna let me know if you get into trouble while you're all trussed up?" he asked.

Jason nodded, no longer trusting his voice.

"Remember what I said before. I'll be right here the whole time, keeping an eye on you."

His tone was so reassuring that the only thing Jason could do was open his mouth and let Henry gag him. Nylon, he decided quickly, wasn't one of his favorite flavors.

Henry turned his attention to the audience and started talking again. Unable to see what he was doing anyway, Jason closed his eyes once more and let himself get lost in the sensation of the tight bondage. The nylon was smooth against his skin; he'd never used nylon rope before. Or, rather, Terry hadn't used it on him. He hadn't played like this with anyone else, not that what he and Terry did was anything like *this*. Terry just used whatever he had lying around his apartment. Sometimes the results were good, and other times, Jason had to wear long-sleeved shirts for a few days so he wouldn't have to explain the bruises and rope burns on his wrists.

Behind him, it sounded like Henry was having the audience members pair off to practice tying each other up while he watched. Jason wished he was turned so he could see what they were doing too. He'd never been to any kind of bondage demo before, and he'd have loved to actually learn something. Sure, he knew there were a couple of fetish groups in the area, but he was too afraid of running into someone he knew to actually go to a munch—a casual meet-up. What if he found out his old algebra teacher was a closet leather daddy or something? It would just be too weird and totally not worth the risk.

Wanting something else to think about, Jason let himself sink further into the situation, into the ropes binding his arms. His mouth. When he was tied up, he didn't have to worry about doing anything wrong. He didn't even have to worry about doing anything right, either. He didn't have to think at all. All he had to do was lie there and accept whatever his partner did. Or at least, that was the fantasy. He had yet to experience it for real, not that Terry didn't try. He just wasn't into it the way Jason wanted him to be.

Henry, though…. Jason wondered what it would be like to be totally at that man's mercy, helpless to do anything but get fucked however Henry wanted to fuck him. His cock throbbed painfully against his jeans. God, he was going to die if he didn't get to jerk off soon. How much longer was Henry going to keep him tied up?

He realized his arms were sore, and shifted, trying to ease some of the tension in his shoulders. It didn't help. He fidgeted. Now it hurt worse. His knees ached and he was pretty sure his feet were asleep. Okay, it was definitely time for Henry to untie him.

Jason opened his eyes, intending to turn his head and get the other man's attention, but he discovered when he tried that he *couldn't* turn it. Shit. Talk about being helpless! And why was the room so quiet behind him? Jason's heart beat harder behind his ribcage as he stared at the ugly yellow wallpaper, trying to figure out what to do. Trying not to give in to the panic that squeezed against his chest.

He tried calling out, but the only sound he could make was a muffled cry. He couldn't even scream for help! He drew in ragged breath after ragged breath. What if they left him there all night? What if…?

"Easy, boy, I've got you." Henry seemed to come out of nowhere, and Jason felt two strong hands on his shoulders. He shuddered and leaned into Henry's touch, desperate for human contact. Henry seemed to know exactly what he needed: he wrapped both arms around Jason and held him tight, warming his chilled skin. "Shhh, you did great," he crooned. "Everybody's gone, I was just seeing the last of them out the door. I'm sorry I left you, but I was only as far away as the other end of the room, I promise. I was watching you the whole time. You were never alone."

Jason heard the words, but they didn't sink in. All that mattered were the strong arms holding him close, making him feel safe.

"I am incredibly proud of you, Jason," Henry said. "I'm going to untie you now, okay? Jason? You with me?"

Jason tried to nod, but he could barely move his head.

"Here, let's start with that."

In almost no time at all, Henry had the rope out of Jason's mouth and was pressing a plastic cup of cold water to his lips. "Drink," he ordered when Jason hesitated.

"I've gotta piss. That'll make it worse."

"A full bladder won't kill you, and I won't untie you until you drink this."

Helpless to do anything else, Jason drank. "I can't feel my feet," he said when Henry eased the bottle away from his mouth.

"Okay, hang on. No, let me," Henry instructed when Jason tried moving on his own. He helped Jason into a sitting position, bringing his legs out from underneath him, and maneuvered him so they dangled over the edge of the table. The pins-and-needles sensation was almost as unbearable as his aching bladder, but Jason didn't care. As soon as he was free of the last of the ropes, he tried to stand—and would have fallen face-first to the floor if Henry hadn't caught him.

"Your bladder can hang on for another few minutes," he said, helping Jason back to the table.

Jason stopped trying to get away the instant he felt strong, skilled fingers massaging first his wrists, then his arms, and finally his shoulders. Jason sighed when Henry moved his hands to his neck. "You're really good at that."

Henry chuckled. "I was a massage therapist for almost twelve years. I'd like to think I know a thing or two."

"What do you do now?"

"You were admiring it this afternoon."

Jason turned to look at him. "You made all of that?"

"Just the gear," he replied casually. "Friend of mine does the leather clothing. You've got some pretty nasty knots in your back and shoulders. If I offer to work on you, will I piss off your boyfriend?"

"Huh?"

"Blond kid, spiky hair? The one glomming onto you in the hallway?"

"Terry is *not* my boyfriend."

Henry smirked. "Well if that's the case, why don't you let me buy you dinner before I work on your back?"

Dinner? As in a date? With *him*? Jason's heart was hammering in his chest again.

"I figure it's the least I owe you for being such a good sport," Henry explained.

So much for it being a date. He ignored the pang of disappointment. "I was only doing what I thought you'd expect your boy to do, Sir." Jason said, trying desperately to be witty. It didn't work. He could tell by the dark storm clouds brewing in Henry's expression that the other man wasn't amused. "It was just a joke. I didn't mean anything by it." Shit. He was an idiot. All he'd had to say was "sure, dinner sounds great" like a normal person.

Henry gave him a long, measured look. "You *sure* it was a joke, boy?" His tone was low, dangerous. It sent shivers up and down Jason's spine. Henry leaned in so close Jason could feel the warmth of his breath on his face. "Because I'm thinking you were serious. I'm also thinking you might be into more than just getting yourself tied up while other people watch. Am I right?"

Jason licked his lips and dropped his gaze. He couldn't answer.

Henry didn't seem to need him to. "I'm going to let you clean up in here—just coil the rope up neat as you can and put it back in the bag. I don't expect it to be perfect. I'll see you in room 412 in twenty minutes. Do *not* be late."

"I—"

"By the way." Henry straightened back up, settling his hands on his hips. "I expect you to hold on to that piss until I see you again."

Jason's stared at him in disbelief. "I'm not into—"

"It has nothing to do with what you are or aren't into. We'll talk about that, don't worry. For right now, you're going to do what I tell you simply because *I'm* the one telling you to do it. Clear?"

Jason lowered his gaze. "Yes, Sir."

"Good boy." Henry cupped the back of Jason's head and drew him into a fierce kiss.

Too startled to do anything else, Jason parted his lips and let Henry ravish his mouth, taking whatever he wanted. It was brutal. Beautiful. Demanding.

When Henry pulled back, Jason felt empty. He wanted more. Judging by the look on Henry's face, he wanted more too.

"See you soon, boy."

Chapter Two

JASON checked the time on his iPhone. Exactly fifteen minutes had passed since Henry left him in the ballroom. He hit the Sleep button. Terry had already called twice while he'd been cleaning up, and the last thing he wanted was Terry calling him while he and Henry were... shit. He had no idea what was going to happen tonight. He could guess, but even though he didn't know what to expect, his whole body thrummed with anticipation. Or maybe it was *because* he didn't know that he was so excited.

The elevator doors dinged open, and Jason swiped his sweat-dampened palms down his thighs. His mouth felt cottony, but he'd resisted the urge to get a drink of water at every fountain he passed along the way because he didn't want to add to the agony of his full bladder. God, he hoped Henry wasn't into weird pee stuff. That would be a total deal breaker, and *that* would break his heart. Or at least ruin his evening.

Or maybe it was what exactly Henry said it was: he was holding it because Henry told him to. Which meant that Henry was definitely into D/s, Domination and submission. Jason took a breath and let it out again. Was *he* into that? He liked getting tied up. He liked it when somebody else took control. He wanted that collar. He hadn't actually minded kneeling at Henry's feet.

And he was out of time to think about it. He was standing in front of room number 412, and there was only one thing left to do: knock. Either that or knock, drop the bag, and run.

But if I do that, I'll regret it for the rest of my life.

Jason rapped his knuckles against the door before he lost his nerve. A fraction of a second later, Henry opened it and greeted him with one of those lopsided grins.

"Nice to see you're not *always* late, boy," he teased. Heat flooded Jason's cheeks, and Henry chuckled. "You're way too cute when you blush. C'mon in."

He stepped aside, admitting Jason into the room. Jason felt like the fly who had been invited into the spider's parlor. But in he went.

There were two double beds, a desk and chair, a wardrobe, a television, and a couple of armchairs and an ottoman over by the window. Piled behind the chairs was enough luggage for a family of four. The drapes were pulled shut and all of the lights were on.

"You can set the bag down with the rest of my gear," Henry instructed. "Then come over here and strip."

Jason balked. "Shouldn't we talk first?" Shouldn't Henry let him fucking piss?

Henry's expression darkened. "You either do what I tell you to do or you leave. Your choice." His tone brooked no room for argument— or compromise. Henry took a step to the right so he was no longer standing between Jason and the door.

Jason's gut tightened. He knew that if he left, he wouldn't be invited back.

But did he *want* to be invited back?

Did he want to be there at all?

Yes. God, yes.

He wanted Henry to tie him up and fuck him senseless. He wanted to forget about his crappy life and just lose himself in mindless kinky sex for a few hours.

More than anything, he wanted Henry to kiss him again.

Jason set Henry's duffel bag down with the rest of his gear and turned back to see Henry watching him. "I.... I don't... I've never stripped in front of anyone before. I mean, you know, with all the lights on and stuff."

Henry smirked. It didn't help. "I'm not expecting cabaret, boy. Just take your clothes off and let me get a better look at you."

Jason licked his lips; they were starting to get chapped. But taking his shirt off wasn't too hard, Henry had already seen his bare chest. It was just the rest of his body he wasn't so confident about.

"Fold your shirt up and put it on the desk," Henry instructed after Jason tugged the turtleneck over his head.

"You should probably know I'm not into watersports," Jason ventured, setting his shirt down on the desk.

"Duly noted. And I believe I said 'fold your shirt'. I do *not* like having to repeat myself, boy." His tone was one of warning.

Shame tinted Jason's cheeks pink. He picked up his shirt and folded it neatly, nibbling on his lower lip. "Look, Henry, about the... the pee stuff—"

"Either you trust me to respect your hard limits or you don't. If you don't, fine, just tell me now and we can quit wasting each other's time."

"I only just met you! How can you expect me to trust you?"

"I only just met you too, Jason. Trust is a two-way street. You have to trust that I'm not a psycho, and I have to trust that you're not gonna go telling all your friends 'bout how some creepy old dude raped you. I have to trust that you're not gonna have second thoughts in the morning and call the cops."

"Why would I do that?"

Henry flashed a rueful smile. "It's happened. Not to me. But think about it—and look at us. You weigh, what, a buck fifty?"

"Not even."

"I weigh about two twenty. Who do you think the police are gonna believe if you cry rape?"

Sobered, Jason nodded. "I wouldn't do that to you. I came here because I *wanted* to." He toed off his shoes and nudged them under the desk with one foot.

"That's where the trust comes in. Inviting you back to my room like this was reckless. It was reckless of you to accept."

"So why did you ask me to come?" Jason pulled off his socks.

Henry hooked his thumbs into his belt loops and leaned against the wall behind him. "When I had you tied up downstairs… damn, boy. You sank into subspace so fast, and that just did me in. Having that kind of power over somebody else's head is a hell of a rush. Before I knew what I was doing, I was telling you my room number."

"Subspace?" Jason questioned, wondering how badly his ignorance was showing.

"It's the name for the place a sub goes inside his own head, where nothing else matters. The rest of the world shuts off and it's just you and your Master. You can't tell me you didn't feel it too, boy."

He balked at the word "Master," but he nodded, remembering zoning out during the demo. He remembered freaking out too, and the way Henry had brought him back, calmed him down. Slowly, Jason undid the zipper on his jeans and slid them to his ankles, together with his underwear. He couldn't look at Henry as he folded the last of his clothing and set it on the dresser. Instinctively, he cupped his hands over his dick.

"Hands at your sides, boy. And eyes front and center. Shoulders squared. There's nothing to be ashamed of."

Heat burned in his cheeks, but he obeyed. He hadn't felt so naked and exposed since sixth-grade gym class, and the first time he had to get undressed in front of a locker room full of other boys.

Henry pushed off the wall and took a couple of steps forward, significantly narrowing the gap between them. "Why are you here, boy?"

"I…." He hesitated. He didn't know what to say. His bladder ached. He wanted Henry to tell him what to do like he had downstairs.

Henry seemed to understand. "Go on and go to the bathroom. While you're in there, take a couple of minutes to figure what you want. And to figure out why you didn't stop at any of the restrooms along the way. It's not like I would have known."

Jason opened his mouth. Shut it again. Henry was right, he could have stopped anytime he'd wanted, but instead, he'd obeyed the orders of a total stranger. What was wrong with him? He didn't know, and he wasn't sure he wanted to think about it. He hurried past Henry toward the bathroom.

"Door open, boy."

Jason stopped dead in his tracks at the threshold. "*What*?"

"You heard me. While you are here, you will obey my rules, and my rule is that the door stays open."

Jason stood there dumbfounded, staring at him, for several very long seconds, but finally the ache in his bladder won out. He left the door open and tried hard not to be embarrassed by how stupid he felt standing buck naked in front of the toilet. It wasn't like he'd never used a public urinal before. *Yeah, but never naked.* At least Henry didn't seem to be watching.

When he was done taking care of necessities, he washed his hands and splashed cold water on his face. What *was* he doing in a strange man's hotel room? It wasn't exactly the first time he'd picked somebody up at a con—or been picked up. But to go back to the guy's room after only knowing him for a couple of hours? Yeah, it was reckless, all right.

Jason looked up to see Henry leaning against the door jamb, studying him. He was still fully clothed; it made Jason feel more vulnerable than ever. Henry's smile told him he knew it too.

"Sorry," Jason apologized as he reached for a towel to dry off.

"For what?"

"Making you wait for me."

"I don't recall giving you a time limit, boy."

"Then what are you doing in here?"

Henry smirked. "Just admiring the view. Hope you don't mind."

Jason nibbled at his lower lip; he doubted it mattered to Henry whether he minded or not. The worst part was that Jason didn't know himself whether he cared or not that Henry was watching him. He *should* care, but when Henry looked at him the way he was now, with heat smoldering in his baby-blue eyes, Jason's cock swelled to its full length and all he wanted was for the other man to bend him over the sink and fuck him into next week.

Henry stepped into the bathroom and came up behind him. He looked like the cat that had eaten the canary.

Or maybe the cat that's about to eat it.

"I'd like to do more than look," Henry admitted. Not waiting for him to answer, Henry leaned in close and wrapped his arms around Jason's waist. When he didn't resist, Henry slid his hands up his chest, his touch so light it made Jason shiver. He grasped hold of both of Jason's nipple rings and tugged. Jason sucked in air, his gaze dropping from the mirror.

"Watch, boy," Henry told him.

Reluctantly, Jason obeyed. It was weird, embarrassing to watch his reflection in the mirror, but by staying, he'd agreed to play by Henry's rules. Henry wanted him to watch—and Jason wanted somebody to tell him what to do.

"Good boy," Henry said when Jason met his gaze in the mirror.

He pulled on both of Jason's nipple rings, hard and steady, until Jason was hissing in agony, gripping the vanity, his cock aching to be touched.

"Keep those hands right where they are," Henry warned him.

Jason whimpered but did as he was told. Before he realized what he was doing, he was grinding his ass against Henry's groin, rubbing his own dick against the counter in the process. He bit his lip and begged, "Please."

"Please what, boy?"

The words stuck in his throat. *Tie me up. Fuck me.* "Please" was all he could say.

Henry eased up his grip and rubbed Jason's sore chest until some of the ache left his muscles. When his thumbs brushed over Jason's nipples, Jason gasped. "Please, that felt so good." God, he was so fucked up. It had hurt like hell, but he wanted more.

Henry chuckled. "You don't need to tell me that, boy." He smirked down at Jason's straining cock. Then he straightened and placed both hands on Jason's shoulders again. "Why don't we both take a second to cool off, then talk—while you've still got a few brain cells left in your head."

Jason couldn't help the cocky smile he flashed over his shoulder. He wasn't the only one feeling a little short on brain cells. Henry was as hard as he was. "Whose fault is that?" he inquired.

Henry gave him a sharp look. "Remember what I said before about lippy boys."

Jason did his best to look contrite. He doubted Henry was buying it.

He followed Henry back to the other room and discovered that while he'd been in the bathroom, Henry had moved one of the armchairs out of the corner and placed it near the center of the room. Henry sat down in it; he leaned back and just... stared. Not sure what he should do, Jason remained standing. He fidgeted and cracked his knuckles.

"What do you want, Jason?" Henry asked after a moment.

Jason licked his lips. This was no time to be shy; he only hoped he could make the words come out right. "I want... I'd like you to tie me up again. Like you did downstairs."

"There anything else you want out of tonight?"

"Could we... I mean... if you wanted to have sex—?"

Henry shot him an incredulous look. "You think I'd invite something as pretty as you back to my room and *not* fuck you senseless? Assuming you want me to."

"Yes! Please."

Henry's smile was hard to interpret, but when he spoke, his voice was soft. Seductive. "Would you like to kneel at my feet, boy?"

"Yes, Sir."

Henry nodded and Jason sank to his knees. Why the hell did it feel so good to kneel in front of another man? In front of this man in particular?

"Unless I tell you otherwise, your hands should be behind your back, boy."

Jason was quick to comply.

"Well, you're obviously pretty submissive—no, don't bristle," Henry chided him gently. "There's nothing wrong with being submissive. It doesn't mean you're weak, Jason." He paused a moment. "But I'm guessing you don't have a whole lot of real life experience as a sub. Am I right?"

Dumbly, Jason nodded. He should have known he was in way over his head, that there was no way to fake it, even for one night. "I was kind of hoping you wouldn't notice, Sir," he said anyway. "I… is… is that okay? I mean…." *Please don't send me packing.*

"There's nothing to be ashamed of, boy. Everybody starts somewhere, even me. You're doing a pretty good job, by the way. The way you kept your eyes down at the demo, the way you sat quietly, waiting for me to tell you what to do. That tells me you've at least done some reading, that you've got some kinda idea of how a sub's supposed to act."

Jason nodded.

"Out loud, boy. If your mouth isn't gagged or otherwise engaged, I expect to hear your voice."

Jason swallowed hard, but the lump in his throat remained. "Yes, Sir."

"How long have you been interested in kink?"

His cheeks burned with embarrassment. How could anybody ask a question like that and sound so blasé about it? How could he answer it? "I guess… I mean… for a pretty long time. I… when I was little…."

"Let me guess," Henry interrupted, saving Jason from further verbal floundering. "When you were a little kid playing cops and robbers with your friends, you didn't want to be the cop or the robber, did you? You wanted to be the damsel in distress who got tied to the railroad tracks." It wasn't a question.

"Something like that, yeah." It wasn't cops and robbers, it was superheroes, and he wanted to be Robin, tied to a chair, waiting for Batman to come save him.

"When I was a little kid," Henry told him, "I wanted to be the villain tying the damsel to the train tracks."

Suddenly, being tied up by the villain sounded like much better proposition than being rescued by the hero. "Would you like me to be your damsel?"

Henry chuckled, but it didn't sound like he was laughing at Jason, he was just laughing. "Let's stick with willing partner for the time being," he said in a gentle tone. "Role playing's a whole 'nother skill set. Sound okay?"

"Yes, Sir." As long as there was tying up involved, fucking, he'd be happy.

Henry leaned in closer and cupped Jason's cheek with one hand, stroking Jason's face with his thumb. Henry's skin smelled of leather, a little of musk. Sweat. Jason feathered a soft kiss to his palm. Then another. And another, until Henry pulled his hand away, causing Jason to look up at him.

"I know you didn't ask for any advice, Jason, but I'm going to give you some anyway: What you do with it is up to you, but I think you need to get out into the scene and meet more people. Doms. Subs. Masters. Slaves. And everything in between."

"Why? Did I do something wrong?"

"No, boy. I just think once you see how other subs are happy, healthy, sane men and women, you'll feel better about yourself."

"I—"

Henry shook his head, silencing him. "It's none of my business and I won't bring it up again. Okay?"

"Yeah, okay. And I'll think about it," he added, even though he wasn't sure whether or not he was telling the truth.

"Good." Henry pressed a soft, sensual kiss to Jason's mouth.

Jason closed his eyes again and sank into it, letting out a happy sigh. God, Henry could kiss him forever....

"You like that, do you?"

"Yes, Sir. Very much."

Henry gave him another one of those half smiles. "I'll keep that in mind, boy. Now, I'm going to ask you again about any medical conditions I ought to know about."

"Nothing, Sir. I get my status checked every year. I mean, I always play safe, but you really can't be too careful."

"Good policy, but I'm not just talking about HIV. I mean, do you have any kind of heart problems, asthma, anything else I should know about before I get you tied up?"

"No, Sir, nothing."

"All right. You should know that I get a physical every year and that I get tested for HIV every six months. I'm negative, but the person I live with is positive and has been for almost ten years."

Jason's head snapped up. Henry *lived* with somebody?

"I didn't say sleeping with, boy, I said *live* with. One thing I will not tolerate is somebody who can't listen to the actual words coming out of my mouth." His tone was one of warning. Jason didn't think he would get a second warning, either.

"I'm sorry, I just... I assumed...." He took a breath. Let it out. "I'm sorry, Sir, you're right. I wasn't listening. I'm sorry about your friend too."

"So am I. But just so we're clear, now that you know a little bit more about my life, are you still interested in playing tonight?"

"Yes, Sir. And thank you, Sir. You... it wasn't something you had to tell me. I mean, it's not something I'd ever find out on my own."

Henry nodded but didn't comment. "You mentioned earlier that I could spank you," he said instead. "That offer for real, or were you just being a smartass?"

Jason hesitated. He knew the answer, but.... "Yes," he admitted. "It was for real."

"And that embarrasses you?"

"Isn't spanking something you're supposed to do to little kids?"

"I guess that depends on your parenting philosophy. But that's not the kind of spanking we're talking here, Jason. What we're talking about is me warming your ass until it's as red as your face is now." His voice dropped to a seductive whisper. "It's about blurring the line between pleasure—" He leaned forward and ran his fingertips lightly over Jason's chest, causing goose bumps to rise on Jason's arms. "—and pain." He grasped Jason's left nipple between his thumb and forefinger, pinching hard enough to make Jason cry out. It was all he could do to keep still, keep his hands behind his back where Henry wanted them. To not pull away. Then, suddenly, Henry let go, and a warm tingle spread through his chest.

And then Henry kissed him again, and Jason had to fight even harder to keep his hands where they were. He nearly toppled forward when Henry pulled away from him.

"Fuck," he swore as he recovered his balance.

Henry chuckled. "I thought we already established that was part of the plan."

"No, I mean yes... *shit*." Of course Henry knew what he actually meant.

Henry just shook his head. "So, are you ready to tell me exactly what you want, boy?"

Jason swallowed hard and forced the words out of his mouth. "I... I want you to tie me up, Sir. Please? Please... please paddle me like you said you would. Please fuck me." *Please kiss me again*, he added silently.

"That wasn't so hard to say, was it?"

"Yes, Sir, it was."

"You should never be embarrassed to tell someone what you want, boy. But since you are, how about I arrange it so you don't have to talk for a while?"

"Please, no more gags. I really hated that."

Henry smirked. "Then I guess you've got extra incentive, boy. I'm going to give you my cock. If I like what you do with it, I won't gag you. If I don't, I will."

Shit, nothing like a little pressure! The last thing he wanted was to spend any more time with rope between his teeth. Then a new thought occurred to him. "Aren't you supposed to give me a safeword or something? What if I can't handle whatever you have planned?"

Henry's smile surprised him. "Did it get too intense downstairs?"

"No, Sir. Well. A little, at the end. I freaked out," he admitted. "But then you were right there and it was okay."

"Have you ever freaked out like that before?"

Jason shook his head.

Henry gave him a sharp look.

"Sorry, Sir. No, Sir. Never. But I've never been paddled before either. Not like what you were talking about. I mean… you know, I've had my ass swatted a few times, but I… I don't know for sure how much I can honestly take."

"Fair enough. We'll talk about limits before I gag you. Or you might surprise me by giving such great head, I won't want to."

Jason was dubious, but the only thing that came out of his mouth was a tentative "Yes, Sir."

"As for a safeword, I like to keep things simple. No means no. Stop means stop. Slow down means to slow it down, give you a breather. All right?"

"Okay."

"Good. Now, first things first. When you kneel in front of a man, it's customary to show him a little respect."

"Sir?"

"Kiss my feet, boy."

Jason gave him a wide-eyed look. He *couldn't* be serious.

But he was. "I'm not asking you to lick my boots, just kiss 'em. Show me you know your place." It wasn't a request. "Start with the left one."

Awkwardly, and trying not to lose his balance, Jason closed his eyes and leaned over to press his lips gingerly to the top of... shit. He shifted so that he was pressing his lips to the boot on Henry's left, rather than his own. "Sorry," he murmured. Henry didn't respond. His boot seemed clean and smelled only of well-cared-for leather. Okay, maybe this wasn't so bad after all.

Jason kissed the other boot and began to straighten back up, but Henry stopped him by laying his hand lightly on Jason's back. "Because you're mine, at least for right now, boy, you can rest your cheek on my boots a minute."

Jason smiled. He liked the sound of the word "mine," even though he'd never, *ever* had any fantasies about being owned by anybody. Hell, the idea of it was absurd. Just the same, he felt happy with his cheek resting against the soft leather of Henry's boots. He didn't move until he felt a light wiggle under the leather—Henry's toes! Taking the hint, he sat back up.

Henry unzipped his fly, and Jason saw not only the outline of an enormous erect cock, but a huge wet spot on Henry's shorts. "You did that to me, boy," he said, his tone low and sultry. "When I told you to get down on your knees for me back at the demo, and you did, I got so damned hard, I wanted to bend you over and fuck you right there in front of all those people. In another venue, I might have, too."

To his surprise, his own cock responded, straining forward, even though he'd never considered himself any kind of exhibitionist. But maybe his dick knew something he didn't—maybe it knew a lot of things he didn't.

"I knew then that I wanted to get you somewhere private, that I wanted you kneeling in front of me, right like you are now." As Henry spoke, he slid his pants and drawers down past his hips, freeing his cock. It was thick and long, beautifully ridged with dark veins. It curved slightly upward, and the tip was deep pink and dripping with pearly fluid.

"See something you like?"

Jason grinned. "Yes, Sir!"

"Then have at it, boy."

Henry didn't have to ask him twice. Jason started at the tip, pressing his tongue against the slit and lapping up the sticky, salty precum. They groaned in unison, and Jason smiled. He took the head of Henry's dick between his lips and swirled his tongue around it several times, something Henry seemed to enjoy, at least if the sounds he was making were any indication.

Jason kissed his way down the length of Henry's erection, teasing it with his lips and tongue. Terry *hated* it when Jason did that to him, but Jason had always thought there should be more to a blow job than mindless sucking. He swirled his tongue over the tender, velvety flesh and leaned in to kiss Henry's balls, smiling as he nuzzled them. Henry smelled musky, but it was a clean sort of musky, and of course he smelled like leather. Jason inhaled deeply and continued his happy exploration until he felt Henry's hand on the back of his head.

Right. Henry wanted him to get on with it. Just like Terry. He couldn't quell his disappointment, but why should Henry be any different from anyone else? Jason took the hint and took the head of Henry's cock between his lips once more.

"You enjoying yourself, there, boy?" Henry asked. He caressed Jason's scalp, carding his fingers through Jason's hair. "Because I sure am. Mouth like yours, so soft, so warm. So talented."

Talented? Henry thought he was talented?

"Blow job's about more than just sucking, boy," Henry continued, running his thumb tenderly over Jason's cheek. "It's nice to meet someone who knows that."

Encouraged to continue as he had been, Jason ran the tip of his tongue around the underside of Henry's cockhead, looking for the sensitive spot and not stopping until he was sure he'd found it.

"Shit, boy. You keep going like that and I might *never* gag you."

Jason grinned. He took Henry all the way to the back of his throat and sucked hard for just a few seconds. Then he pulled back again and slowly kissed his way down Henry's shaft until he reached his testicles once more.

"Feel free to use your teeth if you need to," Henry told him. "I like it a little rough."

Jason worked one of Henry's sacs into his mouth and rolled it around. He scraped the skin lightly with his teeth.

"Powerful feeling, having a man's nuts in your mouth, isn't it, boy?" Henry said. "Sometimes when a guy's got me like you do now, I have to ask myself which one of us is really in charge. Is it me, 'cause you're kneeling there with your hands behind your back, or is it you, 'cause if you wanted to, you could seriously hurt me?"

Jason blinked but didn't lose his rhythm. He'd always assumed that giving a blow job was about the most submissive thing a person could do—except maybe for kissing another man's boots, something he hadn't done before tonight. Now he wasn't so sure.

Henry chuckled. "There's a lot I can teach you about power, boy." He laid his hands on Jason's shoulders and gave him a gentle nudge. When Jason refused to move, Henry gripped him harder. "Enough," he said firmly. "You made your point. No gag for that beautiful mouth tonight."

"But you didn't come," Jason protested.

"You want to taste my cum, boy?"

"Yes, Sir."

"And what's the magic word?"

Heat flared in Jason's cheeks. "Please, Sir."

"'Please, Sir', *what*?"

"Please, Sir, may I taste your cum, Sir?" Jason could barely get the words out.

Henry smirked. "I suppose since you asked so nicely. You, however, are not allowed to come without my permission, understand?"

"Y-yes, Sir."

"Good. I am expressly denying you permission to even *ask* until I've come—even then, I don't think I'll let you. I intend to keep you on the edge for a good long time tonight, boy. Maybe I'll let you come when I'm done fucking you, and maybe I won't. You ready to give up that kind of control?"

Jason licked his lips. What Henry was describing had been a fantasy for... shit. Longer than Jason wanted to admit, even to himself. Now he was being given the chance to do it and he was scared. What if he didn't like it? What if he *hated* it?

Worse, what if loved it? What would that say about him?

Finally, however, he dropped his gaze and nodded. "Yes, Sir. May... may I continue?"

He waited for Henry to say yes before he returned to lavishing attention on the other man's cock, swirling his tongue over the vein-ridged shaft. He nibbled his way back up to the head and ran the flat of his tongue over the slit. Henry's hands tightened in his hair—but then his grip relaxed again.

Jason snuck a peek up at him; Henry was watching him. Smiling. Jason beamed with pleasure too. Knowing he was doing it right made him feel *so* good.

He took Henry's cock between his lips and eased his way down, opening his throat, taking it all the way to the hilt. He laved the shaft and sucked hard, groaning, making Henry moan. When Henry started thrusting his hips, Jason relaxed his throat even more and let him fuck his mouth. In very little time at all, Jason was swallowing a load of thick, salty cum. He took it easily—greedily. He swirled his tongue across Henry's shaft to clean it before sitting back on his heels. His own dick was throbbing, but the satisfied look on Henry's face made his heart swell.

Maybe *this* was why people got off on this. D/s. Domination. *Submission.* Jason lowered his gaze demurely.

"Good boy." Henry pulled his pants back up and tucked in his cock. "Ready to have some real fun?"

Chapter Three

HENRY gave Jason a few minutes to collect his wits—and his breath—before instructing him to lift his ass up off his heels. "You're going to stay that way for a few minutes, and no, it's not going to be comfortable," he warned. "But you let me know if it gets too difficult to hold the position."

"Yes, Sir."

"You want to watch this time while I truss you up?" he offered.

Jason grinned. "Yes, Sir! Thank you, Sir."

Henry chuckled. "Get over in front of the mirror—I did *not* give you permission to *stand*!" he snapped when Jason started to get up.

Jason ducked his head. "I'm sorry, Sir."

"Don't be fucking sorry, just pay attention to what I say. Now get over there."

Jason bit back a second apology. Henry was right. He shouldn't be sorry, he should start listening. He waddled awkwardly over mirror on his knees and waited for Henry to tell him what to do next.

Henry made him wait several long moments before speaking. "Arms at your sides, boy," he instructed.

Jason did as he was told and watched while Henry retrieved several lengths of black nylon rope from another bag.

Henry worked in silence while Jason watched in rapt fascination, marveling at his skill. It was impossible to tell how much time went by, but when Henry was done with him, Jason's arms and torso were bound securely by a latticework of black rope that looked as much like a work of art as it did a work of bondage. He was still "free" from the waist down, but he couldn't move his arms at all. It was a remarkable feeling. *Like I really* am *the fly who stepped into the spider's parlor.* He grinned.

Henry was grinning too. "You like the look of that, do you, boy?"

"Yes, Sir. Thank you."

He chuckled. "You're very welcome." Without warning, he fisted his hand into Jason's hair and pulled his head back. Jason gasped, startled by the sudden roughness, but he didn't resist. He didn't even try to keep his balance; he just gave in, trusting Henry not to let him topple over. When Henry pressed a fierce kiss to his mouth, he gave in to that too, and Henry savaged his mouth. If the man fucked like he kissed…. Jason's cock strained forward. What he wouldn't give for a little relief, but Henry had been clear that he might not let Jason come at all. God, why was that such a turn-on?

When Henry pulled away, Jason snuck a peek his crotch. Henry was hard again.

"You like being able to do that to me, do you, boy?"

Jason blinked. He hadn't thought it had anything to do with him personally. *It probably doesn't.* He smiled anyway. It *was* kind of heady, even though he was pretty sure that every boy Henry tied up made him just as horny. Only the soft kiss Henry pressed to his lips hinted at a different story.

"You can relax a minute," Henry told him.

Jason lowered his butt to his heels, but he couldn't relax. Instead, he watched in anticipation as Henry walked over to the pile of luggage. He heaved the largest suitcase onto the bed nearest Jason and opened it, then turned it so Jason could see its contents.

Jason's eyes widened. The case was packed with over a dozen whips, floggers, paddles… things he couldn't identify. Jason swallowed hard, but the lump of very real fear in his throat refused to go down.

"These are my personal toys," Henry said over his shoulder. "But make no mistake, I might call them toys, but they're not. In the hands of someone who doesn't know what the hell he's doing, any one of these could cause serious damage. Of course," he added with a mischievous grin, "I might have brought more of my toys with me this weekend if I'd known I was going to run into somebody like you."

There was *more*? Shit.

Henry chuckled at his expression. "I made almost all of these myself, but a few were gifts." He began making his selections.

The first implement Henry held up was a thin, foot-and-a-half-long braided brown leather whip. "This is a single tail," he said. "It might not look like much, but a little beauty like this can slice a man's back to ribbons if it's mishandled. Even used right, it's inevitable that the boy getting whipped will end up with a few cuts."

Cuts? Before Jason could voice his concern over getting cut, Henry held up another short whip, this one with two very thin braided tails. "A double tail," he said. "Basically, it'll do the same damage in half the time. The thinner the tail, the more likely it is to break skin."

"And people like that... I mean...?"

"Everybody's got a different pain tolerance, Jason. A different idea of what feels good. We'll go slow, I promise."

Much to Jason's relief, both the single- and double-tailed whips went back into the case—but what Henry took out next scared him even more. The flogger looked brutal. It was made of dozens of long strips of heavy black leather. Henry's smile wasn't reassuring either. "This, on the other hand, will hurt like hell when I hit you with it, but it won't break skin."

When Henry hit him with it? He was seriously going to use that? On him? Jason licked his lips. Maybe coming up to a complete stranger's room and getting tied up *wasn't* such a bright idea after all.

"You still with me, boy?"

Jason nodded. Then: "Yes, Sir," he said, remembering that Henry wanted him to talk more.

Henry set the flogger down on the bed and turned around so he was facing Jason and perched on the edge of the mattress. He hooked his thumbs through his belt loops. "I'm not trying to scare you, Jason. I just want you to understand why you should never play with an amateur. 'Safe' means more than just using condoms. It means making sure the guy topping you isn't an idiot, because all of this stuff can cause real damage. Understand?"

"I'm starting to."

"Good." He brought the flogger over so Jason could see it up close. "This is one of my favorite toys. It's made of bearskin."

"*Bear*skin?"

"Buddy of mine's a hunter. He offered me a quarter of the meat and a couple of yards of hide in exchange for tanning the whole thing for him. It sounded like a good deal at the time, but let me tell you, I don't *ever* want to tan bear hide again."

Jason snickered. It had as much to do with Henry's disgruntled expression as it had to do with the absolute absurdity of the situation. Here he was, tied up, discussing whips and floggers with a man who was about to use them on him, but they were talking so casually, they might have been discussing their favorite authors.

"Find something funny, do you, boy?"

Jason schooled his features and dropped his gaze. "No, Sir."

Henry rolled his eyes. "I'll bet." He set the flogger on the floor next to Jason and went back over to the bed to fish a few more things out of his suitcase.

Jason paled when he held up a thick black leather paddle. It was at least a foot and a half long and six or seven inches across with large metal studs on one side. Jason doubted they were for show.

"What do you think?" Henry asked him.

That I don't want that thing anywhere near my ass! "I think that's a very scary-looking 'toy', Sir," he said, trying to sound respectful.

It was Henry's turn to chuckle. "It's not the toys you need to worry about, boy. It's the man using them who should frighten you. Or put you at ease."

That last statement didn't garner much comfort, especially when Henry went to another case to find a long rattan cane and a brown leather riding crop. "I think we'll keep it light since this is your first real scene."

Jason balked. *This* was Henry's idea of light?

Henry eyed him. "You still want to do this, boy?"

"Is it okay if I say I'm not sure?"

"Having 'no' as a safeword doesn't mean you have to say 'yes' every time I ask you a question. It just means you have to communicate with me." Henry sat back down on the edge of the bed. "What are you feeling unsure about?"

All of it? "I'm afraid it's going to hurt too much, that I won't be able to take it, Sir. I'm afraid I'll have to tell you to stop."

"I'll start out easy, Jason, warm you up right, but by the time I'm done, your ass is going to be hurting something fierce. I'm going to leave bruises and maybe even a few welts. I want to put my mark on you, boy. Nobody who sees that ass for the next week will have to wonder what you've been up to." He paused. "Or, if you'd prefer, we can just fuck now and then go our separate ways. Hell, I'll untie you and you can leave if that's what you want."

"*No.*" God, no. He'd come too far to wimp out now, and he was sure he'd never get another chance like this.

"Then tell me what you *do* want, boy. Tell me *everything* that you want and let me give it to you."

"Do I have to say it out loud again?"

"Yes. I know I said I wouldn't push your limits, but this is one I think I need to push, for your sake. You have got to be able to talk about what you want—and what you don't want. Masters and Doms aren't mind readers."

Jason nibbled at his lower lip. Henry was right. But it was still embarrassing to say it aloud. "I... I want you to whip me, Sir. To paddle my ass until it's red. To use the riding crop and anything else you want to use on me. I am scared. But I want you to kiss me. And fuck me. Let me suck your cock, let me taste your cum." The words tumbled out in a rush, but when he saw the pleased look on Henry's face, he knew he was saying the right things. "More than anything, I don't want to let you down, Sir."

Henry's smile made him feel warm inside. "You won't, boy. You just remember, if it gets to be too much, all you have to do is say one word and I'll stop. Got it?"

"Yes, Sir."

Henry brought the ottoman over and positioned it in front of Jason so that when Jason leaned over it, he could still see himself in the mirror. Henry had him spread his knees wide so that not only was his ass exposed, but so were his dick and balls. That made Jason even more nervous. But before they got started, Henry grabbed a pillow from the bed and put it under Jason's knees. It seemed a strange consideration after everything Henry said about wanting to leave welts on his skin, but he was grateful for the small comfort. "Thank you, Sir."

"You're welcome. Ready?"

"Yes, Sir," he said, despite the mad hammering of his heart and the butterflies in his stomach.

Jason watched Henry in the mirror. The first thing he picked up was the bear hide flogger. Henry took a few practice swings. "Gauging distance," he explained. Jason still jumped at the sound it made, even though the leather never touched his skin. The next swipe barely grazed Jason's ass, but it stung like hell, and he whimpered.

"That was nothing, boy," Henry scoffed. He landed a good solid slap against Jason's skin; it sounded like a thunderclap but actually hurt *less* than the first sting. Before he had a chance to fully process it, Henry hit him once more, this time on the other ass cheek. Jason felt the pressure of the blow, some pain, and warmth, as blood rushed to the place he'd been struck. Henry gave him a few seconds to mull all that over before landing a hard smack against both cheeks at once.

Jason gasped.

"Just breathe," Henry advised him.

Jason nodded. "Yes, Sir," he added aloud.

The next few strokes were lighter, but as Henry ramped up the intensity, Jason began whimpering for real. He squirmed but couldn't move enough to evade the hard blows. He bit back a sob. This had to be the craziest thing he'd ever done! Why was he here? Why was he letting some man hurt him? More than anything, he wanted Henry to stop—but he didn't say so. He tried to just breathe into it, tried to take the pain. This was what he'd wanted, wasn't it?

He squeezed his eyes shut, trying to hold back the tears, but it hurt so much! Finally he couldn't help it, he cried out. It wasn't a word, just an incoherent sob, but it made Henry stop. Made him kneel down and lay his hand gently on Jason's lower back.

"You're doing great, boy." Henry told him. He ran his hand lightly over Jason's ass, sending wave after wave of pain-pleasure radiating through him. Jason shuddered. Leaned into his touch. God, it was fucked up.

Henry's voice cut through his jumbled thoughts. "You with me, boy?"

"Yeah. I'm here."

"How are you feeling?"

"Fine," Jason lied. He looked at himself in the mirror. His face was red, sweaty. His eyes were red and swollen. Black eyeliner dribbled down his cheeks. He bit down on another sob.

Henry wiped the sweat- and tear-soaked hair from his face. "It's okay to get emotional. Nothing you do here is wrong. Talk to me. Tell me how you feel."

"Hideous," he blurted out the truth.

"You are one of the most beautiful young men I've ever played with. And right now, tied up, vulnerable… Jesus. It's taking every ounce of self-control I've got to keep my dick in my pants."

Jason blinked away a fresh outpouring of tears. He had to be kidding! But then Henry pressed another soft kiss to his temple, to his ruddy tear- and eyeliner-stained cheek. To his lips. It was an awkward angle, but Jason leaned into Henry's kiss.

When Henry pulled away, he wiped the tears from Jason's cheeks. "Better?"

"A little, I guess. But I still look like shit," he grumbled.

"How about some water before we continue?"

Jason nodded. Water sounded good. Henry helped him to sit up and held the glass to his lips. When Jason was done, Henry took the glass back to the bathroom and returned with a cool damp washcloth that he used to gently wipe away the black streaks on Jason's cheeks. The soft cloth felt good on his enflamed skin.

"I don't get it," Jason murmured.

"Don't get what?"

"I always thought... I mean, why?" He couldn't put his thoughts into words; everything was still all jumbled up inside.

"You mean why am I taking care of you?" Henry asked.

"Yeah."

"Easy, boy. It's my responsibility. Right here, right now, I am responsible for both of us. Okay?"

"Yes, Sir."

"Ready for more?"

"I... I think so."

Henry eased him back into place and picked up the paddle.

Jason gave him a dubious look.

"It hurts as much as it looks like it does," Henry promised.

Jason licked his lips. He nodded that he was ready, even as his hands clenched into balls at his sides. When the paddle landed, studded side down, against both ass cheeks, he yelped in real pain. People got off on this? He took a shaky breath and tried to get himself together, but Henry didn't afford him the chance to collect his wits.

The second blow landed across Jason's ass harder than the first, causing stars to dance in front of his eyes. He was still shaking, heat and pain radiating through his ass, when the third blow came, and then the fourth and the fifth.... Jason sobbed, howling into the ottoman to muffle his cries, not wanting someone to hear and come running to his rescue—which was crazy. He *should* want someone to come running to his rescue. Except he could stop Henry with a word. He didn't need to be rescued. He just needed to ride it out, only it was like trying to ride a tidal wave!

Then he felt a gentle hand on his backside, caressing his bruised, battered flesh, soothing him. "Shhhh," Henry whispered into his ear. "Take it easy. I've got you, remember?"

Dumbly, Jason nodded. He didn't even realize he'd started crying again until Henry wiped the tears from his cheeks.

"Why don't we take a breather? You probably can't sit on that ass, so I'm not going to move you. I just want you to lay there and relax a minute, okay?"

Jason nodded—but suddenly the tidal wave was back, crushing down on him. He didn't even know what he was afraid of; he was just... *terrified.*

Henry seemed to understand it perfectly. He encircled Jason in his arms and held tight until he stopped shaking. "I'm not going anywhere, baby. I'll be right here. Trust me. Close your eyes. Breathe. I've got you."

Jason closed his eyes for a long moment. His breathing slowed. Some of the tension drained from his shoulders. He felt... maybe not beautiful, but he felt... *special.* Warm. Safe. "Could... could I have some more water, please?"

Henry kissed his temple. "Of course you can." He stood up and stepped into the bathroom; Jason couldn't keep from watching his every movement. Was he seriously afraid Henry would leave him?

Was he that desperate for him not to?

Henry was back at his side, easing him up, holding the glass to his lips, helping him drink. Supporting his weight because he was too weak to support himself.

"Do you want to try sitting?" Henry asked.

"No. Thank you. I... Sir... Henry...."

"Shhhh, don't try to put your thoughts in order right now. Your only job is to *be*. To feel. To experience. I'll do the thinking, okay? All you have to do is be honest with me—with both of us—about how you're feeling."

"Yes, Sir."

"Good boy." Henry eased him back down onto the ottoman before checking his fingers like he had back at the demo. "I'm just making sure you've still got good circulation in your hands," he explained. "Everything feel okay?"

"Yes, Sir." Everything felt better than okay. When he felt Henry's hands on his shoulders, massaging some of the tension out of his arms, he sighed. Henry's touch was sheer bliss. Jason closed his eyes and let himself sink into the sensations he was feeling: Henry's wonderful hands, easing the tension out of his shoulders. His aching, burning ass. He was sure the bruises must be turning black and blue by now.

God, if anyone saw him, if he *told* anyone what he'd done, they'd lock him up for sure.

No, he realized suddenly. It was Henry who'd get locked up for assault and battery, although Alicia might try to have Jason thrown into the nearest psych ward, just for spite.

Jason opened his eyes and looked at Henry. He was the one tied up, the one aching—bruised—but it was Henry who was truly vulnerable. It was like he'd said: if Jason cried rape in the morning, the cops would take one look at Henry, one look at him, and it would be over for the other man. "Thank you, Sir."

"For?" He seemed genuinely perplexed.

"For this. Tonight."

Henry smiled and reached over to ruffle Jason's hair. "I think if you're to the point where you're thanking me again, it's time to continue. What do you say, boy?"

Jason was surprised when he felt a smile tugging at his own lips. "Yes, Sir. I'd like that."

"You think so, do you?"

Jason nodded. "Yes, Sir. The paddle really hurt, but I want to continue. Only maybe with something else? Please?"

Henry laughed. "Fair enough." He hauled himself to his feet and picked up the riding crop.

If Jason was objective—something that was difficult to be with sharp, stinging blows coming down fast and furious on his battered ass—the crop hurt less than the paddle. All the same, he'd rather have the heavy, thuddy pain inflicted by the paddle than the biting sting of the crop.

He squirmed to get away from the blows. "Please... please... ouch! Damn, that hurts!"

"Please ouch?" Henry teased. "Is that 'please, Master, make me say "ouch" some more'?" He rubbed the crop lightly over Jason's battered ass.

"No!" Jason yelped. "Please... no more."

"Some boys like the riding crop."

"I don't think I'm one of them!"

The older man's smirk was terrifying. "Guess I'll have to remember *this*"—he smacked the crop down on the ottoman's leg hard enough to make Jason jump—"the next time you get lippy with me."

Oh God. What had he gotten himself into?

"Of course," Henry went on, thoughtfully, "there's all kinds of ways to use a crop, boy." He brought the wide, flat end of the riding crop down very, *very* lightly on Jason's balls.

Jason flinched—but just as quickly as he'd tensed, he relaxed. "Oh God," he groaned aloud as Henry continued tapping the end of the crop against his testicles. That felt *good.*

"Like that, do you?"

"Yes, Sir." Oh yes! He bucked his hips, pushing his cock against the stool.

"Good to know. However, humping the ottoman will earn you a coupla stripes, boy. Hard ones." He tapped Jason's ass lightly with the crop, driving the point home. Jason stilled his hips at once.

"Good boy. But maybe we'd better remove temptation and move on to something else." Henry swapped out the crop for the rattan cane. "What you've got right now are a few light bruises. I'm going to use this to put some real stripes on that ass of yours, welts that'll be with you for a week."

Jason stared up at him, eyes wide.

"Shhh," Henry soothed. He leaned over and stroked Jason's hair; it was an absurdly tender gesture considering what he was about to do. "I'll start slow, like before. I think you're going to like this."

Although Jason was dubious, he nodded. "Yes, Sir."

With the cane, Henry laid a series of slow, easy blows to his backside and thighs. Little by little he ramped up the intensity, like he had with the flogger, striking Jason harder and harder until he cried out in real pain. Until the endorphins kicked in and he felt... disconnected. It wasn't a scary kind of disconnected, like the nightmares he used to have. It was good. It was good because Henry was there. He still felt the hard slapping of the cane against his skin, but each blow carried him further and further away from himself until he was floating on a wave of euphoria.

Suddenly something cool touched his skin. Jason flinched—but then he realized it was Henry's palm pressing against his ass, and he shifted closer. The caress hurt his enflamed skin. It felt good. He wanted more.

"How're you feeling?"

"Incredible." Jason told him the truth.

Henry's smile made his heart surge. "You *look* incredible, but you're going to have a hell of a time sitting down tomorrow."

"I don't mind." He shifted a little closer, hoping... yes. Henry leaned in. Kissed him. It was a soft, closed-mouth kiss, but Jason shut his eyes and savored the moment—savored how good it made him feel. God, he was so fucked up in the head it wasn't funny, but he didn't care anymore. Nothing mattered to him except for how good Henry's mouth felt on his.

"I don't think I've ever seen anybody do so well his first time," Henry whispered a moment later when their mouths parted. "I wasn't exactly holding back on you, you know."

Jason's heart swelled with pride. "Thank you, Sir."

Henry let him float awhile, let him drift happily in a haze of pain, pleasure—contentment.

When Henry spoke, he kept his tone soft. "I think we should give your knees a break. Can you stand?"

"I might need some help," Jason admitted, feeling a little sheepish.

But Henry didn't seem to mind. He helped Jason to his feet and supported his weight when Jason's knees gave out underneath him. Before Jason realized what was happening, his arms were free of ropes. He blinked, dazed.

Henry just smiled. He pulled the remaining pillows from the head of the bed and arranged them so that when he eased Jason stomach first onto the mattress, the pillows supported his hips, sending his ass jutting into the air. "I'm going to fuck you now," Henry told him. It wasn't a request. It didn't matter; Jason wouldn't have said no if it had been. He felt the mattress sag behind him, and he shivered in anticipation.

"Remember what I said about coming, boy. You have to ask for permission. I may or may not give it. And I would hate to have to punish you after you've done such a good job so far."

Jason shuddered again, this time with dread. But this was what he'd wanted, and so far it totally surpassed his expectations. "Yes, Sir. I understand."

"Good." He caressed Jason's ass. "I'm so proud of you, boy."

Jason's heart swelled at the words of praise. "Thank you, Sir."

Heedless of the bruises, Henry cupped his ass cheeks in both hands and spread them wide, making Jason feel exposed. His cock twitched. He willed himself to relax, to be ready for…. "Oh God!"

It wasn't a cock or even a finger pressing against his entrance, it was the warm, wet flat of Henry's tongue, and it felt *so* incredible. Jason pushed back against the soft lips, silently begging for more as his cock pressed against the pillows underneath him. It was all he could do not to buck against them, because if he did, he'd come for sure.

He moaned into the bedspread. "So good. God, so good, Sir." His moan deepened when he felt the tip of Henry's tongue pushing past the tight ring of muscles. "Oh... oh please... yes... please... oh God, I'm so close... please... can I...?" He'd never come just from being rimmed before.

Henry stopped only long enough to say, "No."

Jason whimpered as Henry's tongue slid back inside. Then he felt the light touch of Henry's fingertip stroking the tender spot between his anus and testicles and a wave of heat washed over him. "Oh God!"

Henry snickered. "Never been touched there, boy?"

"N-no, Sir, I don't think so. Oh," he groaned in pure ecstasy when Henry started tonguing his entrance again. Jason was sure he was going to explode. "Oh, God, please...!"

"Not yet, boy," Henry told him.

He ached—but it felt so good. The bruises, the pain, the pleasure, the fact that he was completely at someone else's mercy. Just when Jason was sure he couldn't take anymore, Henry pressed a finger inside him, seeking out his prostate.

"Please!" Jason almost screamed, fisting his hands into the sheets. "Oh God... Sir... if you...." He squeezed his eyes shut as Henry found what he was looking for. "*Please!*"

"Please *what*, boy?" Henry asked. He'd lifted his mouth away from Jason's entrance so he could speak, but he continued slide his finger slowly in and out of Jason's tight channel, hitting his prostate with every pass. "I can keep this up for hours, boy. Keep you dangling on the edge but not quite taking you over."

"Oh God, please don't! Please let me come!" He was sobbing, ready to promise Henry anything he wanted if only Henry would let him come.

"All right, boy. Come for me," he said as he pushed a second finger in to join the first.

Jason emptied himself onto the pillows with a strangled cry. He continued to spasm with aftershocks, even as Henry reached over for something on the nightstand.

"I'm going to give you my cock now, boy."

"Yes. Yes, Sir! Please."

"You opened up enough, or do I need to—"

"No. Please. Please just fuck me! *Please.*" He whimpered again when Henry pulled away—but then a lube-slicked finger rubbed against his hole, slid into it, made sure he was good and slippery inside. "More, please," Jason begged. A moment later Henry was poised behind him, cock pressing against his entrance. Jason squirmed against it.

"I put a condom on," Henry promised him. That was all the warning Jason got before Henry plunged past the tight ring of muscles and into his body.

The sudden intrusion burned, but in the *best* way, and Jason moaned into the blanket as his cock swelled back to life. "Please, Sir, I might come again… please…? Can I?" he begged.

Henry chuckled softly at his desperate pleading. "Yes, boy, you can come again."

He grabbed hold of Jason's hips to keep him still. He pulled almost all the way out and stayed there a maddeningly long time, then thrust back in fast and hard. He was angled just right to hit Jason's prostrate.

Jason gasped. He tried in vain to meet the frenzied thrusts, but Henry had too tight a hold on him. The only thing he could do was lay there and let Henry pound mercilessly into his bruised ass while Jason moaned in agony—ecstasy.

Jason's eyes rolled back in his head and his toes curled as he shot his second load.

A moment later, he felt Henry shudder as he climaxed.

They breathed in tandem, lying there together, recovering. Henry leaned over and pressed a soft, sensual kiss to the back of Jason's neck. "That was beautiful, boy. Thank you."

Jason turned his head; Henry found his lips and kissed them eagerly despite the awkward angle. Then Henry sat up, rolled Jason over, and pushed the soiled pillows to the floor. He snickered. "I think I owe housekeeping a big tip."

Jason snickered too. "Yes, Sir, I think you do." He settled back onto his stomach with his arms under his head and closed his eyes while Henry stroked his back for a few minutes. He'd never felt so content in his life.

"I'm gonna go clean up a minute," Henry said at length. "Will you be okay?"

"Hmmm? Yeah… yeah, I'll be okay. Thanks."

A gentle hand ghosted across Jason's back one last time. Then he felt something warm and soft covering him up. A blanket. He smiled and snuggled into it.

"I'm only going as far as the bathroom," Henry promised.

Jason nodded. He let his whole world become the sensations around him. Inside him. The soreness of bruises. The softness of the mattress underneath him. The clean, slightly bleach scent that all hotels' sheets possessed. The warmth he felt. He wasn't aware he'd dozed off until Henry laid a gentle hand on his shoulder.

"Sorry," Henry said. "You looked so peaceful I hated to wake you, but I've got some ointment for those bruises. It'll help with the pain."

"Yeah. Okay." Jason didn't fully comprehend what Henry was telling him until he felt the cool balm spreading over his ass and thighs. He tensed a little but then relaxed as it went to work, numbing the worst of the pain.

"Better?" Henry asked.

Jason smiled. "Yeah. Thanks."

"It's my responsibility to take care of you, remember?"

"Yeah."

"You drank an awful lot of water tonight. You probably oughta go answer Nature's call."

Jason nodded. He got up. Even though Henry didn't tell him to, he left the door open while he attended to necessities and washed up.

Maybe he was crazy, but he'd never felt so happy. So alive. He turned so he could see his ass and thighs. Dark-purple bruises were forming around angry red welts. By morning it was going to be spectacular. He was filled with a sense of pride. He didn't know why he was so proud, except maybe that Henry had said *he* was proud of him. That was more than good enough for Jason.

Warmth and pride turned to uncertainty, however, when he stepped back into the other room. All the lights were off, and Henry was in bed, under the covers. It looked like he'd stolen a pillow from the other bed. He probably wanted to go to sleep.

"I guess I should…," Jason began awkwardly.

"Come here." Henry pulled back the blankets so he could crawl in. Then Henry wrapped both arms around his shoulders and pulled him in close. "You doing okay?"

Jason snuggled closer. "I'm better than okay. Thank you. That was… it was amazing, Henry. I… I can't thank you enough," he babbled.

"I'm glad you had a good time. So did I." He feathered a soft kiss to Jason's forehead and closed his eyes.

Jason hoped that meant Henry intended to let him stay, because nothing would make tonight more perfect than waking up in Henry's arms tomorrow morning.

He was almost asleep again when Henry spoke again. "It's still kinda early, at least by con standards. You feel like getting some dinner? You could probably use it after the workout I gave you."

The last of the postcoital haze evaporated. "I wish I could, but I wasn't kidding about being on a pretty tight budget. Unless you want to run up to the con suite and grab something?" Jason suggested hopefully. The con's hospitality suite had free food: chips, fruit, sandwich fixings. It wasn't much, but they could get a bite, grab a couple of sodas, and maybe sit and talk. He'd love the chance to actually get to know the man who had marked him, fucked him senseless—made him feel like the center of the whole universe.

Henry's expression, however, told him what he thought of going to the con suite for food. Jason did his best to hide his disappointment. He wasn't ready to go back to his own room, but it was becoming pretty obvious that's what was going to happen. Reluctantly, he pulled away from Henry's warmth and sat up. He hissed in pain when his butt hit the mattress.

Henry smirked. "I told you it was going to be sore for a while."

"Yeah. I... thanks, again," he offered up, feeling lame. "I... guess I'll see you around the con." Maybe if he was lucky, Henry would want to hook up again before the weekend was over.

Henry cleared his throat. "Let me rephrase my question. It's pretty early yet. You feel like letting me take you out for some dinner?"

"You mean like a date?" Heat flooded Jason's cheeks, and he wondered if he could have sounded any more stupid if he'd tried.

Henry laughed. "Yeah, I know, it's kinda ass-backwards. First I fuck you, then I take you to dinner, but for what it's worth, I did ask you out before I brought you back here."

"Yeah, I guess you did," Jason conceded with a smile.

"So, you interested?"

"Yes, Sir." Did this mean Henry wanted to get to know him better too? God, he hoped so.

"Good. Go on back to your room and get cleaned up, then meet me in the lobby in twenty minutes."

"Yes, Sir." Jason beamed happily. "But, erm, where did you have in mind?" he wondered, not sure what he should wear and hoping he didn't need anything nicer than clean jeans and a T-shirt.

"You choose. I'm not from around here."

Jason nodded, and tried not to feel too unhappy about Henry not being from the area. He'd just had the best sex of his life, and now Henry was taking him to dinner. He didn't want to ruin that by being upset. "See you in twenty minutes, Sir."

"You don't have to keep calling me that, you know."

"It's what it says on your nametag, isn't it?" Jason shot back.

Henry snorted. "Get outta here and let me take a shower, boy, before I tan your hide a little more."

Jason couldn't help his saucy comeback: "Maybe I'd like that, Sir."

"And maybe *I'm* starving," Henry snapped—but Jason could see the twinkle of mirth in his eyes. Henry cleared his throat. "Your twenty minutes started two minutes ago, by the way."

Jason fought back his smile, trying desperately to look contrite. He shimmied into his clothes, wincing with pain as the very tight jeans pressed painfully against his *very* sore ass, and promised Henry he'd see him in… shit, fifteen minutes. He literally ran to his room, grateful that he didn't run into Terry or anyone else he knew on the way.

Chapter Four

DRIPPING from what had to have been the fastest shower in history, Jason surveyed the clothes he'd packed, not liking any of his options. He'd packed for a weekend of trolling for lonely geeks, not a dinner date with a man like Henry Durand.

Man.

The word struck Jason hard. It wasn't that Henry was probably a decade older than him; he didn't mind the idea of being with an older guy. Hell, if this evening was any indication of what older men were capable of, he was never going back to guys his own age again! Fuck, Henry was amazing.

So what the hell is he doing with me? There were better-looking guys cruising the con for a quick lay, and Henry was hot enough to have his pick. *But he wants to take* me *to dinner.* Jason's stomach fluttered as he rummaged around his duffel bag. Finally, he found a well-worn pair of jeans that weren't too tight. Pulling them on carefully over his bruised backside, he wondered yet again why he was so excited. But even after the adrenaline had worn off, after the bliss of the aftercare faded, the answer remained the same: he wanted this. He wanted to be tied up, spanked, and fucked. He wanted somebody to keep him on the edge, begging. He wanted someone tell him when he was allowed to come.

He wanted that someone to be Henry Durand, even if only for this weekend.

AS SOON as the elevator doors opened, Jason saw the object of his desire standing on the other side of the lobby, and his heart started to pound. Henry looked hot as hell. He had on a white collarless shirt, brown leather pants, and a brown leather vest with brass buttons.

"Where do you think you're going?" demanded an angry voice right behind Jason. He recognized the speaker without having to turn around. It was Terry.

He wanted to say he wasn't going anywhere, but he was carrying his leather jacket, so there was no denying he was headed out of the hotel.

"*Well?*" Terry stepped in front of Jason, cutting him off from the lobby. "I waited for you for like, a fucking hour and a half."

"I… sorry. I got… tied up at a panel."

"*What* panel?"

Suddenly Henry was standing next to him. He placed a hand protectively—possessively—on the back of Jason's neck. "You planning on keeping me waiting all night?" he demanded. He sounded pissed. Really pissed.

"I… I'm sorry." Jason met Henry's gaze, silently begging him not to be mad—but then felt a gentle, reassuring squeeze on the back of his neck and realized Henry wasn't pissed at all. "I took longer in the shower than I should have," he said anyway.

"We'll discuss your timekeeping skills later, boy. Please excuse yourself from your friend so we can leave."

Jason turned to Terry. "I'm sorry, but I have to go. I have plans tonight."

"What the—?" Terry looked from Jason to Henry and back again, seemingly caught somewhere between anger and shock.

Jason ignored him and looked up at Henry for direction.

"My coat is over there." Henry nodded toward the other side of the room.

Jason followed his gaze and spotted a long brown overcoat draped across the back of one of the chairs in the sitting area. He blinked, not quite comprehending—but then understood. Henry wanted him to get his coat. He hurried over with Henry following behind.

"I am sorry about that," Jason said quietly when Henry caught up with him.

"Do not apologize for some other guy being an asshole."

Jason nodded. He picked Henry's coat up from the back of the chair—and suddenly realized that Henry didn't want him to *get* his coat, he expected Jason to help him *into* his coat. Shit. He'd never helped a guy into his coat before—or a girl, for that matter. Except his mother. He pushed thoughts of her out of his head as soon as they surfaced.

He didn't think telling Henry he had no idea what he was doing was an option, so, trying not to look like an idiot because Terry was still gawking at him, he did his best to get Henry into the eight yards of heavy satin-lined wool. Henry slid his arms into the sleeves like he was used to being dressed. Maybe he was. Maybe he had a "boy" back home. Jason pushed those thoughts out of his head too. Henry's personal life wasn't his business.

Henry cleared his throat and Jason blushed. He was daydreaming again. "Sorry, Sir," he muttered, half under his breath.

"Either say it loud and proud or call me by my name," came the sharp response. Jason hung his head—and Henry reached out, grasped his chin, and brought it back up again. "Hey, it's your choice. I don't care one way or the other outside the bedroom, but I won't have you straddling the fence. *Boy.*" He was smirking. He knew exactly what Jason wanted.

Jason relaxed. "I'm sorry, Sir," he said more loudly as the world around him, Terry included, vanished from existence. "It won't happen again, Sir."

"See that it doesn't. Now put your coat on, it's cold out."

"Yes, Sir. Thank you, Sir."

Henry quirked an eyebrow.

"For taking care of me, Sir."

Henry shook his head, rolling his eyes—but then he reached out and cupped Jason's cheek. He held it a moment before leaning in to claim a deep kiss.

"It's not much," Henry said as he led the way toward the old white cargo van parked in the hotel's main lot, "but it gets me where I need to go. Or were you expecting me to haul all my gear on the back of a Harley?" he added with a grin, obviously amused by Jason's expression.

"I guess this is more practical," he agreed, even though the van didn't fit with his image of a leather-clad Dom.

Henry gave him another one of those lopsided smiles. "I ride. But not in this cold, and *not* when I'm doing a show." He unlocked the passenger side door, opened it, and helped Jason up. He waited until Jason was settled in (Henry was right, sitting hurt like hell) to close the door and head around to the driver's side. Jason's smiled; on top of everything else, it seemed as if Henry was a gentleman.

The van was clean, no food wrappers or paper cups anywhere—but there were a couple of cigarette butts in the ashtray. Oh well, nobody was perfect. If Henry lit up, Jason would deal with it; it was his van, and he was the one paying for dinner.

Henry climbed in. "How's the ass?"

"Sore. But I'll live."

"A cool bath with some Epsom salts will help."

"Thanks. And thanks for rescuing me back there," Jason added. "Terry isn't usually that much of a jerk. I'm not sure what his problem was."

"I think I might have an idea or two. Which is why I came over to protect my interests."

His interests? Jason stared, agape—but Henry wasn't looking his way.

He started up the van. "Where to?"

"Depends on what you want."

"What I want, huh?" Henry shot over a lascivious grin as he eased the van out of its parking space. "I guess you could call me flexible—at least where food is concerned." His tone was neutral, even if his expression wasn't.

Jason opened his mouth. Shut it again. There were no good comebacks for that. "There's Chinese and Mexican that way." He pointed to the left, toward a line of towering office buildings. "Or if you don't mind driving a little further, there's a Middle Eastern place the other way. It's a little pricy," he warned, "but the food is totally to die for."

"Middle Eastern it is." He made a right turn out of the lot.

And still no cigarette.

Jason settled back in his seat, trying to get comfortable. It had been a very long time since he'd been on anything he would consider a date. It wasn't that he didn't want to, but most of the guys he met only wanted to hook up, to fuck and go. Or they wanted to be friends with fringe benefits, which was okay, but he already had all of that with Terry. He wanted somebody different. Something real.

"Feel free to turn on the radio." Henry's voice interrupted his thoughts. "Or go through the CDs. There's a case at your feet."

Curiosity got the better of Jason, and he reached for the case. "You'll need to make a left at the light," he said as he leaned over, wincing as his jeans scraped along his ass. "That'll put you on the service drive. As soon as you can, you need to get on the freeway, heading north." Jason hoisted the sizeable CD case into his lap and flipped it open.

"I should warn you—I've got some pretty eclectic taste in music."

Eclectic was an understatement. Metal, jazz, disco, steampunk, electronica, everything from ABBA to ZZ Top.

Henry smiled when he slid a Pat Benatar CD into the player; it was the one with "Hit Me With Your Best Shot" on it. "You have a knack for making good choices," the older man told him. "I never woulda figured you for a Pat Benatar fan."

"My mom was."

Henry nodded; he didn't press Jason about the "was" part of that last statement. Jason was just as glad. He wasn't ready to tell someone he'd just met—someone he wanted to like him—his life's story. It wasn't like he was the only guy whose parents had never been married, the only guy whose father wasn't around when he was growing up. He doubted his dad was the only man alive who'd had a kid sprung on him seventeen years after the fact, either. Sometimes life just sucked.

Silence settled between them, but Jason couldn't tell if it was comfortable or not. "I love the vest," he said, trying to fill the quiet. *God, how lame.* Maybe he should have stuck with silence.

"Thanks. I traded it for a custom hood with another merchant at a steampunk expo last month in New Orleans."

"Hood?"

"Bondage hood," Henry clarified.

Jason hesitated. Nodded.

"Something about that make you uncomfortable?"

"No. I don't know. I've seen pictures of stuff like that online and I.... I mean... I don't know why anyone would want to wear one of those things."

"All sorts of reasons. Some guys get off on the whole sensory deprivation thing. Just think about it. Your whole head encased in thick leather, padding over your ears so you can't hear, a heavy blindfold buckled securely in place...." His voice dropped to a seductive whisper. "There's holes so you can breathe, but the only thing you can smell is the leather. Maybe your Master chains your arms over your head, puts a spreader bar between your ankles—or maybe he just ties you up nice and snug so you can't move a muscle. You don't know what he's doing, where he is, if he'll whip you or fuck you. Suck you off. You're completely at his mercy."

Jason shivered. "That sounds...." Horrifying? Exciting? Like something he wanted to try?

"It can be a pretty wild trip. It can also make a very effective punishment."

"Punishment?"

Henry's smile was wicked. "You take a slave—a sub—who craves his Master's attention"—he reached over and stroked Jason's cheek—"and you put him in a hood, sit him in a corner for an hour or two—it's pure agony."

Jason swallowed hard. Maybe he didn't want to try a hood after all.

"I've never done anything to anyone that he didn't…." He paused and then started over. "There's a real fine line between need and want, Jason," Henry explained. "But I promise you, I have never done anything to anyone they didn't want, at least on some level, or anything to cause real harm to the other person. A Master—a Dom—doesn't punish his sub because he wants to hurt someone. That's abuse, plain and simple."

"You seemed to like hurting me earlier."

Henry chuckled. "As I recall, so did you."

Jason couldn't argue, he just wasn't sure how that made him feel about himself. "So what kind of person wants to be punished?" he wondered.

"It's not about wanting to be punished, it's about needing to be disciplined."

"I get plenty of discipline at home. I mean…." Shit. "I don't mean my dad hits me or anything, he just yells. A lot." Which was no doubt way more than Henry wanted to know about his personal life. "Sorry."

"For what?"

Jason shrugged. He wasn't sure. "You need to get off the highway at the next exit. At the first light, make a left."

Henry followed his instructions, then glanced over toward the passenger seat. "The kind of discipline I'm talking about isn't meant to demean a person, Jason. It's meant to make him stronger. When it's over, you should feel better about yourself, not worse."

"I've never had that kind of punishment before."

"What about tonight?" he asked. "It wasn't punishment, but how did it make you feel?"

"Good. I mean, I hated parts of it. The paddle hurt like hell, and I *hated* the riding crop. But when you touched me, the way you talked to me, when you said you were proud of me...? I haven't had too many people say they were proud of me before. Shit. I'm babbling, I'm sorry." Hadn't he already apologized once for boring Henry with unimportant shit? Why couldn't he keep his mouth shut about it?

Henry took Jason's hand in his and gave it a gentle squeeze. "It was a pretty intense session."

"I haven't cried like that since... in a long time."

"You okay with that?"

"I... if someone had asked me that yesterday, I probably would have said no. But yeah. Yeah, I'm okay with it." He held on to Henry's hand a little tighter. "Is it... I mean, do people usually cry like that during a... a 'session'?"

"Sometimes. Emotions usually run high. Sometimes things get rattled loose. Crying's a natural response. It's a pretty healthy release too."

Jason nodded but didn't comment. "This is it—the next driveway up ahead."

Henry turned into the lot, found a parking spot not too close to the entrance, and cut the engine. Instead of getting out, he turned to face Jason fully. "So, if I ask you if you want to play some more this weekend—?"

"Fuck yes."

Henry laughed. "Fuck yes, *what,* boy?"

Heat overtook Jason's cheeks. "Fuck yes, Sir?" he asked.

"Better. Now, I think maybe we'd better talk a little more about boundaries and limits."

"Why? I mean, if no means no...?"

"I'd like to know which boundaries I can push and which ones are hard," Henry explained.

"I thought the idea of boundaries was that you're not supposed to push any of them. Otherwise, why call it a boundary?"

"You tell me."

Jason shrugged. "I don't know. Like I said, I thought it was called a boundary because you're not supposed to cross it."

Henry shot him mischievous grin. "You didn't like that paddle, but if I told you I wanted to use it on you again, would you let me?"

He swallowed back his initial reaction—*no*. That wasn't the real answer, but it was hard to admit aloud that even though he was terrified of that paddle, he was also incredibly turned on by it. He was pretty sure Henry knew it too. Finally, he forced the words out. "Yes, Sir. I would."

"Good. Now, how about the riding crop?" he asked.

Jason nibbled his lower lip. "I *really* hated the way that felt," he said. "But I... I think I could take it, if you really wanted me to. I just might have to ask you to take it easy on me... if I'm allowed to...?"

"You're always allowed to express your needs, Jason. Next question: what if I said I wanted to piss on you?"

"*No.*" Jason didn't hesitate. "You don't—do you?"

"No, I don't. But my point is that some things are negotiable. Others aren't. Got it?"

"Yeah. Okay."

"Good. Now, we've established at least one hard boundary. Any others you can think of?"

"I don't suppose I can say talking?"

Henry gave him a sharp look.

He sighed. Pleading that this was embarrassing wouldn't get him anywhere—besides, given what they'd already done, he shouldn't be embarrassed sitting there, fully clothed, talking about sex. "There's only a couple things I can think of. I read about this thing called a butterfly board online, and I don't think I could ever do *anything* like that." He felt queasy just thinking about it.

"Baby steps, Jason. That's not the kinda thing anybody does as a rookie sub. I'm glad you brought it up, but for what it's worth, I'm not into any kind of serious cock and ball torture, either."

"What *are* you into?"

A slow, seductive smile spread across Henry's face. "I'd like to put you in a hood—I know it scares you a little, but that's half the fun. I've got a St. Andrew's cross at home—ever see one?"

"Only in pictures." Henry *had* one of those things? At home?

"I'd like to chain you to it, spread-eagle." His voice grew low and gravelly. "I'd like to use every paddle and whip in my collection on you, make you scream—wriggle. Fly."

Jason's pulse quickened and his breath caught in his throat.

Henry's grin was wicked. "I'm not sure I'd let you come right away, but I'd like to see how close I could get you. How hard I could make you beg before I fucked you. How long I could keep you on the edge. What do you say, boy?"

He didn't have to answer. His dick was standing painfully at attention, straining against the heavy fabric of his jeans. However: "The hood really scares me, Sir," he admitted.

"Tell me why."

"I've been blindfolded a couple of times. I… I liked it, but back at the hotel, when you had me tied up and facing the wall, when I was gagged, I freaked out because I didn't know where you were. I thought you'd left."

"*Never.*"

Jason loved the firmness of Henry's tone when he said that. "Do you think we could put the hood in the category of 'maybe' for now?" he asked.

"Deal. Now, how about we go in and get some food before they close—and before I decide I need you to do something about *this*." He pulled Jason's hand into his lap so Jason could feel the enormous bulge between his thighs.

Jason took a quick glance at the digital clock on the van's console and smiled. "They don't close until midnight on the weekend. That gives us over an hour. Sir. If there's something you happen to want me to do before we go in…?" He rubbed his palm over Henry's cock. His own was aching to be touched too, but he was pretty sure he wasn't going to get anything in return. *So why am I offering to suck his?*

"Question is, what do *you* want, boy?"

Shit. Of course he was going to make him say it. "May I suck your cock, Sir?"

Henry slid his seat all the way back and unzipped his fly. "In front of me," he ordered. "I'll give you exactly ten minutes to make me come, boy. If I don't, we're going to have a nice long talk about punishment when we get back to the hotel."

The threat sent shivers up and down Jason's spine, made his cock press even harder against his jeans. And of course there was only one answer. "Yes, Sir!" he said before clambering over the console to kneel in front of Henry. He wrapped his lips eagerly around the head of his cock and tasted the salty flavor of precum.

Henry carded his fingers through Jason's hair. "You see what you do to me, boy?"

Jason just smiled and took Henry's shaft all the way to the back of his throat. He pressed his nose into the mass of curly blond hair and inhaled deeply. Henry smelled of musk and leather, and soap from his shower. Jason moaned, knowing what the vibrations would do to him.

"*Fuck*," Henry rasped.

Jason grinned mischievously up at him and pulled his mouth off Henry's cock. "If you'd prefer to fuck me, Sir…," he offered.

Henry glowered but looked like he was having hard time not grinning too. "Time's a-ticking, boy," he warned.

Jason laved his tongue around the shaft, swiping it over every inch of silky skin. He sucked hard, hollowing out his cheeks, and began to bob his head up and down, using every trick he could think of to impress Henry. He knew he'd succeeded when Henry's hips started to buck.

"*Yes*," he grunted as he came hard in the back of Jason's throat.

Jason swallowed it greedily, not losing a drop.

"God damn, boy. I think that was a record." He sounded winded.

Very, *very* slowly, Jason sucked him clean, not letting go until Henry's shaft had gone soft in his mouth. He kissed his cockhead and, feeling the man's hand settle on the back of his head, laid his cheek against Henry's thigh. God, this was so good.

"Definitely gonna have a hard time ever gagging that mouth, boy," Henry murmured as he continued to stroke Jason's hair.

Warmth spread through his chest at the praise. He nuzzled Henry's skin and pressed a kiss into the soft curls around the base of his shaft. "Thank you, Sir. I'm really happy... I mean, I'm glad you like it."

"Shit, boy, who wouldn't? Come here."

"Hmmm?" Jason murmured, but he let Henry pull him up into a kiss. Jason moaned into it. Henry had kissed him earlier after he'd gone down on him, but not *immediately* after. He desperately wanted to deepen the kiss. When Henry responded to his attempt, Jason wrapped his arms around Henry's neck and held on tight. His chest tightened with... something. Need, maybe. He found himself clinging to Henry like he was afraid to let go.

Henry stroked his back. "You okay?" he asked when their lips parted.

"Yes, Sir. I... sorry...."

"Shhh." He pressed another, softer kiss to Jason's lips. "Nothing to be sorry for. Come on, let's get some food."

"Whatever you say, Sir."

Henry smirked. "Whatever I say, huh?"

Jason thought for a second. "Yes, Sir. Whatever you say." He slid back to his knees so Henry could zip himself up—but then on impulse, Jason reached out and took over, tucked Henry's cock gingerly back into his shorts, and zipped his pants back up. Henry's expression was impossible to read—had he done something wrong?

"Was that okay?"

"More than okay." Henry ran his fingers over Jason's cheek, over his mouth, and Jason kissed them. "I swear, you're going to be the death of me, boy."

He opened up the van door and got out, offering Jason his hand. It was an awkward angle to exit the van from—and what anyone watching must have thought! But Jason couldn't have cared less what anyone else thought. As they walked toward the restaurant's front door, Henry laid his hand possessively on the back of Jason's neck again, and that was all that mattered.

Inside, Henry told the hostess it was just the two of them and that he'd like a quiet table—it wasn't a difficult request to accommodate since the place was nearly empty. She showed them to a table tucked away in a corner and left, saying that their waitress would be right over.

Before shrugging out of his own coat, Jason helped Henry out of his. Henry nodded his approval, and Jason laid both coats carefully over the back of one of the chairs. He waited until Henry sat down before pulling out the chair opposite him.

"I'd like you next to me, please," said Henry.

"Yes, Sir."

When the waitress arrived to ask if they'd like anything to drink, Henry ordered a mineral water. "Whatever you've got is fine," he told her. "I'd like a twist of lemon with it and no ice."

She looked to Jason.

"I'm good with water, thanks," he said. He took a sip from his water glass to make it clear he wasn't asking for a bottle of overpriced mineral water.

The waitress took her leave, and Henry leaned toward him. "You remember tonight's on me, right?"

"Yeah... I just... I'm good with water."

Henry searched his face.

"I'm good," Jason insisted.

Seemingly pacified, Henry nodded. "I have a question for you, boy. How far are you willing to play in public?"

"W-what do you mean?"

Henry smirked. "I'm not talking about anything that'll get either of us arrested—or kicked out. I'm just wondering how adventurous you really are. *Boy.*"

Jason's cock throbbed. "There's a lot I haven't done, Sir, but that doesn't mean I'm not up for something new." *Especially with you.*

"There's a bag in my coat pocket. Get it and go to the restroom. But don't open it until you get inside one of the stalls."

Jason shot him a quizzical look.

"Don't worry, I'm sure you won't have any trouble figuring out what to do once you see what's in the bag." Henry reached into an inner pocket of his vest for an antique eyeglasses case. Inside it was a pair of half-moon reading glasses. "Laugh and you're in for it," he warned before slipping them on.

"No, Sir. I mean...." He shook himself. "I think you look kind of sexy."

Henry rolled his eyes. "I know you said the food was to die for, but is there anything you don't like?"

"What?"

"I'm ordering for both of us," Henry clarified.

Jason gave him a startled look.

"Problem?"

"No, Sir. I just... I don't eat meat."

Henry's brows shot up. "But you wear leather?"

"I know it's a contradiction, but yeah. A leather boy wannabe who happens to be a vegetarian."

Henry's response startled him. "There's a difference between somebody who hasn't had much experience and a wannabe, Jason. You don't strike me as someone who only plays dress-up on the weekend. Am I right?"

Jason bit his lower lip. He hated being so fucking transparent. "Sort of. I still have to live at home. I have to pretend to be 'normal' so I don't totally freak my dad out," he explained.

"You're not home now, are you?"

Yes. He felt more comfortable with Henry than he did with his dad. "No, Sir. I'm with you."

"Then I am ordering you to be yourself. Leather boy, submissive, bondage slut, whatever. I want you to be 100 percent true to yourself for the rest of the weekend. For me."

Jason swallowed hard. Nodded. "Yes, Sir."

"Good boy." Henry picked up his menu and began perusing their dinner options.

Jason hesitated. What was he, really? He was definitely a slut for bondage. Pain too, apparently. And he liked kneeling at Henry's feet, doing what Henry told him to do, which he supposed made him Henry's submissive. He wondered what it would be like to do it all the time. *Probably not easy.* But nothing worthwhile was ever easy.

He got up and went to Henry's coat pocket; sure enough, there was a black plastic bag in it. Henry didn't look up from the menu or acknowledge him in any way. Jason took plastic bag and walked to the men's room, his heart pounding harder with each step. He reminded himself that his safeword was still "no." He was pretty sure that applied whether Henry was there to hear him say it or not. If he didn't want to do whatever it was Henry wanted him to, he could back out.

Jason locked himself in a stall and opened the bag. He recognized the bottle of lube for what it was at once, so he ignored that and pulled out the other package instead. The clear plastic contained a string of six balls ranging from about the size of a pea to as large as a pretty big marble—or maybe one of those little bouncy balls he used to get out of the gumball machines as a kid. *Superballs*, he thought they were called.

Then he looked at the label.

Anal beads.

Jason almost dropped the package and had to make a quick grab for it before it fell. Henry had to be kidding! He couldn't possibly expect him to sit through dinner with those things inside him... could he?

Jason's cock twitched. Throbbed. Okay, maybe it wasn't such a crazy idea after all. Or, it was crazy, but it was also a total turn-on. He reached down and started stroking himself through his clothes, which only made it worse. God, he was so fucking horny it would only take a few minutes to make himself come. But Henry hadn't said anything about masturbating. Jason bit back a groan of frustration and tore open the package. What exactly Henry was doing with a package of anal beads in his room, he wasn't sure. Maybe he sold them at his booth? Jason doubted the con would let him put them on display, but that didn't mean he couldn't let adult customers know that he carried other toys as well.

Remembering that Henry was waiting for him, Jason got to work. He pulled down his jeans and underwear, allowing his dick to spring free. When the cold air hit it, he gasped. Whimpered. He fought back the urge to jerk himself off and instead smeared a generous amount of lube onto one of his fingers. The smaller beads would be no problem, but he'd need to stretch himself a little to get the larger ones in. He grunted as he breached the tight ring of muscles; he was still sensitive from earlier. He bet Henry knew that too. He imagined him sitting at the table, ordering their dinner as if nothing unusual was happening in the bathroom. Or maybe he was smiling that odd little half smile of his as he thought about Jason in the men's room, lubing himself up and shoving anal beads into his ass.

Jason inserted a second finger to make sure he was ready before pushing the first bead in. It went in as easily as he had thought it would. The second one too. The third bead took a little more work—he gasped when the beads pushed past his prostate, sending a wave of heat through his already enflamed cock. The fourth bead was larger yet and stretched him almost to the point of discomfort. He knew he'd be fine once his body was used to the invasion, but for right now, he had to force himself to relax as he pushed the fifth bead into his channel. He gulped in air. One of the beads was sitting right on his prostate, rubbing against it, sending fiery pulses to the end of his leaking dick. And there was still one more bead to go. Jason licked his lips, wondering if he could do this, if he could slide the last bead home and then join Henry, sit through dinner as if nothing weird were going on.

He took a deep breath and let it out. He didn't want to disappoint the other man. He didn't want to disappoint himself. Jason added a little extra lubricant, which only made things worse. The last bead was so slippery it was almost impossible to handle. *Shit.* The only way to get it in was to shove it as hard as he could. He gasped and winced as the huge bead slid past his sphincter. For a second, his stomach tightened. Then he relaxed. He took another breath. He could do this.

Jason straightened slowly and the beads shifted around inside him, massaging his channel, rubbing against his prostate, making him moan. How was he was supposed to sit through dinner like this? It was bad enough that his ass ached, but now he was sure he was going to come just pulling his shorts back on! Maybe he *should* jerk off. No. Henry was waiting for him. *And he didn't tell me I could come.* Fuck. What was *wrong* with him? Who was Henry dictate what he could and couldn't do?

He's the guy you're submitting to.

Jason took a couple of deep breaths and tried to think of things that weren't sexy. Like old ladies.

Old ladies' underwear.

Old men in plaid shorts, knee socks, and sandals.

He giggled. Okay, that helped. He kept going with one unsavory ludicrous mental image after another until he was able to get dressed. He was thankful the men's room was still empty when he exited the stall to wash his hands.

HENRY looked up, an impish smile playing across his lips, as Jason made his way back to the table. Jason put the bag with the empty package and lube back in Henry's coat pocket and gingerly resumed his seat.

"How do you feel?" Henry asked.

"Sore—my ass, Sir, from earlier," he clarified quickly before Henry could get worried.

"Anything other than sore?"

"Stuffed like a Christmas goose."

Henry laughed. "If it's any consolation, you're the damned sexist goose I've ever seen."

Heat flooded Jason's cheeks.

"You're not used to hearing that, are you?"

"What, that I'm a sexy goose?" he couldn't help but tease.

Henry gave him a sharp look. "What did I say about lippy boys and gags?" But his expression told Jason he wasn't really angry. Or at the very least, he wasn't likely to pull out a riding crop or gag in the middle of the restaurant.

Jason hoped.

Nevertheless, he lowered his gaze and attempted to sound contrite. "Sorry, Sir. And no, Sir, I'm not used to compliments, at least not like that. I'm the guy people describe to their friends as 'he has a great personality.'"

"Jason, you are a *very* attractive young man," Henry told him with such sincerity that Jason had a hard time not believing him.

Chapter Five

THEIR dinner arrived and the conversation turned to lighter things: books, movies, television. Henry was impressed with Jason's knowledge of classic science fiction and horror, and Jason was pleased to find out that they both loved a lot of the same authors: Robert Asprin, Douglas Adams, Steven Brust, Terry Pratchett. Henry suggested Jason look up Harry Harrison—Jason had never heard of him, but based on what Henry had to say about *The Stainless Steel Rat*, he couldn't wait to read the books.

Henry appeared to derive a great deal of pleasure from watching Jason squirm in his seat as he alternately tried to relieve the pressure from the beads or get them to shift up against his prostate again because when they did, it felt so good he could almost forget how much his ass ached. Every once in a while, Henry would reach over and caress Jason's thigh under the table or shoot him a look that smoldered with such heat…. God, could a man like Henry *actually* want him as much as he said he seemed to? *Or maybe it's just that I give a great blow job*, Jason thought sullenly. Before dinner, he might not have minded, but the more time he spent just talking with Henry, the more he began to dread Sunday morning, when they would each pack up and go their separate ways.

"What are you going to school for?" Henry asked as their plates were cleared.

"Web design. I *wanted* to go to an Art Institutes school, but… well, I'm at Lansing Community College instead."

"Oh?"

Jason shrugged. "It's a long story. It's a great school and I'll probably get into State or something next year." *Fat fucking chance.* He could barely afford community college. He took a sip of his water. His father had never wanted children, never wanted him—he'd never even known Jason existed until Jason was seventeen. Because of that, Dad didn't seem to think Jason's education should be his problem. *Prick.* It would be one thing if his dad didn't have the money to send him to school, but he did. He had more money than Mom had *ever* had. He also had a girlfriend who seemed to hate Jason's very existence. Jason didn't know why. *Maybe it is my existence she hates.* Maybe it wasn't his hair or his clothes—his nipple rings. Maybe what Alicia hated was him, plain and simple.

And maybe some of it really was his mother's fault, because if she'd made better choices, things would be different.

"What about you?" Jason asked. "I mean, how did you go from massage therapy to leather work?"

"There were things I wanted that I couldn't afford to buy, so I learned how to make 'em. Eventually my friends started asking me to make them stuff too, and I decided to turn it into a side business. About eight years ago I realized my 'side business' was sucking up so much of my free time that I started referring my clients to other body workers in the area. I was ready for a change anyway," he added. "I always wanted a job that would let me travel, see the country. Meet new people." He took a sip of his water, staring intently at Jason over the lip of his glass.

"I guess that means you're on the road a lot."

"Two or three weekends a month, usually. The rest of the time I'm working."

"Do you have a shop someplace?"

"Used to. But it didn't last long. I like to set my own hours, work when I want to work, play when I want to play." His brows shot up and he smirked. When Jason blushed at the implication, Henry winked at him, then went on, "It's hard to set your own hours if you're expected to be manning the store six days a week. People who know what I do know how to find me, and when I started doing more shows, I started getting more online orders. I've got more than enough work to keep me in business."

"Where are you located out of?" Jason finally asked what he really wanted to know.

"Just outside Athens, Ohio," Henry told him.

"Never heard of it."

"It's about six hours from here."

Which meant it was probably eight hours south of home, Jason thought miserably. There went his last lingering hope that he'd ever get to see Henry again after the weekend was over.

Henry was still speaking. "It's a small community, but we've got the university, which makes it a pretty progressive little town—or at least progressive enough that no one looked at my shop too funny when I had it."

"Yeah. I mean, I guess that's good."

"It helps. You ready to go, boy?"

Jason forced a smile. He didn't want to leave, but it looked like the restaurant staff wanted to go home for the night. The place had closed ten minutes ago. "Yes, Sir, I'm ready if you are."

"You okay?" Henry asked.

"Huh? No. I'm fine," he lied. But he knew what Henry really meant. The beads were making it impossible to keep his cock down and his ass was sore from sitting for so long, but neither was causing more discomfort than he could manage. "Thanks for dinner, by the way."

"My pleasure." Henry rose from his chair, and Jason stood up too.

He helped Henry with his coat, then put on his own. A frisson of pleasure shot through him when he felt the weight of Henry's hand on the back of his neck again as they walked out of the restaurant.

"So." Henry leaned in close. "You want to drive back to the hotel with those beads in your ass or let me take them out of you in the parking lot?"

Jason bit his lip. He wasn't sure he could take the bumps in the road. Or maybe he wanted to—all that bumping and jostling. But he'd loved the added thrill of being in the parking lot earlier, when he'd gone down on Henry. He knew their chances of actually getting caught were slim, but the possibility still existed.

"I take it by the gleam in your eye, boy, you like taking risks?"

Jason blushed. "Only certain kinds of risks."

Henry got out his keys and unlocked the van's rear door. "Get in." His tone was demanding—it sent a jolt of heat right to the tip of Jason's already aching cock.

"Yes, Sir!" He scrambled in.

"Strip. Then put your coat back on."

Without a word of protest over the cold, Jason peeled out of his clothing while Henry climbed in behind him and secured the doors. Jason's cock was rock hard, throbbing. Leaking. God, he wanted to be fucked again.

"You can keep your socks," Henry instructed as Jason started to take them off.

"Yes, Sir. Thank you." It felt weird putting his coat back on over his otherwise naked body, but he was glad of the warmth. He sank to his knees and placed his hands behind his back before lowering his lips to Henry's boots—left first.

"Very good, boy."

Beaming with pleasure, Jason laid his cheek on the soft leather of Henry's boots and closed his eyes. Never in a million years would he have imagined himself lying at a man's feet, his cheek on his boots, but he couldn't think of anywhere else he wanted to be, except maybe in Henry's bed.

"As nice as this is," Henry said, his tone soft, "there's something else I'd prefer you be doing."

Jason sat up, but he kept his chin lowered, his eyes down. "Whatever you want, Sir." He meant it.

Henry leaned over and pressed his lips to Jason's mouth, claiming a deep kiss that made Jason's toes curl. Then Henry took off his coat and laid it down on the floor of the van.

"On your back. Lace your hands behind your neck," he ordered, and Jason obeyed without question. "You will not move again without my express permission. Do you understand me, boy?"

"Yes, Sir."

Henry slipped something from his pants pocket. Jason's pulse quickened when he realized it was a pair of leather gloves.

Henry put them on and knelt down next to him. "Warm enough?"

"I'm a little chilly, Sir, but it's not bad."

Henry's smile was wicked. "Let's see what I can do to make you forget about the cold." He leaned over to stroke Jason's face with gloved hands. The leather was smooth, warm. Soft. When Henry ran his fingers along Jason's lips, he kissed them, enjoying the flavor of the leather on his lips. His tongue. He closed his eyes and lost himself in Henry's gentle caresses.

A sudden sharp pain in his left nipple made Jason cry out and snap open his eyes. Henry snickered. "Didn't want you falling asleep on me, boy."

"No, Sir," Jason gasped, and his whole body tensed as Henry pinched his nipple so hard it burned. "Oh God. Please, Sir... shit! *Henry*!" Tears stung at his eyes. "That hurts!"

"Breathe through it, boy. We both know you can do this."

"No I can't!"

"That a real no?" Henry asked, easing up just a little.

Jason swallowed hard, but it was impossible to think straight.

"You took more than this earlier," Henry reminded him. "Just breathe through it."

He nodded and tried to breathe through the pain when Henry started pinching again. It wasn't long before tears were trickling down his cheeks as white-hot pain pulsed through his chest. He whined and writhed, trying hard not to pull away because that only made it hurt worse.

"Good boy," Henry soothed when he settled back into place. But then he twisted harder, forcing a ragged sob out of Jason's throat.

"*Please*! Sir! Please! It's too much!"

Henry eased up again but didn't let go. "I know it hurts, but I want you to trust me. I want you to take everything I have to give you, even when it's painful."

"Why?"

"Because I'm the one asking you to."

"I don't think I can. I'm sorry, Sir." Jason let out another sob. This time it was as much over his disappointment in himself as it was from the pain.

"You're doing great, boy. You don't have to pretend you like it, you just have to take it." Then he let go of Jason's nipple and rewarded him with a kiss that made Jason's whole body tingle. He stroked Jason's cheek and trailed his fingers down his chest. He stopped at the right nipple and teased it, caressing it, playing with the ring of surgical steel.

But Jason knew what he was going to do. His heart hammered in his chest so hard he was sure the whole world could hear it. "Please don't," he whimpered. "Please, Sir, I can't take any more."

"Yes you can."

Jason swallowed hard. He shook his head. "No. I can't. Really, I can't."

"Are you telling me to stop?"

Jason bit his lip. He knew if he said yes, Henry would stop. "I just… I'm not sure I can do it," he admitted. "I don't want to let you down."

The soft kiss Henry pressed to Jason's lips startled him. "This has nothing to do with me. This is about exploring *your* limits. You couldn't let me down if you tried. Just being here is enough to make me proud of you, Jason. But I know you can take more than you think. Trust me. Trust *yourself*. Okay?"

Jason closed his eyes for a long moment. Then, finally, he nodded. "Yeah. Yeah, okay."

"Good, boy." With that, Henry squeezed hard enough to bring a fresh cascade of tears to Jason's eyes.

"It hurts!" he sobbed. This was a hundred times worse than when he'd gotten his nipples pierced! He curled his knees up toward his stomach, but it didn't help.

"*Breathe!*"

At the sharp command, Jason tried to lie flat again. He tried to breathe. He knew he could stop it, so why wasn't he saying the one word he knew would put an end to this? He wasn't having fun! It hurt! What kind of a sadist got off on making him hurt this much?

Henry grasped hold of his other nipple so he was pinching both at the same time, twisting them, sending scorching pain through Jason's chest.

He squirmed, struggling, wanting to get away. Wanting to stay where he was, because the harder he pulled, the harder Henry squeezed. "I can't! I can't, I can't!" Jason cried.

"All right," Henry said over his incoherent sobbing. "I want you to count back from ten. Can you do that for me, boy? Count backwards from ten, and by the time you get to one, I'll let go."

"I… y-yes, Sir," he rasped. Count back from ten. He could do that. Count back from ten and by the time he was at one, it would be over and he could tell this fucking *lunatic* to take him back to the hotel! "Ten… nine… eight… shit…."

"That's the blood coming back into your nips. Keep counting, boy. You're doing great."

Easy for him to say! "Seven… six… five… oh God…." His whole chest seemed to be tingling. "Four… three… two… one… oh… fuck, oh." Instead of releasing him, Henry was kneading the muscle around his poor abused nipples. "Oh, fuck," he gasped again. The tingle that had started in his chest spread through his whole body. Then he looked up and saw Henry's smile and those baby-blue eyes, and suddenly the only place he wanted to be was right where he was.

"You did so well, boy. I am so proud of you," Henry told him as he brushed away Jason's tears.

"Please, please, Sir, will you kiss me again?"

"Anytime you like." He pressed a soft, warm kiss to Jason's lips. "You can move your hands now if you want," he whispered, then kissed him again, long and hard.

With a shudder, Jason wrapped his arms around Henry's neck and held on as tight as he could. God, it was crazy, but Henry was so warm, so strong. He made Jason feel so safe. "That was... it was incredible," he babbled. "I hated you. For a few seconds, I really hated you. I'm sorry."

"Shhh, no need to be sorry, boy." Henry scooped Jason into his lap and encircled him with his arms. "You don't hate me now, though, do you?"

"No, Sir." Jason snuggled in close. "I could never really hate you, Sir. It just... it hurt so much." When Henry wrapped his gloved hand around his dick, Jason didn't move or say anything. He simply closed his eyes and enjoyed the feeling as Henry began to slowly jerk him off.

"I want you to come for me boy. I want to see it," Henry said. He slid his other hand under Jason's ass and pressed against his hole. Jason squirmed closer to his touch, grinding his hips down as the beads were pressed against his prostate again. He felt Henry pull the largest bead out, then shove it back in. Then two.... Three.... He stroked Jason's cock harder. Faster. Four beads, out—back in again. It was agony. Ecstasy. And just as Jason's balls drew up against his body, Henry yanked the beads out and Jason came all over both of them with a shout.

"Hands and knees, now," Henry ordered, even as Jason was still quivering with aftershocks. But he didn't argue; he did as he was told because he knew Henry was going to fuck him, and that was exactly what he wanted—what he *needed*.

Jason heard the crinkle of a condom wrapper being torn open, and a few seconds later he felt Henry kneeling behind him, positioning himself. Having the tip of Henry's cock rubbing against his entrance was sheer torture—but it was the best kind of torture Jason could imagine.

"Gonna shoot another load for me, boy?" Henry's smirk was audible.

Jason arched his back, pushing against him. He was already hard again. "Yes, Sir. Please, I want to."

Henry stroked his back. "Good boy. Shoot for me, let me see how good I make you feel." With that, Henry impaled Jason so hard and so fast, he was sure he would have fallen over had Henry not been holding onto his hips. He didn't pause to let Jason catch his breath, he just clutched Jason tighter and rode him more brutally than anyone had ever ridden him before. With each stroke, he slammed into Jason's sore ass and hit his prostate until pain and pleasure were so blurred, Jason didn't know which was which, until he was seeing stars, gasping for breath, crying out, praying no one was around to hear.

He stopped being able to think even that coherently when Henry reached around with one hand to tug first on one nipple ring and then the other. It wasn't the same vicious torture Jason had been subjected to earlier, but it didn't take much stimulation to cause a shockwave of pain—pleasure—to go shooting through his chest, all the way down to his crotch. He whimpered and wriggled, mewling for more. More of what, he wasn't sure; he just knew he wanted… something. Everything.

He shuddered, nearly sobbing, as the second orgasm rocked through him.

Henry's rhythm became jerky, and Jason knew he was about to come too, so he clenched his muscles tight around Henry's cock to give him more friction. He couldn't feel Henry shoot his load because of the condom, but he was sure the other man had come just as hard as he had.

Jason was still panting when Henry scooped him back into his lap and wrapped his arms around him again. Jason sighed, closed his eyes. He feathered a soft kiss to Henry's neck. "Thank you," he whispered. He felt like he could sleep for a week.

Then Henry reached under his chin, tilted his head up, kissed him; it was hungry, a demanding kiss, and Jason gave in to it willingly. Happily. Wholeheartedly. Maybe an eight-hour drive wasn't such an insurmountable obstacle after all. Henry set his own work schedule, Jason's schedule allowed for some flexibility—and hadn't Henry talked about wanting to show him his setup at home? That had to mean he wanted to see Jason again.

"What'cha thinkin' there, boy?"

Jason shook his head, unwilling to admit to the possibilities he was considering. "Nothing much, Sir, just enjoying this."

Henry pressed a soft kiss to his forehead. "Me too."

DESPITE it being well past midnight when the pair arrived back at the hotel, the lobby was crawling with elves, faeries, vampires, airship pirates, Klingons, Vulcans, Stormtroopers, and Time Lords—and the masquerade ball wasn't until tomorrow night. Jason marveled at how every year it seemed like more people dressed up.

"This is nothing," said Henry. "You should see the crowd in Atlanta. It starts on Friday morning and doesn't end until Monday night. Hell, some folks start on Thursday."

"You've been to Dragon*Con!" Jason asked, wide-eyed, because he knew of only one four-day science fiction convention in Atlanta.

Henry chuckled. "Been a merchant there the last five years."

"I am so jealous!"

Henry scoffed. "Don't be. Derrik sticks me with watching the booth while he goes off to all the panels. By the time we close down at the end of the night, all *I* want to do is sit in the hot tub and soak, then go straight to bed. I'm lucky if I get a decent dinner."

Jason blinked. *Derrik?*

"You should think about checking it out some year. It's a lot of fun. Assuming you're not stuck working all weekend."

"I wish I could." Who was Derrik? "But like I said, I'm a poor college kid. Besides, from what I hear, all the hotels are sold out already, so even if I could afford it...." He let his voice trail off. Who the *hell* was Derrik?

"Well, if you find your way down, you *do* happen to know a guy who's got a room." Henry slid his arm around Jason's shoulders and pulled him closer. "I might even make Derrik do his share of the work for a change so I can show you around."

Okay, so maybe Derrik was just his business partner. But it didn't matter who he was or how he'd feel about Jason crashing in on them at Dragon*Con, because Jason wasn't going to Atlanta—or anywhere else—anytime soon.

He and Henry arrived at the elevators, and Jason felt a lump rising in his throat. It was late. He was sure Henry wanted to get to bed, but he didn't want the best date of his life to end. "You, uh, you wanna come up to my room or something?"

"What about your roommates?"

"No roommates, that's why I'm so tapped this weekend. I got sick of sharing a room with twenty of my 'closest friends', so I put the room on my Visa. I'll regret it later," he admitted. But now more than ever, he didn't care about the inevitable bill. He stepped in close and lowered his eyelids coyly. "So as you see, Sir, I'm all alone tonight," he drawled. "And I would really love some company."

Henry's laugh made Jason want to crawl under the nearest rock.

"Right. Good night, then." God, why did he always have to go and ruin everything with his big mouth!

"Hey." All Henry had to do was speak, and Jason stopped dead in his tracks. "I didn't mean it like that. I'm sorry." He tugged Jason by the lapels, pulling him over to a quiet spot where they could talk. "I don't think I'd be the kind of company you have in mind. I'm tapped out—and you did it to me, boy," he added in low, husky tone. "I can't remember the last time I came so many times in one day. You and that beautiful mouth of yours do things to me, boy." He leaned in and gave Jason's lips a soft, tender kiss.

It made Jason's knees go weak, and he felt himself blushing. "We could maybe just hang out if you wanted. I've got a bunch of movies on my laptop. We could watch one."

Henry cupped his cheek, running his thumb gently over it. "As tempting as that offer is—and it is, boy, trust me—the only thing I'm good for right now is crawling into bed and going to sleep. I'm not exactly a kid anymore, you know."

"You're what, thirty?"

Henry hesitated before answering, "Try forty."

Forty? Jesus. "You don't *look* forty."

"So what about you?"

"I'm twenty-two. Twenty-three in March."

"Shit."

"Hey, it's not like I'm sixteen!"

Henry still didn't look happy. Then he sighed. "I knew you were young," he admitted, "but I kept hopin' maybe you looked younger than you really were. Guess I shoulda figured different when you said you were going to community college." He shrugged, sounding genuinely apologetic. "S'pose that's what I get for not just asking."

"But you still want to see me again, don't you? I mean, not *see* me, but you know, maybe we could hook up again tomorrow night?" The words spilled out in a desperate rush.

"Jason, I'm old enough to be your father."

"So what? Look, I don't have any daddy fantasies, if that's what you're worried about. I'm not looking for a surrogate, believe me."

"So what are you looking for?"

A lover. A boyfriend.

A Dom? For someone to show him what it was he was craving— what he needed—because he didn't know himself, at least not exactly. "For some fun," he said nervously, praying Henry wouldn't see through the lie.

Henry studied him a long, nerve-racking moment. "I suppose for a weekend thing, it doesn't matter that I'm way too old for you. *Boy.*"

Jason shivered happily and dropped his gaze once more. "Forgive me if I'm out of line, Sir, but I like... that is, you're experienced, Sir, not old. I like that."

Henry snorted. "You're good for my ego, I'll give you that, boy. All right. I'm going to walk you up to your room, and you're going to give me your key." It wasn't a request.

"Yes, Sir," Jason said anyway.

"You will set your alarm for 7:00 a.m. You will have exactly one half hour to do whatever you need to do in the morning—but I expect to find you showered. And shaved."

Jason blinked. "Sir? I always shave."

"I don't mean your face, boy, although yes, I expect that smooth too. What I'm talking about is your pits. And your pubes."

Jason balked.

"That gonna cause you a problem at home, boy?"

He almost laughed. Like his father would even notice. "No, Sir."

"Good. Then you'll do it. I'll be at your room at exactly seven thirty tomorrow morning. I'll let myself in. What I expect to find is you naked in the middle of the room, kneeling with your back to the door. There will be a chair in front of you and a cup of strong black coffee in your hands. That's for me," he added sharply. "You'll get your morning coffee later. *Maybe.* Can you remember all that?"

Jason's heart thundered in his ears. "Yes, Sir."

Henry nodded. Then he leaned in and pressed a fierce kiss to Jason's yielding lips. "One last thing, *boy*," he added after their mouths parted. "You will not jerk off tonight. You won't touch that pretty little cock of yours tomorrow morning, either, except to wash it. Clear?"

"Yes, Sir."

"Good. Because for the rest of the weekend, that cock is mine and mine only." He reached around and cupped Jason's bruised ass-cheek in one hand and squeezed hard enough to bring tears to Jason's eyes. "Same goes for *this* too, boy." Henry's tone, the implication of his statement, made Jason shiver, made his heart pound faster and blood surge into his dick. Henry's eyes narrowed. "Do we understand each other?"

"Yes, Sir. Completely."

"Good." Henry sealed his mouth to Jason's a second time and didn't let go for a good long while.

JASON was shaky—giddy—when Henry left him in his room. He pulled his wallet and cell phone out of his pockets before stripping out of his clothes. After rinsing the parts of his body that smelled the worst, Jason turned his phone back on and checked his messages. Shit. There were a dozen from Terry. Five from Kendra. He skipped ahead to hers. They all boiled down to the same thing: she was worried sick about him.

Reluctantly, Jason called her back. Maybe he'd luck out and she'd called it an early night.

Luck wasn't with him; Kendra picked up in two rings. "Jason?"

In the background, he heard Terry's voice. "Where the fuck is he? Give me—*Kendra!*"

"No!" she snapped at Terry, apparently retaining control of her own phone. "Jason, where are you, what's going on? Who was that guy?"

"Who was what guy?" he asked, even though he knew the answer.

"Put it on speaker!" Terry insisted.

Then Jason heard a door slam on the other end. Terry's protests became muffled. Kendra must have ducked into a bathroom somewhere. "Who the fuck was that goon Terry saw you with earlier?"

"Henry isn't a goon!" he snapped.

"Look, just tell me you're okay," she pleaded.

Jason heard someone pounding on the door behind her. "Is he drunk?" he asked.

"Fucking—Jason, are you okay!" Kendra demanded.

"I'm fine."

"We're in the con suite—"

"I'm already in bed."

"Alone?"

"Yes, of course alone." Not that it was any of her business.

Kendra was quiet for a long moment. "Terry told me some guy practically dragged you out of the hotel."

"Terry is full of shit."

"Jason, what's going on between you two? The last time I saw you, I thought things were good."

"Maybe you should ask Terry what went wrong," he retorted. "Get him to tell you about how he blew me off two weeks ago." Angry tears stung his eyes. "I sat around for over an hour after work waiting for him to show up—he didn't even fucking call me. When I finally got a hold of him, he said he forgot." And maybe he had, Jason reasoned, but he was sick of being conveniently forgotten every time something better came up. "I'm done being his fallback guy, the one he goes to when he doesn't have any other options."

"Jason, that is not how Terry feels about you! He loves you."

Fucking... he didn't have time for this. It was late and he was tired. "I'm going to bed now," he told her. "We can talk tomorrow if you want, but I have nothing to say to Terry."

"Jason—"

"Good night." He hung up and turned his phone back off. Kendra was supposed to be *his* best friend. Why the hell was she sticking up for the guy who treated him like shit?

Chapter Six

JASON dried his hair without bothering to style it. He didn't have time; it was almost 7:20. He'd winced in pain with every step he took since he woke up. It wasn't just his bruised, battered skin; the muscles underneath ached from the pounding Henry had given him. But every time he winced, he smiled.

He put the coffee—*Henry's* coffee—on to brew, then pulled the chair into place and haphazardly made his bed. The closer it got to seven thirty, the harder his heart pounded, so that by the time he was pouring Henry's coffee into a plain white hotel mug, his hands were shaking and his mouth was dry. The clock ticked over to 7:29. His stomach turned summersaults. His dick was hard. He got into place just as he heard the key slide through the lock. He dropped his gaze to the floor, letting his chin dip a little too.

The door opened. Closed. He thought he heard the deadbolt slide into place.

Soft footsteps fell behind him. It took all of Jason's strength not to turn around and make sure it was really Henry—but who else could it be? His stomach fluttered harder and his heart pounded louder as he waited for Henry to say something.

Maybe I *should say something?* No. Henry's instructions had been clear. Wait.

He took a breath. Let it out. And waited for what seemed like a very, very long time before Henry ran a soft caress over the back of his head. Jason sighed. Then he gasped as that same hand grabbed hold of his hair and pulled his head back. Henry forced a savage kiss onto his mouth. Jason groaned and gave back as good as he got.

When he pulled back, Henry smirked at Jason's erection. "Sleep all right, boy?" he asked.

"Yes, Sir. You?"

"Oh yes." He dropped a heavy duffel bag next to the chair, sat down in front of Jason, and took the coffee cup from his hands.

Jason clasped his hands behind his back and kissed first Henry's left foot, then his right. He was wearing tall brown boots with lots of buckles and straps—definitely steampunk. Or maybe dieselpunk. Jason hadn't noticed enough of the rest of his outfit to know for sure. As he had before, he laid his cheek against Henry's boots and closed his eyes. His heart stopped racing. He felt himself relaxing. He rested there while Henry drank his coffee.

"Stand up," Henry said at length.

Jason climbed to his feet as gracefully as he could with his hands still behind his back. He also got a better look at what Henry was wearing. Definitely dieselpunk. His cap and bomber jacket were totally WWII paramilitary inspired. Jason had never considered himself any kind of uniform fetishist before, but *damn*, Henry looked good.

Henry flashed a mischievous half smile up at him. "See something you like, boy?"

"Yes, Sir." His cock was standing at attention, and much to Jason's embarrassment, a drop of pearly fluid graced the tip.

Henry's smile deepened. Warmed. "Me too. Arms over your head." He laughed when Jason raised his hands straight over his head. "How about you relax a little, bend your elbows—better," he said when Jason assumed a more comfortable pose. "Turn." He ran his fingers over Jason's armpit—Jason wriggled. "Ticklish, boy?"

"A little."

He smirked. "Other side."

Jason turned and Henry inspected the other armpit.

"Put your hands behind your neck and spread your legs."

Jason obeyed. Henry's inspection of the rest of his shaving job wasn't quite clinical, but it made Jason feel like more of an object than a person.

"Turn, boy."

Jason did as he was told—and winced when Henry touched his ass.

"Tender?" He sounded amused.

"A little, Sir." It was all he could do to keep from pulling away when Henry pressed harder, though whether he was checking for serious damage or testing Jason's resolve, Jason couldn't be sure.

"I'd say more than a little. I think I should take it easy on your ass today."

Jason breathed a sigh of relief. He hadn't thought he would be up to any more bruises, but he wasn't sure if that was him wimping out or not. "Thank you, Sir."

"Don't thank me yet, boy."

Jason heard movement behind him. A zipper being undone. Rustling. The soft clink of metal against metal. He felt Henry's hands on his left wrist and allowed the other man to maneuver his arm however he needed. Within seconds, his left wrist was snuggly secured by a thick leather cuff. A moment later, his right wrist was similarly restrained and both hands were placed back behind his neck.

Jason gave a little tug—the metal links between the cuffs gave him very little freedom of movement. It was a delicious feeling.

"Like those, do you, boy?"

"Yes, Sir. Very much." The weight of the cuffs reminded him of the collar he wanted so badly that he was seriously considering charging it to his Visa. If he did, he would end up paying three or four times the actual price—but maybe if he asked, Henry would set it aside and let him make payments? Or was that asking too much of someone he'd just met? Henry seemed generous, but—

The sudden swat to his ass made Jason yelp.

"You wanna tell me where you were, *boy*?" Henry growled.

Jason swallowed hard. He didn't want to admit to the truth. What would Henry think?

"When I ask you a question, I expect you to answer it."

"I'm sorry, Sir. I was… I was daydreaming."

Henry turned him roughly around so they were facing each other. "When you're with me, I expect to be the *only* thing on your mind, boy."

"Yes, Sir."

Henry gave him a long, measured look. "I think what you need is a little *encouragement* to do better from now on."

A tremor of genuine fear rushed through Jason at the way Henry said "encouragement." Surely Henry wouldn't take the riding crop to his ass, but what else was there for him to use as punishment? The crop was the only "toy" Jason genuinely hated.

Henry cleared his throat. "Got something to say, boy?" he inquired.

"No, Sir." He hesitated, then added, "Only that I *am* sorry, Sir."

"This isn't about being sorry. This is about learning discipline."

"Yes, Sir."

Henry pulled a pillow off the bed and set it on the floor in the far corner of the room, over by the window. Jason hung his head at the implication. He hadn't been put in the corner since he was a little kid. It was humiliating.

"I'm sure you've figured out where I want you. Go."

Jason obeyed, slumping miserably to his knees in the corner.

"Since I wasn't *expecting* to have to correct your behavior this morning," Henry told him, "you're going to have a few minutes to sit and think about this while I go get something from my room. You will not move from that spot until I return. Understand?"

"Yes, Sir."

Before he left, Henry unlinked the cuffs so that Jason's wrists were no longer bound together. "Safety precaution," he explained. "But if you move without a real good reason before I get back, you will regret it, boy."

"Yes, Sir."

Jason listened while Henry exited the room. Was this what he wanted? To be treated like a stupid little kid for making one mistake? Or… well, Henry was right, he did have a tendency to daydream. His mom used to say he spent half his time with his head in the clouds.

Despite Henry's order not to move, Jason wiped the tears from the corners of his eyes. He looked down at the heavy brown leather cuffs. They were beautiful, but at the moment, he hated them. He resented Henry. And he put his hands back behind his neck, because it was early enough in the morning that there wouldn't be a line at the elevators. Henry would be back at any moment, and as angry and scared as Jason was, he didn't want to screw this up.

He only wished he knew why he wanted it so bad.

When Henry returned, he showed Jason what he'd gone to get. Jason swallowed hard, but the lump of very real fear refused to leave his throat. The black leather hood looked like a medieval torture device with all its heavy buckles and thick straps. A studded, thickly padded blindfold piece was strapped down over the eye area; a similar piece was strapped down over the mouth area. As Henry had promised when he described a hood the day before, there were holes for the nose—they were ornamented by silver grommets. It looked like there was padding over the ears too. Henry turned it over so Jason could see the thick leather lacing up the back and the heavy clasps that would keep the hood secure around his neck.

"How long?" he asked, his voice barely a whisper.

"One hour."

Jason blinked back the fresh onslaught of tears that threatened to overwhelm him. It wasn't just fear of the hood, although he was completely terrified of it. But it was nearly eight o'clock, and Henry had to be in the dealers' room by nine thirty. If he was in the corner for an hour, there wouldn't be time for anything else.

He searched the older man's face, wondering if there was anything he could say to change his mind. "Please—" Jason began.

Henry cut him off. "I suggest you chose your words real carefully, boy," he warned.

"I… I *am* sorry, Sir. I didn't mean to disappoint you. To make you angry. I don't know how to fix it."

Henry's expression softened. "I am a little disappointed, but I'm not angry, Jason. You need to learn to be still. To focus on what you're doing. Not just for me, but for whoever you're with, because that other person, whoever they are, they deserve your full attention."

"But there's so little time this weekend as it is," he protested. He would rather Henry paddled him than spend an hour in the corner, because come Sunday, Henry would be on his way back home to Ohio, and Jason would be going home to his father's house in Ithaca, near Lansing. He blinked back more tears.

"And that's why I'm disappointed," Henry told him. "But I'll get over it. So will you. That's the thing about punishment, boy. Once it's over, it's over. No anger. No resentment. We just move on."

"Why? I mean…?" How did that work? His dad could yell at him for an hour and still not seem satisfied or any less angry. Dad simply ran out of things to say after a while.

"How about you spend some of the next hour figuring that out for yourself?"

"But when it's over, you really won't be mad at me?"

"I'm not angry now," he repeated. "I have every confidence that spending an hour in the corner like this will go a long way toward helping you learn to focus. We can talk about it afterwards, if you want to, but there's no reason for me to be upset once I've gotten my point across—unless of course you fail to correct your behavior."

"No, Sir. I mean… I mean I'll… I want to do better."

"Of that I have no doubt, boy. Now, please face the wall and put your hands behind your back."

"Sir, will you… that is, if I can ask, what will you be doing while I'm in that thing?"

"What I'm doing isn't your concern." His tone remained gentle. "All you need to know is that I won't leave this room."

Comforted only marginally, Jason turned to face the wall and moved his hands behind his back. He closed his eyes; his heart was pounding. Henry hooked the cuffs together. A moment later Jason's whole face was encased in heavily padded leather.

Henry pulled the lacing at the back of the hood, cinching it up evenly. Jason's heart raced as the leather tightened around his face, seeming to smother him. Even without the straps done up, he could barely move his jaw. He sucked in air, terrified that he wouldn't be able to breathe once the hood was secure. He tried to say "no, stop," but his words came out as muffled gibberish.

A strong hand gripped on his shoulder, stilling him. Henry leaned in close, right next to his head, so Jason could hear him through the thick leather. "Easy, boy. Just breathe. You're okay. I would never let anything hurt you."

Jason drew in a long ragged breath and let it out. Henry was right. He was okay. He wasn't being smothered. In fact, he suspected that he'd only have a hard time breathing if the hood *wasn't* laced tight.

"I meant what I said about not leaving the room," Henry promised. "If you start to freak out for real, I'll let you out and we can talk about it. I won't hold it against you. I might be punishing you for daydreaming, but I would never intentionally do anything to harm you. I only want teach you a lesson. Part of that lesson is learning to trust me. All right?"

Jason nodded. He took another slow, steady breath and resolved to accept this.

Henry finished lacing him in, then buckled the heavy straps into place, and Jason had to force himself to take another deep breath, to keep from flying into a panic again. He couldn't speak. He wasn't even sure he could turn his head. But Henry would be here. He would make sure nothing happened. And when it was over, they'd still have half an hour. How many blow jobs had Jason given and received in less time than that? There was a lot two people could do in thirty minutes.

Henry gave his shoulder a light squeeze, and stepped away, leaving him all alone in dark solitude. Jason strained to hear where Henry went, what he was doing. Was he sitting down on the bed? Did he have the TV on? If he did, he must have the sound muted. Maybe Henry had a book tucked into his duffel bag and was reading it. Or maybe he'd helped himself to Jason's laptop. He wouldn't mind. He only wanted to know where in the room Henry was. He wanted to know he was really watching. But all he could hear was the sound of his own heart pounding in his ears.

Jason squirmed. He wondered how much time had gone by. Probably not more than a few minutes. God. An hour like this? How did prisoners in solitary confinement manage being isolated for days, months sometimes, without going completely insane? He wasn't sure he was going to make it an hour. His ass ached; his shoulders were starting to cramp. This wasn't fun! It was stupid. So what if he'd been daydreaming? Anger roiled up in Jason. He couldn't get the cuffs off, couldn't yank the goddamned hood off his head, but if he got up and walked in the direction of the bed, Henry would be sure to get the hint. He was done. He wanted out!

Or did he?

Would Henry even let him out?

Yes. That was one thing Jason was sure of. If he made it clear that he was through, Henry wouldn't keep him like this. But he doubted he would have any hope of anything else with Henry either, and despite the anger and humiliation, he desperately wanted to get back to the way things had been last night. He wanted to be kissed. Held. He wanted to be kneeling in front of Henry, sucking that gorgeous dick of his.

He wanted to come so hard he forgot his own name.

Deprived of sight and sound, he tried to concentrate on what he could smell. What he could feel. Henry was right: with the hood on, the only scent that reached his nose was well-oiled, well-cared-for leather. It was rich. Earthy. Delicious. The leather hood was cool against his skin. Soft. The hood wasn't actually uncomfortable, it only looked scary.

Jason shifted his arms, trying to relieve some of the pressure on his shoulders. His hour had to be close to being up. He just had to hang in for a few more minutes. Even though the morning was mostly shot, there was still tonight to look forward to, and maybe tomorrow. Maybe Henry would let him hang out in his booth today. They could talk, keep getting to know each other.

He shifted again. He wanted to sit, but Henry had said "kneel."

God, how much longer?

Henry had made his point. Why couldn't he put an end to this already? It wasn't like either of them was having any fun. Jason tried to say as much aloud, but the only thing he could get past his lips was a desperate sounding "hmph!" Damn it! What if he got a charley horse or something?

"Hmph!" he repeated.

Henry continued to ignore him. Maybe the bastard had lied; maybe he wasn't there at all. Oh fuck. Real panic set in and Jason started to struggle, pulling at the cuffs. The clasp between them held fast. *"Hmph!"* he cried.

Nothing.

Trust.

Henry had said to trust him. Jason stilled. Henry was there, he had to be.

"Hmph?" he tried again, more plaintively. *Please just let me know you haven't left me all alone.*

He nearly jumped out of his skin when he felt the light touch of the other man's hand on his shoulder. Jason tried to lean into him, wanting Henry to hold him, but Henry pulled away.

"Hmph!" *Please!*

Henry reached out again and gave his shoulder a gentle squeeze. He didn't tell Jason how long it had been or even say a word, but Jason knew he was there. Henry was watching over him, just like he'd promised he would be.

I'm safe.

Jason settled back into place, determined to ride out the rest of his time as the picture of contrite submission. Discipline, he reminded himself. This was about discipline and focus.

He tried to settle himself in the moment, to just be, but quickly found his mind wandering to places he didn't want it to go. What would his father say if he saw Jason like this? Jesus. Would Dad punch Henry out or walk away in disgust?

Probably walk away. It wasn't a very heartening realization, but Jason knew it was the truth. *God, why won't he just send me away to school so I can get out of his hair?* His father didn't want him, but he made it so it was impossible for Jason to leave. Jason didn't make enough money waiting tables to afford to pay for school and get his own place. He was stuck. His life was miserable.

Until yesterday.

Jason replayed yesterday over in his head. Not just the kinky stuff but all of it, the things they'd talked about at dinner and on the drive back to the hotel. The way Henry kissed him. The fact that despite the huge age gap, they had a lot in common. The way Henry made him feel when he held Jason in his arms. God, did he have any kind of a shot at something real with a guy like him? Henry had been pretty clear about it being only for the weekend, but then he'd invited Jason to Dragon*Con. Or was that just talk?

What do I have to do to get him to want me?

He jumped again when he felt Henry's hands on his shoulders. He hadn't been wriggling, had he? He'd lost track of time. And sensation in his feet.

"You still with me?" Henry asked, his voice muffled by the thick leather.

Jason nodded. He forced himself to remain perfectly still otherwise, even though all he wanted to do was lean into Henry, to have Henry wrap his arms around him.

"Good boy," Henry told him. "You're doing great. I know this isn't easy. It's why I chose this particular punishment. I'm incredibly proud of you right now, I want you to know that."

Jason's heart swelled with joy at his words.

"Your time is half up," Henry went on. "I thought this might make the rest of it a little more interesting. Consider it a reward for doing so well."

Jason gasped when he felt a tug at his left nipple ring. The heavy pressure remained constant. A moment later, he felt a similar tug at the right nipple. Weights? It had to be. They weren't heavy enough to be uncomfortable, but the thought of having his already sore, bruised nipples weighted down for the next thirty minutes was daunting. And how was it only a half an hour had gone by? It felt like days!

Jason took a breath. Let it out. He could do this. He could make Henry proud of him.

"TIME'S up," Henry announced quietly, laying both hands on Jason's arms. Before he loosened the hood, he released Jason's wrists and rubbed some of the tension out of his shoulders. Jason sighed in contentment, especially when Henry told him to sit and take some of the pressure off his knees. Mostly, however, Jason was grateful for Henry's touch. His attention. The soft kiss Henry pressed to his shoulder.

The hood came off quicker than it had gone on—*thank God.* Jason blinked at the brightness of the room. He tilted his head from side to side. Henry reached around and gently removed the weights from his nipple rings and told him to turn around.

"It is customary," Henry went on in a cool, detached tone, "to thank your Master for the time he's taken to correct bad behavior." He stood so that his boots were practically under Jason's nose.

Jason swallowed. Master? But Henry had said his dick and ass belonged to him, at least for the weekend. Jason had agreed. So he leaned obediently over and kissed Henry's boots. "Thank you, Master," he whispered.

"Louder, please."

"Thank you, Master." The word sounded strange coming out of his mouth.

Henry told him to sit up; he pulled the chair over and sat down in front of Jason. "What *exactly* are you thanking me for, boy?"

Jason nibbled at his lower lip. He didn't feel especially grateful for the last hour—but then he remembered Henry telling him how well he'd done, how proud he was. Somehow, that made it all worth it. He remembered the things Henry had said to him before he put the hood on, about learning to focus, being more disciplined. "I was daydreaming when I should have been paying attention to you. You're right, Sir. Master. It's a bad habit. Whoever I'm with deserves my full attention. I'll try to remember that from now on. Thank you for... for helping me get a better handle on it."

"Good boy. Now. How are you feeling?"

Jason considered the question, but he honestly didn't know how to answer it. "Okay, I guess."

Henry gave him a sharp look.

"Physically, I'm fine," he elaborated. "I just... it was hard. I hated it."

"Punishment isn't meant to be easy or fun. Come here, boy." He opened up his arms, inviting Jason into his lap.

Jason curled into the warm safety of Henry's chest immediately, happy to have the other man's arms around him again. "Thank you, Sir."

"For?"

"Holding me."

"I like it too," Henry admitted, feathering a soft kiss to the top of Jason's head. "You're a good fit for me." Then he ducked his head a little, like he hadn't actually meant to say that aloud. Henry cleared his throat. "So. Do we need to talk about anything?"

"No, Sir. I mean, I went through all kinds of feelings when I was in the corner. I was angry, hurt, scared. But I'm okay now." He ventured a shy look up at Henry's face. "And I really have learned a lesson. You're right about the daydreaming thing. I guess I hadn't stopped to think about how it affects other people before. It's pretty rude."

Henry tilted his chin up a little higher and pressed a soft kiss to his lips. "I have something for you, if you want it. It's *only* for the weekend," he cautioned, "but I thought you might like to wear this." Henry reached behind Jason and pulled a slender blue leather collar out of his bag. It wasn't half as beautiful as the gray one, but it was a *real* collar, not some cheap dog collar.

His heart hammered in his chest so loudly he was sure the whole world could hear it—but he didn't care. "Yes. Please. Sir—Master." A collar made the arrangement real. Even if it was only for two days.

Henry chuckled. "Then get on your knees in front of me, boy. And get that fucking mop out of my way," he snapped.

Jason obeyed immediately, although he hated leaving the security of Henry's—no, his *Master's*—lap. He knelt and lifted his hair out of the way. He could barely breathe as Henry secured the thin leather collar around his neck. It didn't have a lock, but Jason had no intention of taking it off until Henry forced him to. He clasped his hands behind his back and kissed Henry's boots, then happily rested his cheek against the soft leather for a long moment.

"Sit up. One of us is going to get off this morning. Have any idea who?"

"You, Master?"

Henry smirked. "Good answer, boy." He unzipped his pants— Jason's breath caught at the sight of the leather thong he was wearing. "Like that, do you?"

"Yes, Sir. But I think I like what's under it better."

Henry rolled his eyes. "That mouth of yours is going to get you into trouble."

"Then I guess it's a good thing you like what I do with it."

Henry drew his half-hard cock out. "You've got fifteen minutes, boy."

Jason went happily to work, ignoring his own aching cock as he concentrated on getting Henry off. When he finished, Henry pulled him back into his lap and pressed a deep kiss to his mouth. Jason returned as good as he got, savoring it. Savoring the warmth of Henry's arms around him. Terry never kissed him after Jason went down on him. He said it was weird, that he didn't like the taste of his own cum in Jason's mouth.

Henry's smile told Jason that Henry didn't mind the taste at all. Maybe he even liked it. "As much as I would love to spend the whole day here with you, I've got to get to work," Henry told him.

Jason sagged in disappointment. "Yes, Sir." It was his fault they hadn't had more time this morning.

"None of that. What did I say about punishment?"

"That when it's over, it's over. We move on."

"Good boy. Now. I want you to get dressed—but do not put that turtleneck back on. I want that collar out where folks can see it."

"Yes, Sir!" That was an order Jason was happy to obey.

"I want you to have some fun today. Catch up with friends, go to a panel, gaming, whatever. However, you are not allowed in the dealers' room for any reason."

"Sir?"

"You don't have a whole lot of money to spend anyway, so there's no reason for you to be shopping, and I don't want you hanging around me all day. I'll take up plenty enough of your time tonight."

Jason felt equal measures of disappointment and excitement—but really, it didn't matter what he felt. There was only one acceptable answer. "Yes, Master."

Henry nodded his approval. "I expect you to knock on my door at exactly seven thirty tonight. We'll be eating dinner around nine. Plan your day accordingly." He gave Jason one last kiss before shooing him off his lap. Henry handed him back his key and picked up the duffel bag. He paused at the door and turned back around. "Just so we don't have any misunderstandings later, who owns that pretty little sex-starved cock of yours, boy?"

Heat rushed into Jason's cheeks. "You do, Master."

"And who is the only person who gets to touch it?"

"You, Sir."

Satisfied, Henry left him.

Jason groaned in utter frustration. Sex-starved was right! Never mind that he'd gotten off several times yesterday and spent an hour in the corner like a little kid this morning. He was hard, horny, and... happy. He closed his eyes and wrapped his brain around that for a minute. *This* was exactly what he wanted.

"Master," he whispered aloud. *Master.*

Jason took several deep breaths and finally went into the bathroom to splash his face with cool water. It only helped a little, but at least he was able to get himself zipped into a pair of comfortable jeans. Obeying Henry's instructions not to wear the turtleneck was easy, at least. He wanted to show off the collar, even though no one was likely to think anything of it at a con. To most people, a collar was simply a fashion accessory.

He'd just slipped into a black pin-striped shirt when someone knocked at his door. Jason frowned. The only person who knew he had a room was Henry, but he should be in the dealers' room.

Maybe he's checking up on me?

Jason couldn't imagine why; it was barely ten thirty.

"Jason?" Kendra called out.

What the hell? He peered out the peephole to make sure she was alone before opening the door. "How the fuck did you know where I was?"

"Hello to you too," she snapped right back.

"Sorry." He stepped aside so she could come in, hastily buttoning up his shirt, hoping she hadn't noticed the dark-purple bruises that were his nipples and areolae. "I didn't tell anybody I was getting a room. How did you find me?"

Kendra flopped down on the bed. She was pretty girl. Woman. She was a year older than him and had long dark hair and a petite figure. Today she was wearing a classic *Star Trek* minidress with knee-high boots—she'd done classic sixties makeup to match.

"It didn't take a rocket scientist, you know," she told him. "When you pulled your little disappearing act last night, I started asking around. Since no one knew where you were, I figured you must've gotten your own room—and I'm pissed at you for that, by the way. You could have stayed with me and Sue. I know you're fucking broke."

"I didn't want to stay with you and Sue." *And whoever you brought back to your room.* Kendra and her girlfriend had a knack for picking up guys, sometimes even couples, to play with. Which was fine, but not if he wanted to get any sleep or maybe have company of his own. "You still haven't told me how you found my room."

She flashed a randy smile. "I batted my eyelashes at the front desk clerk. Poor thing, I probably could have gotten any number I asked for." Even though she was short, Kendra had legs that didn't quit, which meant she got all kinds of attention when she wore miniskirts.

"Shit," Jason cursed.

"I didn't tell anybody," she promised him. "But you owe me an explanation. What the fuck is going on? I'm supposed to be your best friend, remember?"

Jason refrained from reminding her that last night she'd acted more like Terry's best friend than his. He sat down on the floor across from the end of the bed, with his back propped up against the bureau. The floor was hard and his ass hurt, but he couldn't help the smile that played across his lips. "I met someone yesterday."

"I got that part. Terry said he was a real jerk."

Jason snorted. "Like he has room to talk."

"Jason—"

"No. I'm sick of his bullshit. Terry only wants me when he's lonely or horny or both. Why should I keep settling for that?"

"I don't know what happened between you two the other week, but it sounds like you're totally overreacting. He's really upset."

"What about *me*?"

"Jason, *talk* to him, give him a chance to explain."

"He did explain. He said he 'forgot' that we had plans."

She let out an exasperated sigh. "So you're going to break it off with your boyfriend of the last five years for some guy you just met?"

"Terry's *not* my boyfriend. I mean, maybe I started calling him that a couple of years ago, and maybe it was even true, I don't know." He'd met Terry at a con—this one, in fact—the year his mom died, the year he went to live with his father. But his and Terry's relationship had gone through so many different phases—from friends with fringe benefits, to boyfriends, and finally to whatever it was they were now—that Jason didn't even know where they stood half of the time. "All I know for sure is that I'm sick of being nothing but a piece of ass to him—and not even the one he comes to first anymore. I know he's seeing other guys."

"Did he *tell* you he was seeing other guys?"

"He doesn't have to. Look, maybe it's my fault for being busy with school and work all the time. Maybe he got sick of waiting on me. I just know that I'm tired of all the bullshit and I want it to be over."

"Please talk to him before you go and do something rash."

"*No.*" He hesitated. Reconsidered. "All right, maybe." He supposed he at least owed it to Terry to tell him face to face that they were through.

Kendra didn't look happy, but she let it drop, at least for the moment. "You feel like cruising the dealers' room with me? I want to catch up with Sandy and talk to her about a new corset. Something in *white.*"

"You and Sue finally set a date?" he asked. Kendra and her girlfriend had been talking about a commitment ceremony for months, but this was the first he'd heard of actual plans being made.

"October—maybe November. We haven't nailed down the weekend yet, but we're getting close. You've got to promise me you'll be there."

"I wouldn't miss it for anything."

"Good." She stood up, giving him an expectant look.

"Go on without me. I want to head up to the con suite to get something to eat. Then maybe I'll catch a panel or something."

Kendra frowned but didn't argue. "How about dinner, then? My treat. We can go to that Middle Eastern place you like so much. We have a million things to catch up on."

And how much did he want to bet Terry would be there too? "I've kinda got dinner plans already. Sorry."

"The new guy." It wasn't a question, it was an accusation.

"Yes."

"Jason, be careful, okay? I've got a really bad feeling about this guy."

Chapter Seven

THE first thing Jason noticed when he stepped into Henry's room was the number of toys laid out on Henry's bed. Amongst them were the bearskin flogger, the paddle, a couple of canes, and the single-tail whip. That last one scared him to death.

But it was the man himself who really made Jason's heart race. Henry had changed out of his dieselpunk outfit into all leather. All black. The shirt reminded Jason of a cop's uniform shirt, with short sleeves, silver buttons, and breast pockets. He even had on a black leather tie and a pair of motorcycle gloves. The black leather uniform pants were formfitting, and the boots were tall and thick soled.

Jason's cock pressed against his jeans.

"Strip," Henry said instead of the more customary greeting of "hello."

Jason didn't mind. He hoped getting out of his clothes was the first step toward getting laid—getting off—and eagerly unbuttoned his shirt while Henry watched him with keen interest.

Henry took his seat in the chair that stood in the middle of the room, and leaned back. "Have you been a good boy today, or have you been jerking off behind my back?"

"No, Sir. I mean... yes, Sir. I... no, I haven't touched myself, Sir." Heat tinted his cheeks pink.

Henry looked amused. "How would I know if you'd jerked off?"

Jason blinked, trying not to feel hurt and hoping Henry was just testing him. He wanted Henry to trust him too. "You wouldn't know it, Sir." He peeled off his shirt and folded it neatly. "But *I* would."

"And?"

"And my dick belongs to you, Sir. Master."

"How does that make you feel, boy?"

Shit, this *was* a test, just not the kind Jason had thought at first. Henry was making him talk. "I feel good, Sir." He finished undressing and stood in front of his Master wearing nothing but the collar the other man had put around his neck that morning.

"Good, huh?" Henry ran his leather-covered fingers lightly over Jason's hips, his thighs, and back up again, over his chest. The gloves were smooth. Soft. Henry rubbed his thumbs over Jason's bruised nipples until they were throbbing, standing at attention—until his cock ached. Until Jason was whimpering. "Why does it make you feel good to belong to me, boy?"

Jason swallowed hard. He could barely think straight and Henry wanted him to answer a question like that? "I... it just... I like it when you say you're proud of me. I want to please you so much. I like it when you take control. Yesterday you told me you wanted me to be myself, to just be whoever I am, and I'm trying so hard to do that. Only I *don't* know who I am. You're... I'm figuring it out, but only because of you."

"No, boy. I'm just helping you see yourself better, that's all. I'm not so special."

"Yes you are. If... if it weren't for you, I'd be terrified. More terrified than I am already."

"Why are you scared?"

"Because I feel like a total freak for wanting this stuff. Only when I'm with you... when I'm with you it's *not* scary and I don't feel like a freak. With you it all feels right."

"Damn."

Jason looked at him, wondering if he'd said something wrong, but Henry smiled. It wasn't his usual lopsided smirk, it was different. It made Jason's pulse race.

"Kneel," Henry said, and Jason slid obediently to his knees. "I'd like to hear what you did with yourself today."

He shrugged. "I caught up with friends, mostly."

"Did you have fun?"

"Yeah. I mean yes, Sir."

Henry chuckled. "I don't stand on that much protocol, boy. You don't have to end every sentence with 'Sir'." He leaned back in the chair and invited Jason to tell him everything he'd done since they parted company earlier in the day.

Jason decided not to mention Kendra's visit. "There are people here I only get to see a few times a year. I ran into a couple of them in the con suite, and we hung out for a while, just talking. Then I went down to the boardroom and caught a couple of episodes of *Utena*. It's an anime show. Probably my favorite one." Terry hated anime. Or, more to the point, he hated the anime Jason liked and constantly rode him about wanting to watch Japanese schoolgirls.

If Henry thought anything of it, however, it didn't show on his face. "You do anything else?" he asked.

"I went to the art show and walked around." Jason kept telling himself that "next year" he'd hang some of his own work, but somehow "next year" never came. He didn't have enough time to paint, anyway—even when he did, his dad did nothing but bitch about the mess. The smell. How expensive oil paints were and how Jason had better things to spend his money on. "How was your day?" he asked, wanting to divert Henry from the subject of art.

Henry blinked, as if surprised by the question, but then he smiled again, that same quiet, happy smile. "Pretty good. We did about six hundred in sales—that isn't great, but for our first year here it's not bad, either. It usually takes a couple of years for people to get to know you." He shrugged. "I took a couple of commissions for the lady who does the corsetry work you saw in my booth. I got a chance to talk to the corset lady here too."

"She's *really* good."

Henry quirked an eyebrow in Jason's direction. "Might like to see you in one of her creations."

Jason blinked. But then he shrugged. He would wear anything Henry asked him to if meant getting to see him again.

Henry leaned closer and ran his fingertips over Jason's cheek. Jason sighed and closed his eyes, inhaling the scent of the leather glove. He pressed a soft kiss to Henry's palm like he had before. Then he turned his head and started sucking on one of Henry's fingers, treating it the way he'd treat Henry's cock if he had that in his mouth instead.

Henry chuckled softly at his efforts. "You want something, you have to ask for it, boy."

"I... I know."

Henry just smiled. "You ever wear a cock ring?"

Jason blushed bright, hot red.

"That a yes, boy?"

"Sort of."

"Sort of?"

"I bought one about a year ago. I only tried to wear it once. I didn't like it." He could tell by the expression on Henry's face that it didn't matter. Henry was going to make him wear one now.

"What kind was it?" Henry asked anyway.

"Just a plain metal ring, Sir."

Henry got up and went over to where his bags were packed up in the corner. A moment later he was back in his chair and told Jason to hold out his hands. The thing he dropped into them looked more like a leather harness than a ring. The tight woven leather sheath would cover half his penis—or at least Jason couldn't imagine that part going anywhere else, because no way in hell he was letting anybody put his balls in that part of the contraption! There was another band of leather, much thinner, that he was pretty sure *was* supposed to go around his testicles. The last strap had several sturdy D rings on it and looked like it went around the whole package.

"You look nervous, boy."

He nodded. Nervous was an understatement.

"Talk to me, Jason."

At the sound of his name, Jason lifted his gaze to meet his Master's—Henry's—gaze. "I've never seen anything like that before, Sir."

"Do you remember your safewords?"

He nodded.

"*Out loud*, please."

"Sorry, Sir. My safewords are 'no' and 'slow down'."

"All right." Henry took the leather harness from him. "On your feet. Hands behind your back."

Jason did as he was told.

As Henry strapped the leather harness into place around Jason's cock and balls, he spoke, his tone gentle. "This is more of a chastity device than a cock ring—it won't make it impossible for you to come, just damned difficult. Uncomfortable too, although you might get off on it." He winked up at Jason. "Of course if you do get off without permission, what happens next *won't* feel good. Clear?"

"Yes, Sir."

"If we needed to make sure you wouldn't come no matter what, I'd use something a little sturdier. There." He sat back and surveyed Jason's cock, an appreciative look on his face. That, if nothing else, made wearing the thing worth it. "How's the fit?"

"All right, I think. It doesn't hurt, it's just… it feels a little weird, Sir."

Henry nodded. "You'll have to tell me if it gets uncomfortable at any point. The last thing I want to do is damage your dick."

"Don't you mean *your* dick, Sir?" Jason teased.

It earned him a swat directly to the organ in question. He winced even though Henry had only tapped him hard enough so that Jason could feel it, not hard enough to actually hurt. Henry clearly wasn't angry, he was grinning too hard. "What have I said about lippy boys?" he asked.

"Lippy boys get gagged, Sir."

"And are you saying by your backtalk that you *want* to be gagged?"

"No, Sir. I wouldn't want to deprive you of the pleasure of my mouth, Sir. If you want it, that is."

Henry glowered—although Jason didn't miss the good humor twinkling in his gorgeous blue eyes. "On your knees, boy, and give me a good reason not to gag you." His hand was already on his zipper, undoing his pants. He brought out his dick, and Jason went happily to work, taking it to the hilt in one swallow—but then teasing him mercilessly. Playfully. Since he didn't have a time limit, he wasn't in a rush and could pay plenty of attention to Henry's balls before going back to his cock.

At last, Henry shot his load into the back of Jason's throat; Jason swallowed every drop greedily, laving Henry's shaft thoroughly, not letting go until he was completely soft.

Jason, however, was left hornier than ever, even though there seemed little his cock could do about it. The straps of leather encasing him prevented a full erection. Henry was right, it was uncomfortable.

"All right," Henry said as Jason tucked him back into his pants and zipped him back up, "you've earned a reprieve from the gag. *For now*. Get your ass over to the end of the bed and bend over."

Jason hesitated. His ass was already sore.

Henry cupped his cheek and his tone softened. "Trust me, boy. I will never intentionally hurt you beyond what you can take. I will never damage you. I may draw blood tonight," he cautioned. "I plan to use the single tail."

Jason licked his lips nervously. The single tail scared him more than anything else Henry had shown him yesterday, even the hood.

Henry seemed to understand perfectly. "We'll talk about it if we need to," he promised. "But for right now, I want you to trust me enough to do as I say."

Jason swallowed down the lump of fear. "Yes, Master." He got up and positioned himself on the end of the bed. Since Henry hadn't said what he should do with his arms, he used them to cushion his forehead against the mattress.

"Spread your legs, boy."

He did. A moment later, he felt something snug being fitted around his left ankle, then his right. Cuffs. Henry nudged his feet further apart, and... a spreader bar? Jason couldn't see, but it sure felt like it.

"How do you feel?"

"Pretty helpless," Jason admitted. His hands were still free, but there was no way he was going anywhere with his legs spread wide like they were. He couldn't even crawl.

"Not half as helpless as you'd feel if I had real equipment here," Henry told him.

Jason couldn't help but smile, wondering what Henry's play space looked like. His cock strained uncomfortably against the leather.

"How would you feel if I put on some music?"

"You mean I get a say in something?"

Henry's hand came down hard on his ass, and Jason yelped. "No. I asked how you *felt* about it, *boy*."

Despite the stinging pain, Jason grinned. They both knew he was being a smartass on purpose. "Music's fine with me, Sir." He got comfortable again while Henry left him to put something on. Jason was surprised when he heard some sort of string ensemble playing. Metallica? "That's really cool."

Henry chuckled. "Glad you approve. All right. I have one rule for tonight," Henry told him as he sat down on the other bed. "You will not speak except to tell me to stop or slow down. Understand?"

Jason nibbled his lip. It seemed like an odd rule for someone who was always trying to get him to talk more. Maybe he'd been too flippant? But it was hard to believe Henry was annoyed by his occasional smartass remark. He smiled at them too. "Sir—Master—may I ask a question first?"

"You may."

"What happens if I say 'stop'?"

Henry frowned. "I thought we went over this. If you tell me to stop—if you're serious and don't just need me to slow down a minute—I'll stop. "

"No, I mean what happens *after* you stop." Would Henry untie him, send him on his way, say they were through for the weekend? Forever?

Henry's smile was warm. Understanding. It was kind. How could a man who left him black and blue be so kind?

"After I stop, we talk about what happened, why you needed me to stop or slow down. If you need some time to catch your breath or something to drink, I'll give it to you. Then we'll discuss whether or not we're going to continue with what we'd been doing or try something else. Or if I'm just going to untie you and… and let you tell me if you want me to fuck you or that I should just go straight to hell. Okay?"

"Yeah, okay." He couldn't imagine telling Henry to go to hell and actually getting away with it, but he understood the other man's point. If he told Henry to stop, he would stop, and whatever they did next would be up to him. Jason took a breath. Let it out. He could do this. He wanted this. He wanted Henry to be the one to give it to him. "I'm ready, Master."

"Good boy." Henry stood and picked up the bearskin flogger. He trailed the tips over Jason's back, lightly caressing his skin. "Such a very, very good boy," he crooned.

Jason sighed, arching his back into the wonderful sensation.

Henry chuckled. "You won't be making such happy little noises in a minute."

Jason nodded. He knew that. It didn't matter. He turned his face to the mattress, supporting his forehead on his arms, and enjoyed the soft caress of the leather while it lasted.

"I'm going to be working your back, not your ass," Henry explained. "Although I've got a special treat for *that*, later on," he promised. "Working a man's back is a tricky, but I've had enough experience to know where not to hit. Both the flogger and the single tail are short enough that I'll have good control over where they land. But I still need you to lie still." He trailed his fingers lightly, lovingly, over Jason's spine. "Remember. No talking. No begging. Nothing except your safewords."

Jason nodded to acknowledge his understanding.

Just like the day before, Henry started out with slow, gentle strokes. He worked in time with the music, each stroke warming Jason's skin. Jason sighed and felt himself sinking into the mattress, into pure bliss, even though he knew what was coming.

The first genuinely hard thud of leather against his left shoulder made him wince, almost cry out—but there was a new rule. No talking. Jason struggled to obey it, gritting his teeth. He let out only a small whimper when the next blow caught his right shoulder. Henry continued to alternate between his left and right sides, each stroke heavier, louder, more painful, than the last.

"You're doing great, boy," Henry told him softly. "But it's going to get harder, not easier, from here on out. Do you want me to stop?"

Jason shook his head.

"Good boy." Henry leaned over and pressed his lips to Jason's shoulder.

Jason turned his head, hoping—*yes*! Henry met his lips, kissed them. He fisted his hands in Jason's hair and pulled him into a better angle. His kiss was as brutal as the beating he had just given Jason's back. Jason surrendered to it. When Henry released his mouth, Jason met his gaze. Henry's expression was hard to read. Desire. Pride. Maybe... maybe something more? Jason's heart pounded.

JASON was flying so high on endorphins he hardly noticed that the flogging had stopped or that a gloved hand was easing its way over his back. "I need to check in with you, boy." Henry's breath was soft against his ear. "You can speak, but only to answer my questions. You still with me?"

"Yes, Sir." Jason turned so he could look at his Master's face. He was pretty sure he was going to ache all over in the morning, but at the moment he felt…. Fuck, he didn't have words to describe it, he just knew it was good. It was right. This was who he was.

"I'm going to take the spreader bar off for a few minutes," Henry told him. "I want you to sit down and drink some water."

"Yes, Master." The words came easily.

A few minutes later he was sitting on a pillow on the floor, carefully not leaning up against anything. Henry pressed a bottle of water to his lips. Jason drank without hesitation. He didn't realize how thirsty he was until the bottle was empty.

"I'd like to gag you before we start again. I'll be using the single tail, and it's going to be hard for you to keep quiet without it. You'll probably appreciate something to bite down on too. Most people do."

Jason swallowed hard. He'd been pulled down to earth a bit by the words "single tail." "What if I need you to stop? Or slow down?"

"I'll check in with you if you start to sound like you're in distress. Or at the first sign of blood."

"Blood?"

"I'm not going to draw blood intentionally, but it's likely to happen. I'm gonna push you, Jason, but not past your comfort zone. The idea isn't to 'make' you safeword, it's to help you figure out where your limits are. I'll take it slow."

Jason sucked in a breath. Let it out again. The thought of getting hit so hard he bled was terrifying, but his trust in Henry was absolute. "All right. Will you do something first?"

"What do you need?"

"Kiss me again?"

Henry smiled. He cupped Jason's face firmly in both hands and pulled him in for a tender, all-consuming kiss. Jason moaned when Henry's tongue swept into his mouth. His cock ached, but he knew he wouldn't be allowed to come anytime soon, so he didn't bother asking. Instead, he wrapped his arms around his Master's neck and held on tight, rubbing his leather-encased cock against the other man's thigh—driving himself insane because he wanted to come so badly—until Henry pulled away and told him to get back into place.

Still breathless from the kiss, Jason did as he was told—and yelped when he felt the sharp sting of the riding crop on his ass.

"That's for humping me," Henry snarled.

Jason swallowed and stole a look in his direction. He couldn't tell if Henry was actually pissed or not.

"Nothing to say for yourself, boy?"

"It won't happen again, Master."

"If it does, I can promise that you'll regret it. Your pleasure comes from me, nowhere else. You don't take it. You don't even ask for it unless I tell you that you can. Understood?"

"Yes, Sir."

Henry secured the spreader between his ankles once more and told Jason to open his mouth so he could secure the hard rubber ball gag into place. Jason obeyed. It wasn't big, but it wasn't comfortable and it tasted awful. He closed his eyes as Henry—no, his Master—buckled the leather straps behind his head. Jason resolved to take it gracefully. Obediently. His reward was a soft caress in almost the exact same spot where Henry had swatted him with the crop. Jason moaned, started to press back into his hand, but then thought better of it. He lay still and simply accepted the loving touch.

"Ready, boy?" Henry's tone had lost all its harshness.

Jason nodded. He wasn't sure he was really ready. He wasn't even sure why he was there, letting this happen to him, but he was and he wanted to make Henry proud. What he felt next wasn't the sting of a whip. It was Henry's lubed, still gloved fingers rubbing slow circles around his entrance. Jason moaned louder into the gag.

"I wanted to make things a little more interesting for you." With that, Henry slid one finger smoothly into Jason's pliant body. "But I want you to stay still. Try to fuck my finger and you're in for a world of hurt—and I do not mean the good kind," he warned.

Jason nodded. He groaned in pure ecstasy when Henry pressed against his prostate, but he forced himself to lie still. Henry continued to rub the gland, sending wave after wave of heat through Jason's dick. It felt so good it hurt. He was whimpering even before Henry pushed a second and then a third finger into him. Henry was right: without the gag, he would be begging for more. As it was, he was moaning, squirming, as he tried to lie still. He was going to go crazy if Henry didn't let him come!

He cried out when Henry's fingers left his ass.

Then something cool and smooth touched his hole; he turned to see what it was.

"Eyes down, boy, or I'll use the blindfold."

Frustrated, Jason obeyed. Henry slid something into him—a plug maybe? Or a dildo? It felt so good to be filled again, stretched to capacity. God, how was he ever going to be able to go back to self-gratification after this?

The toy grazed over his prostate—and suddenly started vibrating! Jesus fucking Christ!

Henry chuckled. "Like that, do you?"

Helpless to do anything else, Jason nodded.

"Good. Because here's where it's going to start getting interesting." Henry began pumping the vibrator in and out of Jason's ass, sending wave after wave of pleasure shooting to his dick, sending him into a very different sort of orbit than the earlier endorphin rush. Jason squeezed his hands into tight balls in an effort not to thrash around, not to rip the gag out of his own mouth and demand to be fucked. To come.

Then, suddenly, he felt the painful sting of the lash on his upper back. He shrieked into the gag.

"Told you so," Henry teased. He held the vibrator snugly inside Jason's ass—and then suddenly, fire spread through Jason's back once more as the lash came painfully down on his skin. Jason screamed into the gag and tears streamed down his cheeks—but all the while, the vibrator was still buzzing madly against his prostate, and it felt so good!

It was sensory overload: the buzzing, the intense nonstop vibration, the feeling of being so fucking full but unable to move, not being able to fuck himself against the dildo—not being able to come— and the sharp, slicing sting of the whip on his upper back. Each blow came harder and faster than the last. Each one left him gasping, sucking in air, sobbing, but whether it was from pleasure or pain, Jason couldn't tell. Everything was blurring together; he didn't know where one sensation ended and another began.

Henry's voice drifted through the haze of pleasure and pain, but the meanings of the words were lost on him. Then the vibrating stopped. His ass was empty. He cried out in frustration. Need. He wasn't ready for the session to end. Time had lost all meaning. Henry could have been working him over for an hour, or maybe only a few minutes. Jason gave Henry a pleading look over his shoulder. *More. Please more.*

"No, I think that's definitely enough for one night, boy," Henry told him gently, firmly. He ran his fingers over Jason's ass. His hips. His fingers seemed to touch every part of Jason's body. "You're going to be sore as hell tomorrow."

Jason looked up at him through teary eyelashes. *Please don't stop.*

"Shhhh, I know, it was a mind-blowing trip, and you're not ready to come back." His tone was so soft. So comforting. "Just drift there a bit while I get you cleaned up."

Jason blinked at him as he finally comprehended the words Henry was saying to him. Cleaned up. He'd drawn blood.

Henry unbuckled the gag and pulled it carefully out of Jason's mouth, massaging his jaw while he explained, "It's only a little cut, but let's take all the right precautions. Lay there and enjoy the rest of the ride." He stroked Jason's sweat-sopped hair, pushing it back from his eyes. "I'll only be a few feet away. You won't be able to see me, but I'm right here, baby. Okay? I will not leave you."

Jason nodded. He barely registered that the gag was out of his mouth or that tears and drool had pooled under his chin, soaking the blanket. He closed his eyes, floating happily, listening to the music still playing in the background, the forceful thrum of cellos, the passionate voice of violins. He didn't know the song, but it was a good accompaniment to the intensity of the session. He felt light pressure on his back, something soft. Whatever Henry was cleaning him off with didn't sting. He didn't feel it at all, really. Just the cloth. The lightness of Henry's touch. He felt the Band-Aid go on. Only one. It must only be a small cut, just like Henry said.

He was aware of Henry's movements as he removed the spreader bar, as he wiped Jason's face with a cool, damp cloth. Jason flexed his jaw and it popped. He didn't move otherwise until he felt the bed sag. He looked up. Henry was sitting next to him.

"Come on up," Henry encouraged. "Let me hold you a bit."

Somehow, Jason managed to crawl onto the mattress and lay his head in his Master's lap.

Henry pulled a sheet up over him. He stroked Jason's hair. He smiled. "That was beautiful. You were… fuck, you were amazing." He leaned over and pressed a kiss to Jason's temple.

Jason turned his head and Henry kissed his lips too. It was a soft, gentle kiss, but Jason savored it. He loved feeling like he was the center of someone's whole world. He curled in closer, and Henry held him tightly for a long, long moment. This was exactly where Jason knew he belonged.

"I think you've earned something," Henry told him gently. He reached under the sheet and undid the leather straps confining Jason's cock. He'd taken off the leather gloves, so it was his bare hand against

Jason's skin. Jason shivered at his touch. "Come for me, boy," Henry whispered.

After just a few short strokes, the orgasm roared through Jason like a tidal wave. He clutched onto Henry, shaking with aftershocks. Henry kissed him again and held him until he fell asleep.

Chapter Eight

AFTER the sheer bliss of Henry's aftercare, the cool bubble bath he lowered Jason into, and the amazing room service dinner they shared, the last thing Jason wanted was to go back to his own hotel room.

Alone.

Only it wasn't a request. Henry didn't chuck him out on his ear, didn't tell him to get out, but he did make it clear, after applying a second coat of ointment to Jason's back, that he needed to get some sleep and that Jason should go back to his own room and do the same.

There was no promise of anything for tomorrow, only a soft kiss good night.

Fighting back disappointment and dejection, Jason left. It was early yet—well, midnight. But the dance was still going. People were still wandering around. Drinking. Partying. Gaming. Jason considered heading downstairs for a bit, but if he did, he might run into Terry or Kendra, and they were the last people he wanted to see.

Back in his own room, Jason shucked out of his clothes and crawled into the cool sheets of the bed. He very quickly discovered that the only way he could sleep was on his stomach. It took a long time to get comfortable, an even longer time to fall asleep.

STRONG hands held him down. Ropes cut into his arms and legs, his wrists and ankles. Someone pulled a thick leather hood over his face. Jason struggled, tried to call out, to use his safeword, but before he could say it, a thick rubber ball was shoved into his mouth. The gag was cinched painfully tight.

No! Stop! He struggled harder, but the more he pulled at his bonds, the tighter they became, until he was sure his circulation was getting cut off. Until he couldn't breathe.

"You're a fucking disgrace."

Dad? It sounded like his father's voice, but what was he doing here?

"What do you expect, Greg?" Alicia asked. "It's your own fault for sleeping with *that woman*. You can't make a silk purse from a sow's ear."

That woman. Mom. He fought harder than ever—Alicia had no right to talk about his mother that way!

"She was a mistake," his father assured Alicia. "Just like him. A tragic, tragic mistake."

"Mistakes can be corrected," Alicia promised Greg.

Something sharp struck Jason's back—the single tail? Alicia was whipping him? Or maybe his father. The lash struck him again and again, tearing through his flesh, flaying muscle from bone.

JASON woke with the scream still in his throat, gasping for breath, drenched in sweat, his body tangled painfully in the covers. His heart thundered in his chest and his ears. He fought back the blankets, struggling to get to his feet—but he tumbled painfully to the floor, instead. Jason sobbed. Everything hurt. Nothing made sense. He struggled back up to his feet and yanked the sheet off the bed; wrapping it around his shivering body, he ran to the only safe place he knew.

After many long moments of pounding on Henry's door, it finally opened.

"This had *better* be a matter of fucking life or death or so help me—what the *fuck*?" the stranger snarled, glaring down at Jason. He was tall, thin, Asian. Long black hair hung past the waistband of his red silk boxers.

"S-sorry." Jason stumbled backward. How had he gotten the wrong room? Blinking back tears, he sought out the room number next to the door. He bit back another sob. This *was* Henry's room. "I... wrong room," he lied anyway. He turned away from the open door. Of course Henry had a beautiful man in his room. In his bed. Why wouldn't he?

"Jason?" That was Henry's voice.

Jason kept walking. He didn't ever want to see the other man again. Either of them.

"*Boy*! Stop right there."

He stopped. Goddamn it! He started to move again. He wasn't anything to Henry and Henry sure as fuck wasn't anything to him! But by then, Henry had caught up with him and had him by the arm. He dragged Jason back to his room, pulled him inside, and shut the door. "Jesus, baby, what's the matter?"

Jason wiped the tears from his cheeks. "Nothing." Nothing. Everything. It was all such a jumble in his head. What could he say that would even make sense? He looked around the room and saw that the other man was making coffee. Something about seeing that simple act of domesticity brought Jason to his knees—literally.

Henry caught him and carried him over to the bed. He set Jason on it and sat himself down on the floor next to it.

Jason blinked away more tears. He wondered what Henry had told the other man about him. Them.

There was no them.

"Jason," Henry coaxed, "come on, talk to me. Tell me what's wrong."

"Nothing. I... I'm sorry... I didn't mean...." He looked at the clock. Fuck. It was four o'clock in the morning. "I'm sorry," he repeated helplessly. "I should go back to my own room." *Where I belong.*

"Whoa, you're not going anywhere, kiddo," said the other guy. Jason hardly registered his movement, he just felt strong hands gripping his shoulders, keeping him sitting on the bed. It didn't take much effort.

"Thanks—" Henry began.

The other man snorted, the contempt obvious in his tone. "I made your coffee, old man. Now I'm outta here. This is your mess and I don't want any part of it—except to say 'I told you so.'" He shimmied into a pair of jeans and T-shirt, grabbed a leather jacket from the closet, and made his escape, shoes in hand.

Jason closed his eyes, praying that this was part of the nightmare, too, that in a few minutes he'd wake up in his bed and have the chance to *not* embarrass himself by running to a complete stranger's hotel room in the middle of the night.

"Jason?"

So much for that prayer. Jason forced his eyes open. "I… I'm so sorry, Henry. Please tell your… friend… that I…." That he wouldn't do it again? Fuck. He'd never see either of them again anyway. "Please just tell him how sorry I am." He tried to stand, even though he wasn't sure his legs would support him. He sat back down again as he remembered. "Jesus fucking—God damn it!" he swore loudly. "My fucking key…!" He'd left his room without taking his key. New tears fell as frustration overwhelmed him. The last place he wanted to be was Henry's room, but he was stuck.

Henry poured them each a cup of coffee. Jason accepted the cup from his hand without looking up, even when Henry sat down on the bed next to him.

"Would you at least tell me what rattled you so badly that you ran out of your room like this?" Henry asked.

Jason pulled his knees up to his chest. He cradled the coffee cup between his hands for a few minutes, staring at its contents. Henry had fixed it just the way he liked it, with sugar and creamer. "It was just a bad dream," Jason finally admitted. "It was stupid. If I can borrow a shirt or something, maybe I can get the front desk to give me another key."

"What was the dream about?"

"Nothing."

"Did it have to do with our session from earlier?"

Jason shook his head. Nodded. "It wasn't you. I just... I...." He closed his eyes. "I dreamed it was my father tying me up, putting me in the hood. He kept saying.... He told me how useless I am." More tears fell. Jason didn't know how to stop them. "He called me a mistake. A tragic mistake. Alicia was there.... They... it wasn't anything either of them hasn't said in real life." *It wasn't anything that isn't true.*

"You are *not* a mistake."

Jason's laugh was bitter. "That's not what your friend seems to think. What was it he said? That I'm just some 'mess' you need to clean up. That he told you so?" Jesus, how much had Henry told the other guy?

"Sometimes Derrik's an asshole. You don't listen to him, okay?"

Derrik. Of course that was Derrik. Of course Derrik was fucking gorgeous. "I should try to get back into my room."

"Please don't leave like this."

"Why not?"

Henry hesitated. "I fucked up. I knew we only had last night— maybe tonight, depending on when you were leaving. I wanted to give you something to remember me by. In a good way," he added ruefully. "I thought you were all the way back down, but I was wrong. I shouldn't have sent you back to your room like that. I'm sorry, Jason."

He shrugged. "I'm fine. Besides, you needed to go to bed. You have your booth to run. And you have to pack up today. That's gotta be a big job."

"That doesn't matter. I was supposed to be looking out for you. Taking care of you. I took responsibility for you, remember?"

Jason snorted. "According to my dad, I'm old enough to be responsible for myself."

"Maybe out there. But in here it was my job. I failed."

Jason met his gaze. Held it. He shook his head. "It's okay. I guess it's over anyway. It's Sunday morning." He reached up to his neck to unfasten the collar and give it back.

Henry stopped him. "We've still got a few more hours—if you want. Why don't you stay for a while, maybe get some sleep?"

"I don't want to be in your way."

Henry reached over and laid a hand gently on Jason's leg. "Stay." It wasn't a request, but it wasn't an order, either.

Jason nibbled at his lower lip. He *wanted* to stay. More than anything he wanted curl up in Henry's arms and feel safe. Warm. "What am I?"

"What do you mean?"

"If I'm not your mess, am I 'Jason' or 'baby' or 'boy', or… or am I nothing at all?"

"Oh, baby." Henry pulled him into his arms and held on tight. "Boy. Jason. You are *so* special. I wish we had more time so I could show you *how* special." He kissed the top of Jason's head.

Fresh tears fell as Jason clung to him, as he clung to what felt like a lifeline. "We could. I mean, I live about two hours north of here, but…." *Please?* "I want to see you again. I don't want it to be over."

"Shhhh, this isn't the time for talking about stuff like that. Let's just get some sleep, okay?"

Jason nodded. Staying was what he wanted. And maybe Henry would decide that eight hours wasn't too far away, maybe…. *God, please.* At Henry's direction, he slid under the covers and tried to get comfortable. He couldn't lie on his back, so he rolled onto his side, facing the wall.

"Will you be okay if I turn out the light?" Henry asked.

"Yeah. Sure." A moment later there was darkness. Then Henry crawled in under the covers and spooned against Jason like he had on Friday.

"Is this okay?"

Jason nodded. He scooted back against Henry's warmth. His strength. "You're going to think this is stupid, but the only person I've ever actually slept with was my mother. When I was little. When I had nightmares. Or... later. When she got sick and we both had nightmares."

"Why would I think that's stupid?"

"Isn't it stupid?" He'd been with Terry on and off for five years, but he'd only ever crashed over at Terry's place a handful of times after they'd fucked.

"No, that's not stupid." Henry wrapped his arms around Jason's shoulders, and Jason began to relax. "What happened to your mom?"

"Diabetes. She did the best she could, but like the asshole in the emergency room told us, 'Poor people die.'"

"*What*?"

Jason shrugged. "No insurance. They didn't want to admit her. The doctor told us that poor people died."

"Fuck."

"Yeah." He rolled over in Henry's arms, snuggling into his chest. "Less than a year later, she died, so I guess they were right."

"How old were you?"

"Seventeen. I'd just started my senior year of high school. My best friend...." He swallowed hard. Kendra. "She graduated the year before. I... it was always me and her. When she wasn't there... it didn't end up mattering. After Mom died, I got shipped off to live with my father. I'd never even met him before the day I moved in with him. I know somebody called him or something to let him know, but he never called me, just to say hi or... or anything. I know I was this huge inconvenience to him."

"You're his son."

"Like I said. I was this huge inconvenience."

Henry sighed. "I'm not gonna say it's okay. It's not. But the worst of it's over."

"Sometimes I'm not so sure."

"It is. Trust me."

Jason nodded. He trusted Henry. Even if didn't, he was too tired to argue about things that didn't matter, things he had no control over. Instead, he closed his eyes and listened to Henry's breathing, to the soft thud of his heart. "Thank you, by the way," he whispered after a while.

"For what?"

"For not saying it's okay. That's what everybody said after my mom died. Only it wasn't okay. I hated that. I hated my dad. I even hated my mom. I hated everything. Everyone."

"That when you got your nips done?"

Jason peered up at him in the dark. "How'd you know?"

Henry chuckled. "Just a guess."

Jason snuggled deeper into his embrace. "I cut class and drove into Lansing on my eighteenth birthday. My dad couldn't stop me. My teachers couldn't say dick."

"Must've gone over like a fart in church."

He laughed. "Yeah. I... Henry, I, um, I want to come into the dealers' room today. I mean, I won't bug you or anything but I... there's something I want to buy."

"I thought you were strapped for cash."

"I am. But some things are worth it."

Henry pressed another soft kiss to the top of his head. "Yeah. Some things are."

Jason tried very, very hard not to read anything into that.

HE WOKE disoriented. It wasn't that he was in a strange bed, all hotel room beds felt strange to Jason. It was the sound of the shower running in the other room, the gritty feeling in his eyes.

And then he remembered.

Fuck, was it Henry or Derrik in the shower? *Please let it be Henry.*

He glanced at the clock. Nine thirty. Knowing the time didn't give him any better of a guess as to who was in the bathroom.

The water turned off. Jason shut his eyes and pretended to be asleep. If it was Derrik… Jesus, he didn't want to face the man again after last night. He barely wanted to face Henry. He just wanted to crawl under the nearest rock and die.

Soft footsteps came out of the bathroom. Fabric rustled. Then someone leaned over him and pressed a soft kiss to his temple. Jason smiled. It was Henry. He opened his eyes.

"Sorry if I woke you."

Jason shook his head. "What time is it?"

"Almost ten. You want me to walk down to the front desk with you, see if we can get you back into your room?"

"Yeah. Sure. I mean… you don't have to…." The dealers' room opened at ten, and even if Henry didn't have to be there right on the dot, he needed to get there soon.

"I want to come with you, Jason. I'd like to take you to breakfast too, if you feel like having me around."

"What about your booth?"

"Derrik's going to cover it this morning."

God. "He must either hate me or think I'm the world's biggest flake." Or both.

Henry's smile surprised him. "I know he was a jerk last night—"

"I'm the one who showed up pounding on your door at four o'clock in the morning, sobbing like some kind of basket case."

"That wasn't your fault, Jason. It was mine. I should have realized you were still in a delicate headspace when you left. I should have kept you here."

Jason shrugged. He didn't want to argue about it. "Do you have a shirt or something I can borrow?"

"You'll swim in just about everything I own, but this shouldn't be too bad." He handed over a royal-blue terrycloth bathrobe.

"Thanks."

Getting the front desk manager to believe his story wasn't as difficult as Jason had feared. She did make him dig out his ID and show it to her before she left him alone in the room, but at least she agreed to let him in, in the first place. Jason sank down on the tangled mess of sheets on his bed; he felt more childish than ever.

"You okay?" Henry asked him.

"Just thinking about what kind of an idiot I was last night. You really don't need to stick around." He reached for the collar to unbuckle it.

"Let me," said Henry. "I put in on you. I should take it off."

Jason fought back a fresh wash of tears. This was it. The end of his weekend. And it wasn't even ten thirty. "Thank you," he murmured. He closed his eyes. A second later, his neck was free of the thin band of leather and he felt completely naked.

"Why don't you keep it?" Henry suggested, startling Jason into opening his eyes back up.

"Sir?" He shook himself. They weren't in those roles any more. Were they?

"Just keep it." He pressed the collar into Jason's hands. "If you do go out and start playing, which I think you should, by the way, you can use this."

"I'm not sure I understand."

Henry sat down on the edge of the bed. "If some guy starts hassling you, you tell him you've got somebody looking out for you, that you're under my protection."

Jason's eyes widened at the implication.

Henry smiled. "It doesn't mean too much in the real world, but on the scene, anybody hears that and they'll back off. Or if they don't, some other Dom'll make sure they get the clue, fast. Being under someone's protection isn't the same thing as being collared, but it means you've got somebody watching your back, even if he's not there physically. We're a small community. We tend to look out for our own."

"Thank you, Sir."

Henry leaned in and gave his forehead a soft kiss. After straightening back up again, he dug his wallet out of his pocket and pulled out a brown and gold business card. He grabbed a pen from the nightstand and wrote a number on the back. "That's my home number," he explained. "If you ever need anything—and I do mean anything at all—you call me, okay?"

Jason swallowed back the lump in his throat. He tried not to feel too hopeful. "Yeah. Yeah, okay. Thank you. I... it's been an amazing weekend, Henry. I'm... I can't tell you how glad I am I met you."

"Me too."

There was a brief moment of awkward silence, then Jason slid out of Henry's robe and got dressed. He made sure to tuck Henry's card into his wallet where he wouldn't lose it.

WHEN they got to the hotel restaurant, Henry reiterated that he was buying breakfast and that Jason should get whatever he wanted. As soon as their waitress asked if they wanted coffee, Henry started ordering for both of them. Then he ducked his head apologetically. "Go on," he said to Jason, indicating that he should speak for himself today.

Well, that answered one question, at least: they were no longer Master and boy, they were just... what? Friends? Lovers? Acquaintances who fucked? Jason had no idea. But at least they fell back into easy conversation like they had the other night at the Middle Eastern restaurant. After breakfast, Henry paid the bill, but when Jason offered to get the tip, Henry let him.

"I wish I could hang out," Henry began as they stood to leave.

"You have to get to work," said Jason. "I understand. I, erm, I guess I should get my shopping done and then get packed up. Checkout's in an hour."

Henry nodded. They walked together to the dealers' room, stopping just inside the door. "Come say bye before you head out, okay?" Henry asked.

"I will. I…." Jason hesitated. Should he offer his hand? Try to get a kiss? Just a hug?

"I'll see you before you go, then." Henry ended Jason's internal debate by simply walking away.

Trying not to feel too hurt, Jason watched him go over to his booth. He didn't follow. He had every intention of buying the gray collar, but he didn't want Henry to know that was what he was really after, although maybe his fear that Henry would refuse to sell it to him was childish. Why should Henry care how Jason spent his money? Just the same, he took a leisurely turn of the room, stopping to talk to a couple of people he knew, keeping an eye on Henry's booth. As soon as someone came up to ask Henry a question, Jason made his move. By then, Derrik was through with the customer he'd been helping, so the timing was perfect.

Except for the part where he had to talk to Derrik. Well, really, all he had to do was hand Derrik the collar and his credit card. The implication would be obvious.

Jason scanned the merchandise quickly. Shit. He didn't see it. And Henry had already glanced over at him twice since he'd walked up to the booth. If Henry got rid of his customer before Jason could find it…. He had no choice. He had to ask Derrik for help.

Derrik shot him a dark, questioning look as he approached. "Need something?" he queried.

"Erm. Yeah. Hi. Sorry about last night."

"Don't you mean *this morning*?" he corrected.

Jason hadn't noticed the thick tribal tattoos that went all the way around both of Derrik's forearms or exactly how incredible the man's physique was. How beautiful his face looked.

Jason ran a hand over the back of his neck. He felt completely naked. "Yeah. Sorry. Look. I was here on Friday, and…."

Derrik quirked an eyebrow at him.

"And there was a collar. A gray one. Four hand-forged D rings. I'd like to buy it, but I don't see it."

Derrik shrugged. "If you don't see it, it must have sold. Sorry, kid."

Jason's heart sank. He should be glad someone else had bought it. He was dreading his credit card bill as it was, but he'd wanted it *so* badly. It was *his* collar.

Henry got rid of his customer and came over to where he stood. "Hey. Heading out?"

Jason forced a smile. "I just… yeah. I'm about to head out." It was easier to lie than tell him why he was really there. Besides, as soon as Jason got his gear packed up, he would be leaving. Only saying good-bye now meant he wouldn't be able to come back down later for one more kiss. One more anything. God, this really was it.

Henry didn't question his statement, he simply took Jason's hands in his and leaned in to press a tender kiss to his cheek. "Drive safe, okay?"

"Yeah. You too. I mean… you know. Tomorrow. When you head out." He would give *anything* to stay one more night with Henry.

But no invitation was issued.

"I, erm… I guess…. Will you be here next year?" Jason asked, not quite ready to let go.

"I think so. It's been a pretty good show. Better in some ways than I'd expected," he added with a grin.

Heat flooded Jason's cheeks. "Are you coming back for Penguicon?" April seemed like forever away, but it was better than January.

"We've got a leather show in Chicago that weekend."

"Ah." Jason bit back his disappointment. "I guess… I guess I'll see you next year."

"Count on it, boy."

JASON shouldered his bag carefully—his whole back ached—and headed toward the lobby. Kendra caught him just as he got off the elevator. "I'm glad I found you before you left," she said.

He smiled. It was a forced effort. "You're not heading out?"

"We didn't want to drive all the way back to Houghton tonight. Hey, you want to stay over one more night? We've got room."

For a moment, Jason considered saying yes, but if he stayed, it would only be to see Henry. He doubted that would go over real well with Kendra, who probably only wanted him to stick around so she could try to get him and Terry back together. "I've gotta head home. I have class tomorrow."

"Look, I'm sorry about yesterday, okay? I know it's none of my business, I just... you and Terry are so great together."

"Yeah." He didn't feel like telling her how wrong she was; she didn't seem to want to listen, anyway.

"How're things at home?" Kendra asked, changing the subject.

"Dad's a prick, Alicia's a bitch. So status quo, I guess."

"Something'll work out, just hang in there, okay?" She pulled him into a fierce hug—Jason hissed in pain and pulled away from her, dropping his bag in the process. "Jason, my God, what's wrong with you?"

"Nothing." He picked up his bag but didn't hoist it back over his shoulder.

"Look, if something's the matter, if you need help—"

"I'm *fine*," he snapped. She didn't look like she believed him. "Look, I'm sorry we didn't get more time to hang out this weekend, but I've gotta run. I need to get home."

"Call me, okay?"

"Yeah. Sure."

Chapter Nine

AFTER the best weekend of his life, "home" seemed even more dismal than ever.

Jason knew it was stupid; he should love his dad's house. The three-bedroom ranch was located in a well-to-do subdivision on the outskirts of Ithaca, and it was a million times nicer than the dinky trailer Jason and his mother had lived in, in Troy. And Dad had all the little luxuries: a widescreen TV, DISH Network, DVR, and a shiny, hardly used kitchen. But Jason hated it here.

"Hello?" he called when he walked in the front door. Dad's car wasn't in the driveway, but that didn't mean much. He usually put it in the garage. Jason didn't "need to park in the garage," according to Dad. Jason's little hatchback was already covered with rust patches; there wasn't much sense in trying to protect it from the rain or snow.

"Dad?" he hollered a little louder. Still no answer. That meant Dad was probably at Alicia's.

Jason snagged an apple from the fruit bowl on the counter. He noticed that the note he'd left for his father was still on the fridge. He wondered if his father had even seen it. If he cared.

Jason trudged down the hall to his room, eating his apple. He unpacked his bags and flopped down stomach first onto his bed. He resisted the urge to call Henry, even though he was desperate to hear the other man's voice. The dealers' room would be closed by now, but Henry was probably packing up. Or maybe getting ready to go out to dinner.

With Derrik.

Derrik, who was beautiful.

Derrik, who was closer to Henry's age.

Derrik, who was his friend, who knew what Henry liked on his pizza and what his favorite flavor of ice cream was.

Derrik, who was hopefully only his business partner.

Dear God, please....

Jason heaved a sigh. It didn't make any difference what Henry and Derrik were to each other. Derrik was with Henry. Jason was home. Alone. Lonely.

He sat up and pulled the textbook for his Web design class out of his backpack. He tried to reread the chapters for Thursday's test, but no matter how hard he tried, he couldn't concentrate on cascading style sheets and HTML coding. After an hour of reading the same few pages over and over, he gave up and got out his sketchpad. He spent the rest of the night drawing pictures of men in bondage while listening to string quartet versions of his favorite songs on YouTube.

Before he went to bed, Jason tucked the blue leather collar under his pillow. His dreams were filled with images of leather and rope. He woke up in the middle of the night with the world's worst hard-on and jerked off, wishing it was Henry's hand on his dick instead of his own. He wondered if he was ever going to see him again.

"MORNING," Jason said to his father as he wandered into the kitchen wearing sweatpants and an old flannel shirt.

Greg Saunders looked up from his paper and frowned. "You're going to school in that?"

He shrugged. "Why not? Half the kids in my class show up in sweats or pajama bottoms." Jason poured himself a cup of coffee.

"Your generation has no respect for the education you're getting."

"What does what you wear have to do with respect?"

Greg sighed. He went back to reading.

Jason stirred sugar and milk into his coffee cup. Sometimes it was hard to believe he was related at all to the straitlaced man sitting at the breakfast table in a suit and tie, drinking his coffee, reading the business section. Jason was just glad that male pattern baldness was passed down through the maternal line, and that in every picture he'd seen of Mom's dad, the man had a full head of bushy black hair. Jason's father was fighting going bald with every expensive shampoo on the market, but it was clearly a losing battle.

Jason sat down at the kitchen table. He was careful not to lean back in his chair. "Can we talk about next semester?"

His father looked up from his paper again, his expression souring. "What about it?"

"Work's been slow lately, and I need to buy new tires before it gets too bad out there." So far the winter had been mild, but it was only January. Last year, they'd had three snowstorms in February and another in March. "When I was driving home from Detroit, my engine light went on. If it turns out to be something major, I might not be able to afford more than a class or two next semester."

"You're only taking two classes now."

"I've got three—"

Greg let out a rough, angry sigh. Right, Jason had almost forgotten. Life Drawing didn't count as a "real" class. Art classes were electives—and yes, Jason had to take a certain number of electives to graduate, but he should be taking Japanese or at least Spanish. Or maybe Chinese, since all the schools were starting to push it now.

"Anyway," he went on, "I was wondering if I could borrow enough money to cover my classes next semester."

"No."

"I'm talking about a *loan*, Dad," Jason implored. "I might not even need it, I just want to know that I can register for next semester."

"Maybe"—his father folded his newspaper and stood up—"you should have thought about *that* before going off to some stupid convention over the weekend."

"I only need seven or eight hundred bucks—"

"The subject is closed, Jason. I'm not a bank. If you want a loan, I suggest you go talk to Financial Aid." He left the table but called over his shoulder, "And don't forget to wash up your dishes. I found two plates in the sink when I came home from Alicia's Saturday morning. We have a dishwasher. You'd think after living here for five years you'd have learned how to use it."

Jason blinked back the angry tears that threatened to overwhelm him. It would be one thing if his father couldn't afford to float him a loan, but he *had* money. He wasn't poor like Mom. What the fuck had she ever seen in his father, anyway? Jason's mother was warm. Creative. Funny. She was everything his dad wasn't. *Was that the reason you never told him about me?*

When he was ten or eleven, Jason asked his mom about his father—he'd asked before that, but finally he got an answer, or at least as much of one as she was willing to give. She'd smiled when she told the story. She met his father in college—she was an art student and Greg, his father, was majoring in political science. One day she was sitting by some trees with her sketchpad and this poor lost-looking guy asked her for directions to Barnard Hall. It was clear across the campus. Instead of giving him directions, she walked over with him; they chatted. He showed up the next day at her work—just to buy a cup of coffee, he claimed. A month later, he asked her out.

They dated for a while, then broke up. She never said why, only that some things weren't meant to be. Then she smiled at Jason and said that maybe the only thing that was meant to be was him.

"God, I miss you, Mom."

Jason drank his coffee and made sure to wash out his cup and put it away before leaving for class. The check engine light glowed orange at him the whole way there.

After class he headed for the nearest garage, where, after waiting for over an hour, he was told that there were six things wrong, but if he didn't get at least one of them fixed now, he wouldn't make it around the block, let alone all the way back home. The repair completely wiped out his checking account, but at least he was able to get to work without breaking down on the side of the road, something the mechanic was astounded hadn't happened already.

Before Jason left the shop, he made an appointment to come back in a couple of weeks to get the next most pressing issues dealt with. Hopefully by then, he'd have enough money to pay for it. The mechanic warned him to expect to spend at least a thousand bucks the next time he came in.

JASON spent the next two and half weeks working every shift he could get, even to the point of cutting class a couple of times—which wasn't going to do his grades any favors, but it would be a moot point if he wasn't able to get to school at all. Besides, the more time he spent working, the less time he had to spend at home. When he was working, he wasn't worrying about Derrik or wondering if he should call Henry—or staring at his phone wanting to call him and then chickening out.

When he was working, he was too busy to wonder what was wrong with him, why he wanted to be on his knees, taking orders from a man he barely knew.

"SERIOUSLY, dude, you'd be better off buying a new car than sinking any more into this piece of shit," the mechanic told him when he showed up for his next appointment. "Your car has three tires in the grave."

"Yeah. I know."

"I've got a buddy selling an old Trans Am. The body has some miles on it, but we just put a new engine in her last year. Five thousand and she's yours."

Jason could only shake his head. "Sorry. I've barely got what I owe you for today." He had exactly eight hundred and twenty-two dollars in his wallet, which wasn't enough to pay for everything he'd been hoping to get done today, but he could at least get a couple of things fixed. After that, he'd have five dollars and whatever change he could scrounge from under the seats leftover for gas.

"You're going to be putting more than five grand into this thing before summer," the mechanic warned.

Jason sighed. He wasn't surprised at the prognosis. "Just fix what you can, and I'll see you again in a few weeks."

"It's your money."

"Yeah." He sat down in the reception area with his Web design book and laptop to do his homework. His back didn't hurt anymore. The bruises had all faded. Even the welts were gone.

He found an unsecured WiFi connection—it was amazing how many places had WiFi that they left unsecure—and surfed over to Henry's website. Jason still hadn't called him, but sometimes he looked through Henry's site just to see his face and remember the weekend he'd spent at Henry's feet.

His dick pressed uncomfortably against his jeans.

Jason clicked off Henry's site and went to work on his homework. If anything was guaranteed to get rid of a hard-on, it was cascading style sheets.

He was interrupted thirty minutes later when his cell phone rang. He glanced at the caller ID—Kendra. He'd been ducking her calls for over two weeks and didn't honestly want to talk to her now, but he didn't want to do his homework either. He flipped open his phone. "Yeah, hello?"

"I was getting ready to drive down there! Are you okay?" She sounded frantic.

"I'm fine, just busy." He repeated the same story he'd told her in the e-mail he sent two days ago about how work was crazy and his teachers were all piling on the homework. It was the truth, but it wasn't the real reason he was avoiding her, and he was pretty sure she knew it.

"How's that big project for the Web class coming?" she asked anyway.

"I'm working on it now."

"Look, Jason, I know you're going to get mad at me, but I did some checking up on that guy you hooked up with at con."

"*What?*"

"I'm sorry, but I was worried about you, so I talked to Sandy. She was right across from him in the dealers' room, and they got to talking about some pretty sick shit. I mean, look, I know you and Terry fool around a little with tying each other up and stuff, and that's cool."

Heat flooded Jason's cheeks. He hadn't brought up bondage with Kendra since they were kids and she made it perfectly clear that she was *not* going to tie him up when they played superheroes, never mind that Robin had gotten tied up on the *Batman* cartoon the day before. So if Kendra knew he still liked getting tied up, it meant that Terry must have told her.

"Kendra, my sex life is none of your business—"

"I'm not trying to make what you and Terry do my business. I just don't want to see you getting hurt by some pervert."

"What are you talking about?"

"You know exactly what I'm talking about. He hit you."

"You're making it sound like something it isn't."

"I knew it! Jason, listen to me, I *know* your dad's done a number on your head, and maybe you don't think you deserve any better because of the shit he keeps telling you, but that's all it is: *shit.* Your dad doesn't know you, and you do not have to let some surrogate father figure turn you into his personal punching bag or… or his *doormat* to get him to *like* you! There are lots of guys out there who will like you just the way you are. That BDSM crap isn't healthy. The people who get into it, they've got problems, Jason."

"You don't know what you're talking about." He knew exactly how defensive he sounded, but he didn't care. "You don't understand," he insisted.

"Jason, honey, please listen to me. The people who get into that stuff, they do it because they're bullies or control freaks. Or because they just get off on making other people hurt. And that's abuse. This guy is what? Twice your age? What could he possibly want with a twenty-two-year-old, anyway? He's *using* you. He thinks you're easy prey, that's all. You *can't* see him again."

"Kendra, the last time I checked, my mother was still buried at St. Anne's Cemetery. You're not her. You don't get to lecture me or tell me who I can go out with."

"I'm not trying to be your mother. I'm trying to be your friend. You're so sweet, but you can be so naïve. I don't want you to get hurt by some freak."

"I have to go, I have work to do—"

"Jason, please just call Terry. He misses you so much. He knows he screwed up. He really wants to fix things up with you."

"That makes one of us. I'll talk to you later." He didn't wait for her to say good-bye, he simply hung up. If Kendra didn't want him to get hurt, she wouldn't be trying to get him back together with Terry. She wouldn't be calling Henry a freak, because…. *Because I'm just as big of a freak as he is. I wanted it.* He still wanted it. He wanted Henry.

Jason got up and got a drink from the water cooler on the other side of the room. He needed something a lot stronger. When he got back to his seat, he got out his wallet, found Henry's card, and dialed his number before he lost his nerve.

"Hello?" a woman answered.

Jason blinked, too surprised to speak.

"*Hello?*" she repeated.

"Uh. Hi. Sorry. Is Henry there?"

"Hang on."

Jason heard movement on the other end of the line and then a muffled "Hank! Phone." Silence. "How should I know? Just pick up already!" Another pause. "Oh fer…! Fine. But I'm tossing it down." Feet stomped. There was another moment of silence. Then a soft thud.

Finally: "Hello?" Henry said into his end.

"Henry?"

"Yeah."

"Hi. I—sorry, it's Jason. Jason Kennly? From ConFusion? In Detroit?"

"Hey." His tone was reserved. Maybe even a little chilly.

Jason chewed on his lip. "Did... did I catch you at a bad time?"

"Not really."

"I... I just... are you up to talking?"

"If you want. How've you been?"

Awful? Lonely? Missing you? "Okay, I guess. You?"

"Busy."

"Yeah," Jason agreed, wiping his hand over the back of his neck. "Me too. Busy, I mean."

A moment of uncomfortable silence stretched between them.

Jason pulled his knees up to his chest. "How is everything? I mean, you know, besides busy."

"Jason, was there something you actually *wanted*?"

"Just to talk."

"Okay. So talk."

"I... it just... is something wrong?"

On the other end, Henry sighed. "It's been almost three weeks, kiddo. I kinda figured you'd changed your mind—or maybe you took my advice and found somebody local to hook up with. Which I suppose is for the best." Hurt. Henry sounded *hurt*.

"No, Sir! I...." He lowered his voice. "I mean no, I haven't hooked up with anyone else. I just... I would've called you sooner, but I didn't want to bug you."

"It's not bugging me when I invite you to call."

"I know. Or, I should have known. I must've wanted to dial your number a hundred times in the last three weeks. I've wanted... God, will you think I'm stupid if I say I missed you?"

"Why would I think that's stupid?"

Because I'm half your age, just like you said. Like Kendra said. "I don't know," he lied.

Henry didn't press him for a better explanation. What he did ask, however, wasn't any easier to answer. "So, what's eating at you?"

Jason took a breath and let it out as he tried to gather up the scattered shards of his thoughts. "It's a bunch of stuff. But mostly it's my best friend... or, I mean, I've known her forever, it's just that right now I'm not sure...." He shook his head as if to clear it, but it didn't work. "I'm not sure about a lot of things. All I know is that Kendra went checking up on you, talking to some of the merchants in the dealers' room. She knows... I mean, you know. About what you're into."

"It is absolutely no secret that I'm involved in the leather community or that I'm into BDSM, Jason. If that makes you uncomfortable, I'm sorry." He sounded more peeved than sorry.

"No. I mean. Not really. Not exactly. It's just... she thinks... she said some stuff to me and I guess it's getting under my skin. I know you're right and that I should go out and meet other people. Other submissives."

"But?" Henry coaxed.

"I'm terrified."

"Of what?"

"Being a freak. Being new. Being naïve. Running into my eighth-grade math teacher."

"What?" Henry chortled.

"It's not funny!"

"Yes it is, but I'm sorry for laughing. I suppose running into your eighth-grade math teacher would be pretty horrifying—for both of you," he added. "All right, so if you're not up to getting out and meeting people—*yet*—how do you feel about reading?"

"I've already done some."

Henry snorted. "I know what kind of crap is out there, kiddo. How about this: you go to my website—the URL is on my card. I've got a list of recommended books. I know money's tight—"

"No, that's okay. I mean, yeah, sure, money's tight, but I... I'm okay. I mean, you know, I can afford a couple of books. What ones should I read first?" He didn't want to admit that he'd already looked at Henry's list of recommended books, but there were so many of them, he couldn't figure out where to start.

"Start with anything by Jack Rinella or David Stein; they're both gay men, that might help. There are some het titles you should read too, just start with whatever appeals. Everything I've got listed is a good book, one I've read myself. And don't be afraid to call me if you have questions, Jason. I'm here for you." The sincerity in his tone was impossible to ignore. It made Jason feel warm. Safe.

Connected.

"Thank you. I... is it okay if I still call you Sir?"

"I guess that depends on what you want. *Boy.*"

Jason's heart thumped in his chest, and he couldn't help the wide grin spreading over his face. The mechanic walked through the door. "I probably picked one of the world's worst times to call, Sir." He didn't lower his voice but kept it conversational. "I'm afraid I have to cut this short."

"Oh?"

"I'm at the garage getting some work done on my car. It looks like the mechanic is done—or has more bad news."

"Don't you go spending money on books you can't afford, boy."

"I won't," he lied.

"*Boy.*"

"I really won't spend more than I think I can afford."

Henry sighed. "Don't wait another three weeks to call me."

"I won't, Sir." At least that was a promise he could honestly keep. He hung up.

Jason settled up with his mechanic, made an appointment to come back in a couple of weeks, and drove to work feeling better than he had in three weeks.

Chapter Ten

IT WAS almost midnight when Jason got home from work. Alicia's car was in the driveway, right where he usually parked. He sighed; what else was new? He parked on the street and trudged through the snow to let himself in.

"Please take your shoes off *at* the door," Alicia called from the kitchen. She stepped into the front room carrying a cup that probably had tea in it. She was dressed for bed in a green bathrobe and white silk pajama bottoms, her long dyed red hair pulled up into a white silk scarf.

Jason nodded hello and toed off his work shoes.

"You're going to ruin your shoes, Jason," she told him, not for the first time. "And would you *please* hang your coat up in the hall closet for a change? I realize your mother was a bit... bohemian, but you've lived here for long enough to know what coat closets are for."

"I keep my coat in my room." He told her what she already knew.

She scowled at him over the rim of her cup. "Everyone *else* uses the coat closet."

"I'm not everybody else." He shuddered as the memory of the nightmare came back to haunt him. *You can't make a silk purse out of a sow's ear.* The only sow's ear he could see was staring at him disdainfully from the other side of the room. Yes, Alicia was beautiful, but as far as Jason was concerned, her beauty was strictly superficial.

"Your manners are going to get you into trouble," said Alicia.

"I really don't know what I ever did to you, but I'm not in the mood for your shit today. Good night." He brushed past her and went to his room. He was sure he was going to get an earful from his father tomorrow, but he didn't care.

He closed his bedroom door and slumped against it. He missed the feeling of bruises on his back. Of welts. Well, maybe he didn't actually miss the *welts*, but he missed the man who had given them to him. How fucked up was that?

He wasn't sure.

Jason dropped his book bag to the floor next to his desk; it landed with a hard thud. He set his laptop down far more gently on bed. He figured it was too late to call Henry, but he could at least shoot him a text message to say hi. He considered for a minute before tapping out a few carefully chosen words and hitting Send. Smiling, he headed to the bathroom at the other end of the hall for a shower. He liked almost everything about his job, *except* that he came home smelling like garlic and tomato sauce every day.

When he got back to his room fifteen minutes later, wearing clean sweats and a T-shirt, Jason discovered he had a new text message waiting for him on his cell phone.

His heart raced—but it was from Terry. *Call me. Please. I'll make it up 2 U. I'll do anything just 2 hear UR voice.*

Biting back the disappointment he told himself he had no business feeling anyway, Henry was probably sound asleep or something, Jason booted up his laptop. He went straight to his e-mail, just like always. There was all the usual junk mail, some list mail. And an e-mail from Kendra with an attachment. He clicked it open.

Jason, please read this. I know it's fiction, but it was written by a woman desperate to impress her lover. I don't know what kind of man he must have been if she thought a story like this would impress him, just that men like this make me ill. You're better than this, Jason. You deserve better. You're not weak. Don't let this Henry guy make you think that you are. And if this so-called "classic" doesn't make you sick, then I don't know what to say to you anymore.

Frowning, Jason clicked open the attachment. *The Story of O.* Okay, he'd heard of that. It was an erotic BDSM classic, and it was on his list of books to read, he just hadn't gotten around to it yet. *No time like the present...* and he really didn't want to look at HTML coding anyway.

Only Kendra was right, it was repulsive. The story revolved around a spineless woman named O who was taken by her so-called "lover" to a strange house, prettied up, gang-raped, whipped, raped again, and then locked in a cell until the next time somebody wanted to "play" with her some more. Jason was sure he was going to be sick—and he wasn't even a quarter of the way through the story.

He jumped when his phone chirped with a new text message. It was from Henry. *I ever tell you I get insomnia? Call if you want.*

He licked his lips and swallowed hard. Of course he wanted to call Henry, to talk to him, but what if Henry told him *The Story of O* made some good points about BDSM? What if it was one of Henry's favorite books? What if Henry wanted him to be more like O?

Jason hit the Call Back button before he lost his nerve.

Henry picked up on the first ring. "Hello, boy," he greeted Jason, his tone sultry. Soft.

Any other time, Jason would have gotten an instant hard-on. Tonight, he just curled his knees up to his chest. "Hi, Sir."

"What's the matter?"

"I... nothing," he lied. "I mean... something. I just... maybe it's nothing, I don't know."

"You wanna tell me what 'it' is?"

"Kendra sent me *The Story of O* and I started reading it."

"Jesus. Jason, look, you've gotta take that story into context."

"*What* context? O never fights back. She isn't given any kind of safeword. He fucking makes her say 'I love you' before she goes down on him in a room full of strangers—the same men who already raped and whipped her!"

"Do you want to talk, or do you want to yell at me?" Henry's tone was sharp.

"I'm sorry, Sir."

"Better. Now. Like I said, you have to take it in context. You also have to take it as a work of fiction—written by a woman, by the way."

"That's the part that I don't get. What made her think her boyfriend would like something like this? What kind of man was *he*?"

"That's not exactly the point of the story. Look, it's not a book everybody likes."

"Do you?" Jason wanted to know.

"When I'm in the right mood, yes. It's a good novel." He was completely unapologetic. "But it's not real life. I suggest that if you decide to finish it, you keep that in mind. You might want to read up on the author too, because I'm guessing your friend Kendra slanted the facts to try and prove a point. It sounds like she succeeded, but only because you didn't do your own homework. You just took her word on what the book is really about."

Feeling fully chastised, Jason hung his head. "You're right. I just… Kendra's always been so much smarter than me."

"Jason, you and me, we just met. You don't know me from Adam. You've been friends with Kendra for a long time. Right now I might have some opinions about her, and she sure as hell seems to have some about me. But the thing is, you two have a history, and I don't want to come between you and her, or you and anyone else, for that matter."

"No! I mean… God, I don't know what I mean or what I want anymore."

"I'm afraid I can't help you there, kiddo. Only you can figure your life out. Only you can live it."

Jason closed his eyes. "My father's always telling me how to live my life. Him. Alicia. Now Kendra. I don't know who to listen to anymore."

"It's *your* life, Jason. What do *you* want?"

Jason was quite for a long time. "Sir," he finally said. He let the word hang between them for a few minutes as he mulled it over in his head. "It feels really right to call you that, Henry. Sir." *Master.* "I like the way it sounds. The way it feels."

"And that scares you."

"Yes, Sir. I don't want to be somebody's doormat."

"Good, because I've got one of those already. It sits right outside my back door. What I want is…." He hesitated.

"Is?" Jason prompted.

"What I want is complicated."

His heart thumped hard in his chest. "Does it involve me?"

"That kinda depends on what *you* want. Contrary to popular fiction, I can't just whisk you off to some isolated chateau. Even if I could, it wouldn't be to a place like that."

"What kind of place would it be?" Jason asked.

"Someplace real quiet, someplace we could be alone. Someplace where I could tie you up, spank you until you were squirming—screaming—without having to worry about anybody running to your 'rescue'."

Jason's cock strained against his zipper. "What about fucking?"

"You *want* to be fucked, boy?"

"Only by you." The words were out before Jason realized he'd said them. He reached under his pillow, found the collar, and laid it across his lap so he could look at it. It was true. Ever since he'd meet Henry, he hadn't looked at anybody else, at least not seriously. Henry was who he thought about when he jerked off.

"So," Henry said in a low, gravelly tone, "if I were there, or maybe if you were here, what would you ask me to do right now?"

"What… what do you mean?"

"Would you ask me to tie you up? Paddle you? Would you ask me to use the cane? The flogger? The crop?"

"Not the crop!"

Henry laughed. "I think it's a good thing you're not here, boy. That kind of disrespect would earn you a few stripes—and I would use the crop to give 'em to you too, *just* because I know you don't like it."

Jason ducked his head. Then: "Sir, can I ask you a question?"

"Anything you want, boy."

"I just… what *is* the right response?"

"Come again?"

"I mean, if I don't want something but I don't actually want to say 'no', I don't want to safeword out, I just want to tell you how I feel, how do I say what I want without getting into trouble?"

Henry's chuckle was a low, wicked rumble in his ear. "For starters, I'm a very hard man to please. My boys are always getting into trouble over something."

His boys?

"But to answer your question, the 'right' response is always a respectful response."

"Please not the crop?" Jason tried to rephrase his response.

Henry laughed again. "Better."

"But not perfect?"

"Nobody's perfect, boy. Listen to this." He cleared his throat. When he spoke again, he didn't sound like himself at all. He sounded like a submissive. "Master, if it pleases you, Sir, could you choose something else tonight?"

"Wow."

"What, that I can pull off 'sub'?"

"Something like that. Okay. Thank you, Sir. I'll… I'm not sure I can be that eloquent, but I'll try."

"It's not the words, it's your tone, boy. Although phrases like 'if it pleases you' and 'with your permission' are pretty useful."

"Yes, Sir."

"All right, back to my original question. If we were together, what would you ask me for?"

Jason opened his mouth. Shut it again. He nibbled on his lip. He thought about *The Story of O*, about Kendra. About Henry and the weekend they'd shared. "If I really had a choice—that is, Sir, Master, if it would please you, Sir, I'd ask you to put me on your St. Andrew's cross and use the flogger on me." Just thinking about it made his cock twitch.

"Very nicely done. Now, why those two things?"

"I've never been tied to anything, except maybe a chair when I was a little kid playing superheroes with my friends," he admitted. He licked his lips and heat flooded his cheeks. But at the same time, his dick stood straight at attention as he imagined what it would feel like to have Henry tying him up, arms and legs spread wide, wrists and ankles bound tight, so he could barely move.

"And I take it you liked being tied to a chair, boy?" Henry's voice had dropped to a husky whisper.

"I think I'd like the St. Andrew's cross more, Sir."

"You trust me enough to try something like that? You'd be completely helpless," Henry warned.

"I trust you, Sir. You're nothing like the asshole in that book."

"That's the difference between reality and fiction, boy. 'Sides, I prefer someone I can actually *talk* to. Someone with an opinion. Someone who keeps me sharp. If I wanted a blow-up doll, I'd get one."

Jason smiled. He rubbed himself through the fabric of his sweatpants, but it only made him hornier.

"You getting hard, boy?"

"Yes, Sir."

"Have you let your hair grow back, or have you been shaving?"

"I've let it grow back."

"*Tsk.* Lazy. Tell me something, boy. If I told you to do something—or not do it—would you?"

Yes! "I… if I can, Sir. I would do anything I could to make you… to please you, but—"

"Shhh, stop fretting. I'll do my best not to ask you to do something you can't do, and I'll take you at your word if you tell me I've misjudged, okay?"

"Yes, Sir. Thank you, Sir."

"Good boy. Now. Laziness is not something I tolerate. So until you can shave yourself—pits and pubes—you're not allowed to masturbate."

"Oh, God," Jason breathed, pulling his hand back.

"You were touching yourself, weren't you?"

"Yes, Sir," he admitted sheepishly.

Henry merely chuckled. "You're not now, though. Are you?"

"No, Sir!" Jason wrapped his hand around the collar. He took a breath. He let it out. "Sir, may I ask… you said I could masturbate after I shave, but may I come?"

"Very good question, boy. Yes, you may come. But after that it's back to hands off, except to wash up."

Jason ran his thumb over the soft leather of the collar. The gray collar had been so much softer. Silky almost. Thicker. But the one in his hand was a gift from the man he wanted more than anything in the world to please. "Yes, Sir."

"You are an amazing boy, Jason. I know you're not going to 'cheat', that you're going to do exactly what I say."

"Yes, Sir."

"By the way—you're not going to be jerking off anytime soon, but I am. I've got my cock out, and I'm stroking it as we speak."

"You're cruel." But he was grinning.

Henry chuckled. "Just now figuring that out, boy?"

"No, Sir. I suppose I just felt like stating the obvious." Jason licked his lips again. He'd never done this, but…. "Sir… if I were there, I would ask permission to kneel in front of you so that you wouldn't have to stroke yourself, Sir. I'd much rather… that is, if it pleases you, Master, I would love to take you into my mouth. I'd love to run my tongue up and down your shaft, around the head of your cock. Is there anything for me to taste, Sir? Are you getting sticky?"

"Oh yeah. You know it, boy."

"I'd love to taste you, Sir. I'd love to swallow your cock whole. Kiss your balls. Roll them around in my mouth. I…." He drew a blank. What else? Jason closed his eyes and tried to imagine it, tried to remember what it had been like going down on Henry. "You're so good to me when I suck you off, Sir. When you stroke my hair, I only want to please you more. I want to find that spot right under the tip of your cock and run my tongue around it because it makes you squirm. I want to slide my tongue over the slit. I want to take your cock all the way to the back of my throat and—" He was cut short by a loud grunt on the other end.

"Shit, boy."

"I hope *that* wasn't what I inspired you to do."

There was a moment of stunned silence where Jason feared he might have seriously crossed a line—and then Henry burst out laughing. "Boy, I swear, I don't know whether to whip you senseless or kiss you when you say shit like that!"

"Well, I know what I'd prefer, Sir. If it pleases you, that is. Your kisses are to die for."

"Brat. Okay. I need to go clean myself off and you need to get to bed."

"Yes, Sir."

"And boy, thank you."

"You're welcome, Sir." *Master.* He hung up; his balls ached, but he was afraid that if he went to the bathroom again, someone— Alicia—might notice and ask why he was taking a second shower. Reluctantly, he got under the covers and turned out the light. He went to sleep holding on to the collar.

A BLACK sedan stood waiting at the corner.

"Get in."

Jason blinked. Henry? How had he gotten there?

"Get in, boy."

Jason obeyed, sliding into the backseat. Henry was his Master, wasn't he?

"You're wearing too many clothes. Take off your jeans. Boxers, too."

"I—"

"Silence, boy! Unless you want to wear this." From out of nowhere, Henry produced a wicked-looking gag with a mouthpiece bigger than a grapefruit. "You gonna deprive me of the pleasure of that mouth?"

"No, Sir." He ducked his head. He'd been told not to speak.

Henry grabbed him by the hair and began wrestling the gag into place.

"No! *Please*! I can be quiet! I'll be good—!" But before he could get out another word, the sour-tasting rubber was lodged between his teeth, stretching his jaw uncomfortably wide.

Tears streamed down his cheeks as he finished stripping. Rough hands dragged him out of the strange car and bound his wrists behind him. A blindfold was secured over his eyes. He was taken inside, bent over something hard, maybe a stool. An ottoman.

"Oh, nice," said a voice. "I've wanted this for so long." It sounded like Terry.

Jason wriggled but the bonds held tight.

He heard other voices now, men he didn't know but who made it clear exactly what they were going to do to him while Henry watched.

JASON woke in a tangle of sheets and sweat. He clutched the collar tighter, squeezing back tears. Henry would never do that to him.

Slowly, his breathing evened out. His heartbeat slowed back to normal.

Too unnerved to go back to sleep, Jason pulled his laptop back onto his bed. He didn't bother with the light—he didn't want anyone noticing he was up. He surfed over to Henry's website and his list of recommended BDSM books. He couldn't afford to buy them full price, but he had enough experience buying textbooks online to know where to go for used books.

By the time he was done shopping, Jason had charged six titles to his credit card. He considered e-mailing Kendra to thank her for the nightmare, but it wasn't really her fault he was a mess.

After a few minutes' debate, he padded quietly down the hall to the bathroom. He didn't get in the shower. Instead, he stood in front of the sink with the water trickling out of the tap. He lathered up with soap and shaved his pits first, then his pubic hair. Then he stroked off as quietly as he could, wondering what it would be like to have Henry going down on him.

But he doubted Masters sucked off their slaves. Still, having Henry's hand around his cock, Henry's dick up his ass... *God, it was so good.* Jason came with a loud grunt. He caught himself on the sink and drew in a ragged breath, praying no one had heard.

"Master," he whispered aloud. He smiled. It felt *so* right. He cleaned up after himself and went back to his room just as the sun was starting to come up.

When he got there, he shot Kendra a quick text: *Read the book. You made your point.*

It wasn't a lie. She had made her point. He just didn't happen to agree with it.

"YOU got something in the mail," Alicia informed Jason as he walked past the family room, where she and his father were eating Chinese takeaway in front of the television.

"Oh?" He tried to act nonchalant, praying his father hadn't suddenly decided to start going through his mail.

"Kitchen table," Dad said.

"Thanks." It had only been a week; he hadn't expected anything so soon.

"Jason." Alicia called him back to the family room.

He stuck his head back through the doorway. "Yeah?"

She fixed him with a disapproving glower. "I'm a little surprised that with all your car problems you're able to buy… whatever… through the mail."

God, please don't let her *have opened it.* "I needed some stuff for class," he lied. "It was cheaper to buy it online than at the bookstore. Night, guys."

He breathed a sigh of relief when he found the unopened brown cardboard box waiting for him in the kitchen. For once, he was grateful for his father's apathy.

He made himself a sandwich and carried the box to his room.

By the time his dad and Alicia turned off the television, Jason was halfway through the first book. By the time he heard footsteps padding down the hall—the telltale sounds of springs bouncing in his father's bedroom—he'd nearly finished it. By the time all was quiet in the house, he'd read the whole thing and he felt… scared. *Terrified.* Confused.

His head was buzzing with questions, but he wasn't sure he wanted all of them answered, because what if he didn't like what Henry told him?

Jason reached for his phone and punched in Henry's number—by now he had it memorized. He'd called Henry nearly every day the past week. Most of the time they just talked about life, school, and work, and mostly it was Jason who did the talking while Henry listened. Sometimes Jason talked dirty while Henry masturbated. Henry hadn't allowed him to touch himself again except to wash. It had been… frustrating. Amazing. Frightening, because it felt so right. So good. And now he was afraid—

Henry picked up after four rings. "Jason?"

He blinked. Henry hadn't used his given name once in the last week. It was usually boy, occasionally baby. Jason looked at the clock. "Shit. Sorry." It was nearly midnight. "I didn't realize the time." Even though Henry suffered occasional bouts of insomnia, Jason didn't like to call after eleven without texting him first to make sure he was up.

"You okay?" Henry asked.

"Yeah. I, ah, I got some of those books you suggested."

"Ah." It sounded like Henry was shuffling around a little, maybe sitting up, getting comfortable. "And?"

"I think I'm a little overwhelmed," he admitted. "I mean… *total* power exchange?" He used the words from the book.

"Every relationship involves some kind of power exchange, Jason. I'm just—okay, this is going to make me sound like a real prick. I'm going to say it anyway. I'm honest enough with myself and the people I get involved with to know what I want. To express what I want, in *words*, not with frickin' head games. And I'm enough of a prick to expect to *get* what I want."

"A slave. A real slave. Not just in the bedroom. Like in *The Story of O*." Which Jason had finished but hadn't liked, no matter how objective he tried to be. "You want someone who's at your disposal 24/7." He couldn't help sounding bitter. Angry. Cheated, because Henry had convinced him that that *wasn't* what it was like at all. "You want someone who drops whatever their plans are just because *you* say so. Someone… someone who keeps their eyes down and never talks back, someone… Jesus, Henry! You *lied* to me!"

"I have *never* lied to you." Henry's tone was frighteningly calm. "Slave is the natural counterpart to Master, Jason, and no one lives their life exclusively in the bedroom."

"Yeah. Yes, Sir. Sorry." Fuck, why was he sorry? For forgetting to call Henry "Sir"? For getting angry? For believing the bullshit?

"Why don't we drop the 'Sir' for a while and just talk, okay?" Henry suggested.

"I didn't think we could do that."

Henry snorted. "One, you don't belong to me, and two, even if you did, the answer would still be yes. We can do whatever we want."

"Don't you mean we can do anything *you* want?"

"Can I ask you a question?"

Jason blinked. Nodded. Realized how stupid that was. "Yeah. Sure."

"When we went out to eat or ordered room service, who did the ordering?"

"You did. Except for Sunday morning." After Henry took the collar off him, Jason ordered for himself.

"All right. And how did you feel about me ordering for you?"

"It was...." He hesitated. "I guess I kind of liked it," he admitted. "But it wasn't like you ordered something I didn't like. You even asked me if there was anything I didn't want."

"Why would I intentionally get you something you wouldn't want?"

"Because you could."

"Not if I wanted you to go out with me again."

"Yeah, but maybe that's exactly my point. We were sort of on a date, weren't we? So if you wanted to see me again, you wouldn't act like a prick. But if I was... if *someone* was your slave, then it wouldn't matter what you did. You'd order the food and he'd eat it. He wouldn't have a choice."

"You think so, do you?"

"Total power exchange," Jason repeated. Total. Complete. Absolute.

Henry sighed. "How about this: Let's say I had me a slaveboy and I told him he had to take math classes and become an accountant, because I wanted someone to do the books for my business. But what if my slave wanted to be an artist, take art classes. What do you think he'd do? Especially if he didn't have an aptitude for math."

"I don't know. If he's your slave, he should do what you tell him to, right?"

"What would *you* do? And I expect an honest answer."

Jason nibbled at his lower lip. "I'd have to tell you I couldn't do it." And that made him feel like a failure. "I suck at math and would make a lousy accountant." And more than anything, he wanted to take art classes. He hated fucking Web design.

"Thank you."

"For what?"

"It's not always easy to be honest, Jason. Especially… well, it's just not. Okay, so carrying on with the scenario where my slave has just told me that he's very sorry, but he sucks at math and would make a lousy accountant, what do you think *I* should do?"

"I really *don't* know. If you're the one making all the decisions, he can't just tell you no."

"Like hell he can't! If I completely ignore my boy's limits and desires and try to force him into something that's no good for him, then I don't deserve his service. If he was smart, something I know *you* are, he would take my collar off his neck and throw it in my face. He'd tell me where to go and how to get there and in *exactly* what position I should fuck the horse I rode in on."

"But then I—he—wouldn't be your slave anymore!"

"That's my point, Jason. If I pushed you that far, you'd walk out on me and I wouldn't own you anymore. It would be my own damned fault for abusing the gift of your submission."

"So why call it slavery if the slave can leave whenever they want?" Jason demanded.

"Why get married if you can get divorced?"

He blinked. "I… I don't know. I guess… because it's a promise. It means two people love each other and want to make it work, no matter what."

"What do you think a collar is?"

"I… it's not about love. Is it?"

"It can be. Every couple—every arrangement—is different. The people involved set their own rules. *Their own rules*, Jason," he repeated. "Not the Master's rules. Unless you skipped all those chapters about negotiation."

"No, Sir. Henry. I just… shit." He swiped his free hand over his face.

"Why don't you take some time to sit with it a bit? To think about what you really want."

He sagged against his headboard. "Yeah, okay. And thanks. Again. You must think I'm a basket case."

"No, I don't. I think you're figuring out some scary truths about yourself. And that's the thing: this is stuff only you can figure out. I can't tell you what to do. No one can. I'm only going to ask you for one favor before we hang up."

"Anything," he promised without hesitation.

"All I want is to still be your friend in the morning. I want you to know you can call me anytime, for anything. Okay?"

Jason licked his lips. "Okay. Thank you."

"Good night."

"Night, Henry." *Sir.* Master.

It felt right. And that terrified him.

Chapter Eleven

JASON woke up the next morning to find a text message from Henry waiting for him on his phone.

Just wanted to check in, make sure you're okay. XO Henry.

Jason blinked. XO? What kind of short hand was—*Kiss and hug.* His stomach fluttered. He texted Henry back quickly:

Doing better. Still thinking but less freaked out. Thanks for checking in. He hesitated, then tapped in, *XO Jason.* He hit Send before he lost his nerve.

He went to the kitchen for coffee and something to eat. It was late enough that both his father and Alicia were gone for the day, but just the same, he carried his cup and plate back to his room, closed the door, and buried himself in the other book that had come yesterday. He was a quarter of the way through it when his phone chirped, alerting him to a text message.

It wasn't Henry. It was from Terry.

I'm not going 2 let up til U agree 2 talk. I'll show up at UR work. UR house. I'll keep showing up.

Fuck. Angrily, Jason typed back, *Fine. Have the night off. Pick a place. We can talk.*

A moment later, Terry typed back, *Applebee's. Cedar St. Lansing.*

Jason blinked. Applebee's was his favorite "American fare" restaurant, and Terry wasn't asking to meet in the middle, he was willing to drive all the way to Lansing.

Jason's phone chirped again. *Time?* Terry had texted.

7, he tapped in and hit Send. God, he hoped he wasn't making a mistake.

His phone chirped. *I'll B there. I miss U.*

Jason typed back. *I have 2 study. C U 2nite.* He turned off his phone and went back to his book.

THE knots in Jason's stomach tightened as he pulled into the Applebee's parking lot. He spotted Terry's car—and parked as far away from it as he could so that when they left, they wouldn't end up walking in the same direction. He couldn't begin to count how many times Terry had used that as an excuse to end up together in one backseat or another, making out. Fucking.

Jason did a double take when he got to the table to find Terry wearing a button-down shirt instead of one of his usual T-shirts. Terry smiled up at him. He got to his feet and gave Jason a light hug. "I missed you."

"Yeah. Missed you too," Jason found himself lying. Or was it a lie? He was sour about the way things had been the last while—maybe even the last year—but there must have been a time when he enjoyed getting together with Terry. Why else would he have kept seeing him for so long, even after things got bad? "Sorry I've been so hard to get ahold of," Jason told him. "Life's been a little crazy."

"Kendra told me you were picking up extra shifts. Sorry to hear about your car."

"Yeah, it sucks," Jason agreed. He shrugged out of his coat and sat down. "How about you? How's work?"

"I quit."

"You're shitting me."

Terry smiled. "Nope. I got the manager's job I applied for at the video store. It's not glamorous or anything, but it's forty hours a week, salary and benefits."

"I'm glad," said Jason. He meant it.

The waitress came by to get Jason's drink order.

"Water's good," he told her.

"Get what you want," said Terry. "I asked you out, dinner's on me."

Jason's licked his lips. He hadn't intended for this to be a date. "That's okay. And water's fine," he said to waitress, who wisely left them alone for a few minutes.

"Come on," said Terry, "I've been dying to celebrate with you. I got a real job."

"And I'm happy for you," he repeated, "but I can get my own dinner."

Terry's jaw tightened—then relaxed. "Maybe you'll let me buy next time."

Jason frowned. Shrugged. He wasn't sure he wanted a next time.

DINNER was pleasant. They talked about nothing, everything: the new season of *Doctor Who*, movies and television series coming out they both wanted to see—wanted to avoid.

Terry didn't bring up Henry or the con.

When the waitress dropped their bill, they split it up and each left a tip. For a change, Terry left a decent tip without Jason having to goad him into doing it.

"I had a nice time," Jason was forced to concede as they made their way toward the door.

"I'm glad." When they got outside, Terry turned to him. "Maybe we could do it again sometime?" he asked cautiously.

Jason nibbled his lower lip. "I… yeah. Sure. I'd like that."

Terry smiled. "Me too. Well, ah, I guess this is good night. Drive safe."

"Thanks. You too." Jason walked to his car. With every step he took, the knot in his stomach got tighter and tighter. He'd expected to leave tonight angry with Terry, never wanting to see him again. But he'd had a good time, and he did want to see Terry again. He was remembering why they'd started dating in the first place, how funny Terry could be, how easy he was to talk to, at least when he wasn't being a jerk.

But what did that mean for him and Henry?

As Jason was pulling onto the highway, his phone rang. He felt an immediate stab of guilt—but it wasn't Henry, it was Kendra. He let her call go to voice mail and phoned her back when he pulled into his driveway at home. Kendra wanted to know every detail of his "big date" and was so happy to hear that he and Terry were "working things out."

"I know it's early to start thinking about spring break," Kendra went on as Jason made his way to his bedroom, "but me and Sue just moved into our own place, and we'd *love* to have you and Terry come visit. We have a guest room," she added. "And no more fucking roommates from hell."

Jason shrugged. Which was pointless, she couldn't see him. "I'll have to see how things go around here," he hedged. He flopped down onto his bed but didn't realize he'd reached under his pillow for the collar until he closed his hand around it. The leather felt good in his hand. He missed Henry.

"Jason, I know I came down on you pretty hard about that guy from con, but when you get here, Sue wants to talk to you about her ex. He was just like Henry, and he really hurt her. It wasn't just the bruises either, it was… he made her feel like shit, like she didn't deserve any better. She'd gotten that so much already at home, just like you do from your dad, that she believed him. By the time he was done with her, she hardly had any friends, because he cut her off from everybody with all these stupid rules he made her follow, and it was hell, Jason. I don't want to see you go through the same stuff she did before she finally got away from the creep. You just… you've been through fuck and back already with your mom's diabetes and your dad's bullshit. You need somebody who'll treat you right."

"Yeah. I know." He pressed the leather to his nose and inhaled deeply. "I have to go. I have to study for a test next week." What he really needed to do was sort out what he wanted. *Who* he wanted. Because he could fall so easily for Henry, and he knew it.

Only Henry lived in Ohio. Hadn't it been hard enough trying to maintain a long-distance relationship with Terry, who only lived two hours away? How could he ever have anything with somebody who lived as far away as Henry did?

But Terry would never tie him up the way he wanted, he would never—

Jason's phone chirped again. It was a text message from his father, reminding him about dinner with Alicia and her family on Sunday:

Please do not forget that it's Amanda's birthday. A gift from you would be nice. She's turning 22. Get something nice.

He groaned but texted back that he'd be there with a "nice gift" for Amanda, Alicia's youngest daughter. Not to show up would be risking more shit than he wanted to deal with, and showing up without a gift would be even worse. He just wished he knew what the hell to get Amanda for her birthday. He'd only met her a couple of times and didn't have a clue what she was into.

Before he went to bed, Jason shot Henry a quick text. He didn't mention Terry. He tucked his phone under his pillow so that if Henry called, it would wake him up.

JASON and Henry played phone tag all the next day; every time one called, the other was busy. Jason played phone tag with Terry too, but it wasn't so accidental.

ALICIA lived in Lansing, in one of those twisty-turny subdivisions that were easy to get lost in. Jason missed her house every time he visited, which admittedly wasn't often. By the time he arrived, Alicia was putting dinner on the table. Her oldest daughter, Valerie, answered the door; she took Jason's leather jacket with a dark, disdainful look and ushered him into the dining room, where she introduced her fiancé, Lawrence Belamy, a fourth-year law student at U of M in Ann Arbor.

"Nice to meet you." Jason extended his hand.

Lawrence accepted with a tight smile. "You're Greg's son, then?"

Duh. "Yeah. Hi," he said to the rest of the table. "Sorry I'm late, I missed your street," he added with an apologetic smile in Alicia's direction.

"Honestly. How long have I been a part of your father's life?"

Jason shrugged. *Too long?* Probably not the best answer. He took his seat quietly. He was wearing a button-down silk shirt that he'd picked up at the thrift store, dark jeans, and dress shoes; his hair was pulled back in a neat ponytail. Lawrence and his father were both wearing suits. Ties. Crisp white cotton shirts. Alicia and her daughters were dressed up too, and he was certain the rock on Valerie's finger wasn't a cubic zirconia.

Jason's mom had never dressed up for family dinners; it was always "come as you are." Mom said family shouldn't care what you're wearing, just that you show up. Alicia didn't seem to agree. Every time she looked at Jason, he got the feeling she was completely disgusted by what she saw. He did his best to shrug it off. She was Dad's girlfriend, not his. She didn't have to like him any more than he had to like her, they just had to put up with each other.

Jason turned to Amanda. "Happy birthday, by the way," he said.

Amanda was plainer than her sister, she wore lighter makeup, and her hair looked like it was naturally that particular shade of blonde. Her smile seemed more genuine too. "Thanks. You have one coming up soon too, don't you?" she asked.

Jason nodded. "Yeah, March second."

"So soon?" Amanda seemed surprised. "I hadn't realized it was right around the corner. We'll have to get together, do something special for you."

He forced a smile. That would be a first.

"Let's not talk about Jason's birthday, Amanda. This is your big day, not his," Alicia said with a disapproving glance his way, as if it was somehow Jason's fault for being born so close to Amanda's birthday. "Greg, would you say grace, please?"

Speaking of firsts…. Dad never prayed over meals, at least not that Jason had ever seen. But when his father bowed his head and started to pray aloud, Jason followed suit and quietly went through the motions. He wasn't exactly against religion, but he had never quite been comfortable with it, either. Too many people used their religion as an excuse to condemn guys like him, women like Kendra and Sue. Since Jason's mom had never adhered to any particular faith, it had never been an issue for him. *Until now.* He muttered "amen" along with everybody else when his dad finished speaking.

As food started to make its way around the table, Lawrence piped up, "So, Jason, your father says you're going into Web design."

"Yeah." Jason surveyed the meal. There was a standing rib roast, baby red and yellow skin potatoes and carrots that had obviously been baked with it, gravy, biscuits, and salad. Right. Salad and bread it was.

"What made you decide on computers?" Lawrence asked amiably as he passed Jason the potatoes.

Jason passed them on to Amanda, who was seated next to him. "I really wanted to go into art—" he began.

Across the table, his father cleared his throat.

"But there's no money in art." Jason told Lawrence what his father had told him when they first started discussing school. "So I— we"—he gave a nod to his dad, who appeared pleased by his little speech—"figured Web design was the next best thing. Everybody needs a website, and it'll still let me be creative."

"Jason, why on earth aren't you eating anything?" Valerie interjected as he passed on the carrots as well.

"I'm a vegetarian." He kept his tone carefully neutral.

Valerie frowned. "Carrots aren't meat."

"I'm fine with salad," he told her. It was pointless getting into an argument.

"Oh, I'm so sorry," Alicia said, although to Jason's ears, she didn't sound sorry at all. "I keep forgetting you don't eat meat. I can open up a can of vegetables or something if you'd like. I've got corn, probably some green beans."

"It's no big deal," he lied. The food wasn't the big deal; the big deal was that she never remembered.

"It's really no trouble," she insisted. "I don't want you to feel left out."

"It's fine, Alicia," Jason's father told her.

Jason flashed him a smile that was half gratitude, half apology. It wasn't actually fine—not for Alicia or for him, or even for his dad—but at least the conversation was over.

JASON was on his way home when his phone chirped, letting him know he had a new text message. He glanced at it—his heart thumped. Henry. He pulled off on the next road crossing the expressway so he could read the message.

Tag, you're it. XO.

A smile spread over his face. Henry signed every text with XO.

Jason considered getting back on the road, calling from the house, but after the last few hours, he needed to hear the sound of Henry's voice more than ever. He dialed his number and waited.

"I was starting to think you were avoiding me, boy," Henry teased when he picked up on the other end.

Jason tried to laugh, but he was too drained. "Never, Sir."

"You okay?"

"Yeah. I just left Alicia's house, that's all. It was her daughter's birthday. Amanda, the younger one. The one who's almost human."

Henry snickered at his description. "How bad was it?"

"I got to eat salad, bread, and cake."

"Not much of a meal."

"Yeah, well." Jason shrugged. "The worst thing is that I'm sure I'm going to get an earful from my father later."

"Over…?" Henry queried.

"He pretty much made it mandatory that I get Amanda something for her birthday—you know, like I can afford to go out and buy stuff for a total stranger. I mean, I've met Alicia's daughters a few times, but it's not like we hang out or anything. I don't know what kind of music she likes or if she has any hobbies or what."

"So what'd you end up getting her?"

"A fifty-dollar gift card for Bed Bath & Beyond."

"Sounds good. My sister and mom love that store and keep hoping they'll open one up around here somewhere. Nearest one is over an hour away, by my aunt's place. My stepdad's pretty happy 'bout that. He says if they could, those two would be in there every week."

"Well, I guess if I ever have to get anything for *your* family, I'll know where to go," he said sourly. And then blushed. That was a pretty presumptuous statement. He also realized it was the first time Henry had talked about his family except to clarify that it was his sister who had picked up the phone that day, and yes, she was the one with HIV. Henry hadn't told Jason how she got it, and Jason hadn't asked.

But now he wondered why Henry was so closemouthed when it came to talking about himself. Maybe he was just private? Or maybe it meant he wasn't really serious about whatever it was they were doing. Jason doubted that Henry's family even knew he existed. Why should they?

"I take it your gift didn't go over so great?" Henry asked him.

"I probably didn't spend enough." Maybe if he'd made it a hundred-dollar gift card or a card to somewhere else, like Niemen Marcus or something, his Dad would have been happier with him.

"A gift isn't about how much money you spend."

He snorted. "Dad got Amanda a gift certificate for a whole day at some fancy spa in East Lansing. It had to have cost him five or six hundred bucks, easy. Then Alicia promised to take her shopping afterwards, for 'whatever she wanted'—and I don't mean at Walmart."

"Jealousy isn't pretty on you, Jason."

"I'm not jealous! I just… nothing I do is good enough for these people. *Nothing*. I would have spent more money if I'd known I was supposed to, but I didn't know. Nobody told me how much to spend or what to buy or what to wear or anything!"

"You sound like a six-year-old."

Jason stopped just short of pouting. Henry had a point. "They never tell me anything, Henry," he said, his tone more subdued. "It's like… sometimes I think Alicia *wants* me to fail, and Dad… Dad doesn't notice anything but my mistakes."

"Come on, fifty bucks is what you bring home on a good day. I'm sure your dad knows that, and I'm sure Amanda appreciates it. Nobody wants you to fail. If you weren't sure what to get Alicia's daughter— and if you really *cared*—you could have asked your father or Alicia for some kind of direction instead of just guessing."

If Henry knew them at all, he wouldn't say that. But what were the chances of Henry ever wanting to meet Jason's "family"? "Maybe," he said, instead of arguing. "But it doesn't feel like any of them gives a shit about me. My dad spent more time talking to Lawrence—Valerie's fiancé—than he did to me. I sat in the corner watching the clock, waiting until I'd been there long enough that I could leave without looking rude."

Henry was quiet a moment. "So I take it you're alone now?"

"I… sort of. I'm in my car."

"Not on the road, I hope."

"No, Sir. I pulled off the road because… because I wanted to talk to you." He'd wanted Henry to cheer him up, not make him feel worse.

"Where are you?"

Jason frowned. He'd just answered that. "On some little road off the expressway."

"Anybody around?"

"Not really." The stretch of highway between Lansing and Ithaca was pretty empty, just a few farms, a country club. Lots of nothing.

"Perfect. I want you to do something for me, boy. You feeling up to it?"

Jason could almost hear the lascivious grin in Henry's voice. "Sir?" he asked.

"Push your seat back a little to give yourself more room. Then unzip your fly and take out your dick."

Jason licked his lips.

"Problem hearing, boy?"

"N-no, Sir." Jason eased back his seat and unzipped his fly. His cock was already getting hard. He freed it from his boxers.

"You're getting hard, aren't you?" It was barely a question.

"Yes, Sir. What if someone sees me?"

"There anybody around?"

"N-no, but—"

"Then you will do exactly what I say. Do you understand me, boy?"

"Yes, Sir."

"Good. Can you put me on speaker so you can use both hands?"

Jason gulped down a lump of fear. "Yes, Sir. Just a second." He didn't know why the idea of having Henry on speaker was so scary. It wasn't like anyone else would hear. He hit the speaker button. "Can you still hear me okay?"

"Loud and clear, boy. Pull your pants down past your hips. Then lean back and put the phone on your lap. I want to be right next to that pretty little cock of yours."

Jason's face burned, but he did as he was told. "All set, Sir," he said when he was done.

"I think I might have to get you one of those video phones," Henry crooned. "I would love nothing more than to be able to see you right now, your pants down, your cock dripping… it is dripping, isn't it?"

"Oh yeah," he breathed as pearly fluid began collecting on the tip of his cock.

"Good. I want you to touch your dick, boy. Just the head. Just that sweet, sticky fluid. Run your finger over the tip, across the slit."

Jason couldn't help the groan of pure pleasure he felt touching himself like this. It had been forever since Henry had let him masturbate. "Oh God, please tell me I get to come."

"It's Master, not God. I don't need *that* kinda promotion."

Jason couldn't help but laugh. "Yes, Sir. Master." It wasn't such a hard word, was it?

"Have you been good? You been keeping yourself shaved?"

"Yes, Sir. I shave every couple of days."

"Good boy. You still rubbing your slit?"

"Yes, Sir."

"Good. Now I want you to put that finger in your mouth."

Jason balked.

"What, never taste your own cum before?"

"I… no." Heat flooded his cheeks.

"Go on, then."

Nervously, Jason glanced left—then right. No cops. No people out walking their dogs. Just him. And Henry. He stuck out his tongue and gave his precum-coated finger an experimental lick. It tasted… well, it tasted about like anyone else's precum.

"If I was there, it would be me licking your fingers, boy. I tasted your cum once, you know."

"You did?"

He chuckled at the shock in Jason's voice. "You were a little too preoccupied to notice. But yeah. I wanted to know what you tasted like. And let me tell you, I've tasted lots of cock in my day, lots of cum, but you... damn. Maybe it's that vegetarian diet of yours, but you taste better than anyone I've ever had. I could suck your cock all day long."

"You... you'd... I thought...."

"What? You thought that because I'm a top, I don't like cock? I just never got around to sucking yours, that's all. Tell me, boy, would you like me to suck you? Would you like me to take your cock into my mouth, all the way to the back of my throat, and suck you dry?"

Jason shuddered. "Oh God. Master. Yes, Sir, please." He could almost see it, almost imagine how it would feel to have Henry's mouth around him, hot and velvety. "It would be so good."

"Yes it would. You're such a good boy, Jason. So easy to please. Now. I want you to stick your whole finger in your mouth and suck hard. Get it nice and wet. You're gonna want it wet for where it's going next."

Jason's eyes widened. Henry couldn't be serious!

Henry laughed, a low-sounding rumble, almost as if he could see Jason's expression. "That's right, boy. You're going to fuck your ass for me in a minute. But right now, while you're sucking your fingers, I want you to take your other hand and unbutton your shirt."

"Yesh-Shir," Jason said around his fingers.

Henry laughed some more. "I want you playing with those nipple rings, boy. Pull. Twist. Pinch your nips. I want you playing with yourself the same way I like to play with you. I'm not there, so you have to be my hands. Got it?"

This time Jason took his fingers out of his mouth before he answered, "Yes, Sir." Then he went back to sucking, pretending it was Henry's fingers, Henry's cock. With his other hand, he pulled his nipple rings. He twisted. He pinched each nipple as mercilessly as he knew Henry would if he were there. Henry didn't tell him to stop until he was whimpering. Panting. Mewling as pleasure and pain got all mixed up together in his head. His body.

"Now take that finger you've gotten all nice and wet and juicy and fuck yourself with it. Move the phone if you have to."

Jason's heart pounded so loudly in his chest he was sure Henry could hear that too—but he obeyed without hesitation. He moved the phone to the armrest and shoved his hand between his thighs, past his aching cock. He scooted farther forward and found his entrance.

"Take it slow, boy," Henry told him. "Relax. Let me know when you're inside."

"I've never done this before," Jason admitted. "Not with my hand."

"What *do* you use when you fuck yourself, boy?"

Jason blushed. "A butt plug, Sir."

"How many do you own?"

"Three, Sir."

"Any dildos?"

"Two."

"Good to know, boy."

Jason licked his lips. Then he let out a soft moan as his finger pressed past the tight ring of muscles. "I... oh...."

"That feel good, boy?"

"Yeah. It burns a little without lube, but I wish it was you, Sir. I wish you were inside me."

"Me too, boy. If you didn't live so goddamned far away, it would be me. But I'm here and you're there, so you're gonna have to use your imagination. Pretend it's me fucking you, boy. My finger. My dick."

"Can I use two fingers, Master?" The word slid out easily this time.

"Can you take two?"

"Yes, Sir."

"Then go ahead—but take it slow. I'd never harm you, so you're not allowed to harm yourself, either."

Jason's heart thumped harder, his eyes rolled back in his head, and his toes curled as he pressed a second finger into himself. He pushed both fingers deeper... deeper... and cried out when he hit his prostate. He rubbed it, sending wave after wave of heat to the head of his cock. "Please, Master... please... I... if it pleases you, may I touch my dick?"

"Very good, boy," Henry told him. He sounded so pleased. "And yes, you may touch your dick, just as long as you keep fucking yourself with your other hand. But you ask for my permission before you come, you hear me, boy?" he warned.

"Yes, Sir. Oh, God, Sir... feels so good. It's been so long... God... shit... close... please?"

"Not yet."

Jason shuddered. He kept pumping his hand up and down on his shaft, his other hand rubbing against his prostate. He was *so* close. "Please, Master, I can't hold it... please, please let me come? Please, Sir!" he cried.

"Come for me, boy."

The orgasm rocked through Jason's whole body. He came loud and hard and didn't stop fucking himself until he was shaking. Finally he sagged against the seat, panting, sated. Then he opened his eyes and looked out the window. "Oh, fuck."

"You okay?"

"Yeah. I just... I have to clean the windshield."

Henry laughed. "That's my boy. Did you have fun?"

"Yes, Sir. Master. Thank you."

"You're welcome, boy. Now, get yourself cleaned up and go home. Have yourself a nice cup of hot cocoa and take a nice long shower—but before you do that, send me a text so I know you got in okay."

Jason smiled. Even from hundreds of miles away, Henry was still taking care of him. "Yes, Sir."

It wasn't until he got back on the highway that Jason started to feel guilty. He should have told Henry about dinner with Terry... but... it wasn't like they'd gotten back together. It was just dinner. Jason paid for his own meal. He and Terry were just friends.

Jason blinked in surprise when he walked out to the parking lot after class to find Terry leaning against his car. "Happy birthday!"

"Hi. I...." He didn't know what to say. Terry was holding a single red rose. Jason accepted it. "I...thanks."

Terry laughed. "Well, somebody isn't going to win any awards for eloquence, that's for sure," he teased.

Jason ducked his head. "Yeah. Sorry. I just... didn't expect to see you."

"I know. But I know your old man can be kind of a dick about your birthday, and I wanted to make sure you knew somebody cared."

"Thanks." He'd gotten a card from Kendra and Sue yesterday. His aunt in California sent him a check for twenty bucks, and much to his surprise, Amanda sent him a fifty-dollar gift card from Amazon. The note inside was sweet: *I don't know what you're into, but Amazon has everything*, and a smiley face. He hadn't received anything from Alicia or Valerie, but he hadn't expected anything from either of them. His father had handed him three fifty-dollar bills that morning—no card— and mentioned that if he still needed tires, maybe they could go shopping over the weekend or something. It wasn't exactly a trip to the day spa, but he needed new tires more than he needed a massage.

Jason turned his attention back to Terry. "You want to go get a cup of coffee or something? I don't have to be to work for a few hours."

"Only if you'll let me buy."

Jason nibbled his lip.

"Come on, it's your birthday."

"Yeah. Okay. Thanks, Terry."

When Jason got home from work, he found another package of books waiting for him on the kitchen table. Under it was a thickly padded oversized envelope from New Marshfield, Ohio. It was too small to be books, and he was pretty sure he hadn't ordered from anyone in Ohio, anyway. He only knew one person who lived in Ohio.

He opened it right there in the kitchen, his heart beating rapidly in his chest.

The envelope contained a jewel case with a CD inside. The disc was labeled in black marker in loopy, scrawling handwriting.

String Quartet Tribute to Metallica and More, Happy Birthday. XO Henry.

Jason's heart swelled with emotion, and a smile blossomed across his face. He dialed his phone as he walked to his room, packages in arms.

Henry picked up in four rings. "Happy birthday," he said instead of hello.

Jason was still grinning. "I got the CD. Thank you, Sir."

"I know it wasn't a gift card to some fancy spa." Henry sounded almost apologetic.

"No, Sir, but I love it." *I think I might love you.*

"I'm glad, boy. How was work?"

Jason shimmied out of his pants one-handed. "It was all right. I made a little over fifty bucks. And I had that test today in my world history class."

"How'd you do?"

"I think I passed."

Henry chuckled. "That good, eh?"

"Yeah. Well." He didn't want to tell Henry how many classes he'd cut or how much homework he hadn't done so he could pick up extra shifts at work.

"Do I need to give you extra incentive to do better?"

Jason licked his lips nervously. "What sort of incentive did you have in mind, Sir?"

"Well...," he began thoughtfully, "I know Web design isn't your best subject, so I suppose a B or a C would be acceptable, but you're way too smart not to be able to read and regurgitate for history."

"Shit," he muttered without meaning to.

Henry cleared his throat.

"That is, I... Sir... I mean... maybe I'd better just shut up."

"Good choice, boy. So. How about one week in a chastity device—a real one, not like what you wore for me at the con—for every grade below an acceptable grade?"

"And acceptable grades are...?"

"There is no reason for you not to get an A in art. I checked the link you sent me to your deviantART page. Your work's real impressive."

Despite the threat of a chastity device, Jason beamed with pleasure at the compliment. "Thank you, Sir." Jason had e-mailed him the link last week, when Henry asked if he could see some of his artwork sometime. "Most of it's pretty old stuff, but I'm glad you like it."

"You're a talented artist, boy. You ever decide to change your mind about Web design and get back into art, there are some people I want you to meet."

Jason barely knew what to say. "You really think I'm that good?" His mom had always liked his work, and his friends and even teachers said it was good, but wasn't that what they were supposed to do?

"You've got real talent, boy. *And* I believe you're trying to distract me."

Heat rose in Jason's cheeks, pooled in his groin. "No, Sir. Not intentionally."

He chuckled. "Good, because that will get you a few stripes."

Jason shivered. "The crop, Sir?"

"Yup."

"Yes, Sir. I'm sorry, Sir. You were saying about my grades?"

"There's no reason for you not to ace that art class," Henry repeated. "No reason not to get a B in history and at least a C in Web design."

Jason licked his lips. He was getting a C in history and not sure he was going to pass his Web design class at all. However, "Yes, Sir" was all he said into the phone. Then: "I think I need to go study."

"I think that might be prudent." It sounded like he was trying not to laugh too hard. "Happy birthday, boy," he said again, his tone full of warmth and sincerity.

Despite everything, Jason smiled. He felt good. "Thank you, Sir." And he still didn't mention Terry.

Chapter Twelve

JASON shivered, wishing he'd brought his coat when he went outside to take a quick break after the lunch rush *finally* died down. Normally by this time, he'd have been cut from the floor and on his way home, but when he walked in the door to start his shift, Melissa, the new hostess, asked him if he could stay through dinner. They'd had two call-ins and she had a full book of reservations for the night. Jason wasn't about to turn down the money to be had on a Friday night, even though he *should* be studying for his Web design test next week. Except he wasn't sure it would matter; even if he aced next week's test, there was no way he was going to get better than a D in that class. But one week in a chastity device wouldn't be that bad. Would it?

He'd pulled his history grade up, at least.

And guilt continued to needle at him, but he called Terry anyway, because he'd promised he would, and when Terry asked him to go out clubbing tomorrow night, Jason agreed. They'd had dinner a couple of times in the last few weeks and gone to a couple of movies. Terry kept finding excuses to pick up the tab: he made more money than Jason, his income was more reliable since he wasn't dependent on tips, Jason's car still needed a ton of work, Terry didn't have school to pay for like Jason did…. Sometimes it was easier to let Terry pay than it was to argue. Besides, Jason had paid for so many of their dates over the last year or so, it seemed fair enough to let Terry buy him dinner once in a while. He knew he was making excuses, but he liked this side of Terry. He wanted to see more of it.

Behind him, the heavy back door opened, and Melissa stepped out of the restaurant. Her cigarette was lit before the door was even shut behind her. She inhaled deeply and leaned back against the brick wall, holding her pack out to Jason. For once, he wished he did smoke— maybe it would make him feel better—but he shook his head. Today wasn't the day to start a habit he couldn't afford to keep up. Into the phone, he said, "I gotta go. See you tomorrow."

"I can't wait to see you, Jason."

"Yeah, me too." He didn't know if he was lying or telling the truth anymore.

Jason hung up and pocketed his phone. "How's it going in there?" he asked his coworker.

"Lull between storms. Thank God, too. If I didn't get a smoke, I think I was going to fucking kill someone."

Jason snickered. Melissa was about his age, cute, petite, blonde. She'd only been at the restaurant for a month or so, but he liked her. They didn't have the usual things in common—TV, movies, books— but she liked a lot of the same music he did. They had gone out for coffee a couple of times after work and he enjoyed her company. But every time she asked about the man in his life, he told her it was complicated and changed the subject. "Can I ask you kind of a weird question?" he ventured tentatively.

"Sure, shoot."

"What if you were dating this guy, this real jerk, and then... then suddenly you met someone else... someone... I guess no one's perfect, but what if you met someone you thought was *everything* you ever wanted?"

"I'd say: 'What's the problem?' Dump the jerk and go for Mr. Wonderful."

"That's the thing. Sometimes... I mean... Henry's... God. He's so incredible, and I think I really want to be with him. But some of the things he wants... it's so fucking intense, maybe more intense than I can do. And my best friend thinks he's a total freak and that makes me feel...." He hesitated. Kendra made him feel like there might be something seriously wrong with him. "She says Henry's just a creep using me to get his rocks off. And I can't even tell her she's wrong, but I like it." He closed his eyes. He couldn't look at Melissa. "And on top of all that, Terry—the jerk—wants to get back together with me. Which would be so much easier than trying to be with Henry because what Henry wants is so complicated. So hard. But then we talk and no matter what he tells me to do, I do it. I *want* to do it." And that scared him more than anything else. He wanted so badly to please Henry, he wasn't sure he could ever tell him no.

Melissa took a deep drag off her smoke. "Can you fill in a couple of those blanks, honey?" she asked cautiously.

Jason faced her. "I just… I don't want you to think I'm weird."

"How weird is weird?"

"I… it's kinda personal."

"What, like diapers and fuzzy animal costumes personal?"

"No! Jesus."

She snickered. "Dressing up in women's underwear?"

"No." Except that Henry wanted to see him in a corset, but he wasn't going to tell Melissa that.

She shrugged. "Okay, so it can't be that weird. Spill it."

"I… it's kinda whips and chains personal."

She grinned again. "You go, girl! Keep talking!"

Jason stared straight ahead at the dumpster on the other side of the alleyway. "I just… okay, so I've always had… you know…."

"Smutty little fantasies?"

His whole face felt hot. "Yeah. And Henry… oh my God, Melissa. It's like he can read me like I'm a fucking book. But I've only ever wanted… I mean, like you said, 'smutty little fantasies'. He's way more serious about it than that, and it's one thing to get tied up for fun, but to *live* that way? I don't know if I could handle that."

"Is he asking you to move in with him?"

"I wish."

She quirked an eyebrow but didn't actually call him on what he'd just said. "So what exactly is the problem?" she asked instead.

Jason sighed and met her gaze once more. "I started hanging out with Terry again, and… and we're just friends, but I know he wants more. And he's acting… it's been really *nice*. He's reminding me of the guy he used to be, the one I used to love hanging out with. And… and maybe Kendra's right, you don't just walk away from five years with someone over some new guy. Do you?"

"That depends on the new guy. Besides, you said you loved 'hanging out with Terry', you didn't say you loved *him*."

Jason bit his lip. "I know. I mean, I *thought* I loved him. He was the first guy I was ever serious about. But then… then things just got bad between us, I guess. Or maybe I got busy with school and work and he went off and did stuff."

"Stuff?"

"I know he was seeing other people—which wouldn't have bothered me so much except that when I asked him about it, he kept denying it. If he'd just told me the truth, I wouldn't have cared. I mean… fuck, I don't know what I mean anymore."

"Well, if you want my opinion, the bottom line is that tigers don't change their spots overnight."

"Tigers have stripes."

"That's my point." She put out her cigarette on the wall behind them. "If your ex is suddenly acting the way you want him to after how long?" she asked.

"About a year, I guess."

"If he's suddenly acting like Prince Charming, I'd start looking for a toad, if I were you."

Jason had to laugh. "Maybe."

"Look, Jason, maybe it's not his fault any more than it's yours. Priorities change. You're probably not the same person you used to be either."

Jason licked his lips. That was an understatement. "What about the other stuff?"

"What, you mean getting tied up?"

"It's a little more intense than that."

"Honey, does he make you happy?"

A broad grin spread across Jason's face, and his cock swelled against his pants.

Melissa smirked. "Looks like part of your anatomy is happy, anyway."

"It's not just the sex," he told her. "It's the way I feel when I hear his voice, the way he kisses me…. God, his kisses are to die for." He missed kissing Henry more than anything else.

"Well then, what's the problem?"

"He's forty."

"So?"

Jason blinked. She was completely unfazed. "Sometimes I'm not sure I even know who he is. I mean, he's twice my age and I don't know what his favorite flavor of ice cream is!"

"Have you tried *asking*?"

TERRY pressed Jason into coming straight to his place after work on Saturday so they could grab dinner together before going dancing. He suggested Jason's favorite Middle Eastern restaurant.

"Why don't we do something closer to your apartment," Jason offered instead when they talked about it. Somehow it felt weird—wrong—going with Terry to the same restaurant where Henry had fucked him senseless in the parking lot. He wasn't sure he'd be able set foot inside the place without blushing—and he was sure he wouldn't be able to use the men's room.

Maybe that was the reason Jason ignored Henry's text message asking him to call when he got a chance.

Stepping into Terry's apartment after so long felt comfortable. More comfortable than Jason had expected it to. It didn't hurt that it looked like Terry had finally discovered what a vacuum cleaner was for and that there wasn't a sink full of dirty dishes in the kitchen. The apartment smelled like lavender-scented air freshener, and Adele was in the CD player.

"Well, what do you think?" Terry asked, greeting him with warm smile.

"It looks good." Terry looked good too. He was wearing a button-down shirt and snug jeans. It was sexy, but not his usual "come hither" style.

"Why don't you jump in the shower?" Terry suggested. "Feel free to help yourself to whatever you want from the closet when you're done. And you can use anything in the bathroom too. Take your time."

Jason nodded. Hesitated. Padded into the bathroom. Every other time he'd come over to Terry's place before going out, they'd ended up making out, fucking, sometimes not going out at all, regardless of their original plans. Which was why Jason kept expecting Terry to barge in on him in the shower, ask to join him, but he didn't.

After a very long, very hot shower, Jason shaved and did his hair. He took his time. Terry didn't bark at him to hurry it up or come in to see about getting a pre-dinner blow job. He stayed completely out of Jason's way.

Maybe tigers could change their spots after all.

Knives twisted in Jason's gut. But Henry had said it himself, Jason wasn't "his." He didn't know what he was to the other man. They had phone sex—a lot of it in fact—but so what? And yeah, if Henry told him to, he would probably wear that chastity device for a week, but if he didn't, it wasn't like Henry would ever know. Despite Henry talking about things like Dragon*Con and that St. Andrew's cross he had at his place, they hadn't actually made plans to see each other again. Henry hadn't invited him down for a visit, and he wasn't coming back up to Michigan before next January.

And besides, all Jason was doing tonight was having dinner with a friend and then going to the bar. Terry wanted more, but Jason hadn't agreed to more. He hadn't even kissed Terry.

Jason walked to Terry's bedroom, got dressed, and joined Terry in the living room.

As soon as he came into the room, Terry muted the TV. "Damn. I think I'd forgotten how sexy you are." Terry grinned up at him. "So, you ready?"

"Yeah. Sure."

"You okay?"

"Yeah, I just... I don't know what to make out of all this."

"All what? Me wanting to prove to you that I'm not a complete asshole? I know I can be a jerk, okay?" He crossed the distance between them and took Jason's hands in his. "I know how close I came to blowing it with you, but I swear, I never meant for you to think you were anything less than the most important person in my life. I love you. Maybe it took seeing you with that other guy for me figure out how much I need you."

Jason swallowed hard, not knowing what to say to that. "I—"

"You don't have to answer me. I know I have to earn this." He leaned in and pressed a soft, sweet kiss to Jason's cheek. Then he stepped back and got Jason's coat. "Come on, let's get some dinner, then go have some fun."

Six hours, a bottle of wine, and a half a dozen cosmopolitans later, Jason found himself back in Terry's apartment, on his knees, his mouth around Terry's dick. He wasn't even sure how he'd gotten there. He only knew that his own dick ached. He wanted...

Henry. He wanted Henry's voice in his ear telling him what to do. He wanted Henry's smoldering gaze on his body. He wanted Henry's mouth on his lips.

But Henry was a gazillion miles away, and Henry had been so clear when he'd said Jason wasn't his. Terry was right here, and he'd promised to give Jason everything he wanted tonight.

"Oh yeah," Terry grunted, jerking, bringing Jason violently up out of his thoughts. "Oh God, I missed this. Oh fuck." He fisted both hands into Jason's hair and held on tight, keeping him still as he began hammering his dick in and out of Jason's mouth. "Oh fuck... fuck yeah," he muttered, thrusting harder.

Jason looked up. Terry's eyes were closed; his head was tilted back. He wasn't even looking at the man whose mouth he was fucking!

Jason's gut clenched, but before he could do anything about how wrong everything felt, Terry came into the back of his throat and he swallowed it.

"Jesus, you're good at that."

Jason blinked. Good at what? Kneeling there while somebody fucked his mouth? Anyone could do that!

Terry sat back on the sofa. "Give me a minute to recover, then I've got something for you."

Jason didn't speak. He realized that when he'd knelt, he'd put his hands behind his back without even thinking about it. Terry didn't seem to notice. Jason shifted, resting his hands on his knees. He wanted to leave, but he was too drunk to drive. Had Terry kept buying him drinks on purpose? Jason hadn't bought a single drink for himself all evening—but Terry wouldn't really get him drunk just so he'd be stuck there. Would he?

"Come on." Terry stood up again. "Let's go to the bedroom."

Dumbly, Jason followed after him. Nothing in the bedroom seemed out of the ordinary—but then Terry pulled a length of hemp rope out from under the bed.

"Why don't you get comfortable," Terry crooned. "Then I can make you nice and *un*comfortable."

Jason hesitated. "Do... do you even know what you're doing?"

"What's to know? It's rope. You tie it in knots. You want me to blindfold you?"

Jason swallowed hard. He leaned in for a kiss, but Terry pulled back. He didn't make a big deal of it, but it was no secret he didn't like kissing Jason after Jason had gone down on him. He said it was too weird to taste his own cum in his lover's mouth.

Terry kissed his cheek. "Get undressed. I want this to be good for you, Jason. I swear I'll do anything you want tonight. *Every* night. I want you so bad. I love you so much. If you tell me what I did wrong before, I swear, I'll never do it again."

Jason's stomach clenched and bile burned the back of his throat. He ran to the bathroom and heaved the contents of his stomach into the smooth porcelain bowl.

"Jesus! *Jason!*" Terry was on his heels. "What the fuck? Are you okay?"

Jason leaned back from the toilet. He hit the handle. His breath was ragged. "Can I have a minute? Please?"

Terry blinked. Nodded. He left without a word, closing the door behind him.

Jason sagged against the cool tile wall and closed his eyes, shaking with the effort not to sob out loud as hot tears trickled down his cheeks. He didn't even know which one of them he was cheating on, who he was being more unfair to.

Terry loved him, wanted him. He was making an effort, even if it was falling short.

It was falling short because Jason wanted *Henry*. No way Terry could compare to *him*.

Only after Jason told Henry about tonight, he doubted the man would ever speak to him again.

Still shaking, Jason hauled himself to his feet. He rinsed out his mouth with mouthwash. He still tasted bile. Cum. His stomach heaved again. Thankfully nothing came up. He took deep breath. Let it out. He washed his face with cold water and resigned himself to losing both Terry and Henry. Maybe even Kendra, because he'd let her think he wasn't still in touch with Henry. He needed to tell her that he was. He needed to come clean with everybody, no matter the cost.

Jason crossed the hall to the bedroom and changed back into his own clothes before going to the living room, where Terry was watching television. Terry turned it off as soon as Jason came into the room.

"You feeling any better?"

Jason shook his head. "I'm going to head home."

"Please don't. I'll take the sofa, you can sleep in my bed. Or whatever. If you want the sofa, you can have the sofa and I'll take the bedroom. We can talk in the morning."

"There's nothing to talk about, Terry. I'm sorry. Please don't call me again."

"What? *Why?*"

"Because I don't want to see you anymore."

"Is it that other guy?"

"Yes. No. It's a lot of things. I'm not who I was five years ago. Neither of us is. I'm sure there was a time when I did love you, but... but I don't love you now. I haven't in a long time."

Terry was quiet for a long moment. Finally, "Don't call me when he hurts you, Jason," he said, his voice thick with anger. "If you don't want to see me again, that's fine, but don't you *dare* call me when he fucking hurts you."

"That's fair."

HE DIDN'T get far. He pulled over to the side of the road only a few blocks away from Terry's apartment. He wasn't in any shape to drive, although he was pretty sure most of the alcohol was no longer in his system. More than anything, he wanted to hear Henry's voice, but no way was he going to call him at two o'clock in the morning. There was no one he could call. So he sat there for an hour, watching the snow fall, until he felt up to driving home.

JASON counted the rings... six... it was early, barely 9:00 a.m., but surely—

"Hey, you're up early," Henry said by way of greeting.

"Hi. Yeah."

"You okay?"

"No. I… I have something to tell you." He'd gotten in at seven; salt trucks hadn't been out yet, and the roads were impossible, covered with snow, so what should have been a two-hour drive ended up being almost a four-hour drive instead.

When he walked in the front door, he discovered his dad was home for a change. Awake. Waiting for him. He ripped Jason up one side and down the other for being out all night, said he was irresponsible, disrespectful. Arrogant. He said Jason was no better than his mother, believing he could do whatever he pleased and not have to face the consequences. God, if his father had any idea…. Finally Jason escaped, but only because Dad was running late; he was supposed to have breakfast with Alicia before going to Sunday service at her church. When his dad had gotten so religious, Jason wasn't sure, but he didn't care. Dad's exit meant he could shower, make himself some coffee, and then slink off to his room. By then he figured Henry might be up—or maybe he'd hoped he wouldn't be. But he was. And this was it.

"I think this is going to be the last conversation we ever have," Jason told him, biting back another sob.

"Baby, talk to me. What's wrong?"

"I… I'm a total fuckup, Henry." He sat on his bed, clutching the phone in one hand, Henry's collar in the other. "Please don't hate me." *Please say I've still got a chance.*

"There is nothing you could do that would make me hate you, boy. Now come on, what happened?"

"I… I went out to dinner with Terry about a month ago. I… I've kinda been seeing him."

Henry was very quiet for way too long. "All right," he finally said, his tone frighteningly calm. "You certainly have every right to see whoever you want to, Jason."

He squeezed his eyes shut. It would be easier if Henry *did* hate him. "We didn't do anything before last night," he promised, as if that somehow made it better.

"So you're back together?" It was only barely a question.

"No. I told him I didn't want him calling me again. He agreed not to."

Henry let out a long, heavy breath. "So what is it you're *not* telling me?"

Before he could answer, his phone beeped, letting him know someone else was trying to call. "Hang on. Please?"

"I'm not going anywhere."

Jason nodded even though Henry couldn't see him. He looked at his caller ID. Kendra. Fuck. He hit Reject Call and put the phone back up to his ear. "I'm back."

"I'm still here."

Jason let go of the collar to take a sip of his coffee. "Terry wanted to go out dancing last night. Like we used to. I... I've been... the last month we've been really reconnecting. It was like it used to be. He came and saw me on my birthday, *just* to see me. Just to take me out to coffee, and I know I should have told you. I'm sorry." Tears streamed down his cheeks.

"You don't owe me anything, Jason. I just want to know that you're all right."

"I got pretty trashed last night. We split a bottle of wine and then went to the bar. And... I didn't get drunk on purpose, but I... Terry kept buying me cosmos, and I kept letting him, and when we got back to his place, I... I don't know what happened exactly. I wasn't thinking straight, I guess. Or maybe I wanted it. All I know is that I got down on my knees and sucked him off." He'd never felt so ashamed of anything in his life.

There was silence on the other end.

"Nothing else happened, I swear. I got sick. After I threw up, I left."

"Please do not tell me you drove home drunk."

"No. I drove a couple of blocks and parked and just sat there."

"How are you feeling now?"

Jason almost laughed. "Like I've totally screwed up the best thing…." He shuddered. How could he call Henry the best thing that had ever happened to him? He didn't even know what they really were to each other.

"Have you slept?" Henry asked.

"No."

"All right. You're going to go get yourself a great big bottle of Gatorade or something like it, and you're going drink the whole thing."

"I hate that shit."

"I don't care. You're going to drink it. You're also going to cook yourself three scrambled eggs and some dry toast. Then you're going to sleep."

"If I eat, I'll throw up."

"If you don't put something in your stomach, it'll be worse. Put a bottle of water next to the bed before you crawl in. You're probably going to wake up thirsty."

"Does this mean you're not mad at me?" Jason asked hopefully.

"I'm fucking *pissed* at you." His tone left no room to question exactly how angry he was. "But not for going out with Terry, not even for not telling me about it. I'm not your mother and I'm not your father. Who you go out with and what you do with them is your business, not mine. But it was fucking careless as hell to go out and get drunk with someone who you *knew* wanted you in his bed. Maybe he got you drunk on purpose and maybe he didn't, but he sure as fuck didn't stop you. It's a wonder… Jesus, boy, you could have gotten yourself seriously hurt last night."

"Yes, Sir." Jason wiped the moisture from his cheeks. "What… what do you want me to do after I do everything you told me to?"

"Call me. I don't care how late it is when you wake up. We'll talk about the rest of it. I think maybe it's time to put some labels on things."

"Yes, Sir. Sir, I—"

"No," Henry cut him off before he could finish his sentence. "Go take care of yourself. We'll talk later, after you're feeling better."

"Yes, Sir. Thank you."

JASON decided to walk to the store instead of driving; there was a gas station less than a mile from the house, and the fresh air would probably help his head. He got down half the bottle of awful-tasting sports drink on his walk home.

As he walked, he thought about what Henry had said about Terry. He wasn't sure if he was ready to believe Terry had gotten him drunk on purpose, but he had let it happen. Mostly, however, Jason blamed himself; he shouldn't have gone out with Terry in the first place. When he got back home, Jason made himself three soft scrambled eggs and a piece of toast. He ate. He finished the drink. Nothing came back up.

Kendra called three more times before he finally turned his phone off, refilled the Gatorade bottle with water, and crawled into bed. He felt completely wrung out, like there was nothing left inside—at least nothing that wasn't raw and bleeding. But Henry was still taking care of him. That had to mean something.

Chapter Thirteen

IT WAS dark when he opened his eyes again. He'd woken a couple of times during the day, drank his water. Fallen back asleep. He still felt like shit, but he'd slept as much as he knew he was going to be able to. He looked at the clock; it was six thirty.

Fuck.

He'd lost the whole day. His stomach growled, but more than he wanted food, he wanted to hear Henry's voice, to have him say that things were okay between them. Or that they would be, eventually. Only there was no guarantee he would say that. He might tell Jason to go to hell.

He wiped the moisture from his cheeks and dialed Henry's number, ignoring the fact that he had a dozen voice messages. Chances were they were all from Kendra.

Henry picked up after an agonizing six rings. "Just get up?"

"Yes, Sir."

"Good. I was afraid I might have to wake you up if you didn't call me soon."

"Sir?"

"Assuming my directions are correct, I'll be pulling into your driveway in about twenty minutes."

Jason nearly dropped the phone. "But... but it's an eight-hour drive!"

"Seven-hour drive," he corrected. "Some conversations should be had in person, boy."

"I...." He didn't know what to say.

"Why don't you hop in the shower and put on some clean clothes? I'm starving. You probably are too. I'll pick you up and we'll go get something to eat."

A million things ran through his head, but the only two words that came out of his mouth were "Yes, Sir."

"Do you want me to knock or just call you when I pull up?"

"I...." Jason hesitated. He slipped out into the hallway. The house was quiet and when he checked, his dad's car keys weren't sitting on the table or hanging up on the hook by the back door. "You can come up if you want. No one's home. Unless you'd rather just call—"

"Jason," he said sharply. "When I ask you a question, it's because I want an answer. Clear?"

"Yes, Sir."

"If you're going to keep calling me that, you're going to have to let go of whatever it is that makes you doubt yourself so much. Now go get cleaned up."

"Yes, Sir." Jason hung up. He showered. He shaved. He pulled his wet hair into a ponytail because he didn't have time to do anything else with it. He was just getting dressed when the doorbell rang; the sound of it made him feel weak. Queasy. Henry was here. Henry had driven seven hours just to... fuck.

Probably not to fuck.

Hopefully not to break off their... their whatever it was, either.

Jason tucked in his shirt and answered the door, his heart pounding in his ears.

"Come here, boy." Henry drew him into his arms at once, wrapping him in warm strength.

Jason clung to him. "I'm sorry. I'm so sorry," he sobbed.

Henry held him tighter. "Shhh. You have nothing to be sorry for."

"I screwed up."

Henry sighed. He nodded against the top of Jason's head. "Yeah. You did. And so did I. Now get your coat—and bring the collar."

Jason looked up at him, startled. Afraid. "Please don't take it back."

"We'll talk after we've eaten."

"Henry... Sir... *please*...."

"Shhh, it's all right. Trust me. I didn't drive almost four hundred miles just to take back my collar, boy. I drove up here so we can sort out what went wrong, where we *both* screwed up. And to figure out how we're gonna fix it."

Jason swallowed hard but did what Henry told him to. He went to his room and got the collar from under his pillow. When he offered it over, Henry took it and put it in his coat pocket. Despite what Henry had said about wanting to fix things, Jason found himself blinking back more tears.

"Do you trust me?" Henry asked him.

"Yes."

"Then let's go get some food. We'll talk after we eat. I promise. I'd like to figure this out with you, boy. Okay?"

Dully, Jason nodded. He wasn't going to be able to eat, and it wasn't because of the alcohol he'd drunk last night, but he didn't want to argue, either. So he followed Henry out to his van, and climbed in. He gave Henry directions to the nearest restaurant—one of the few places in town that wasn't fast food.

A SHORT ten minutes later, they were sitting in a little pizzeria in downtown Ithaca, Henry with an iced tea and Jason drinking water, waiting for their dinner. Henry had ordered without asking Jason any questions—but the choices were limited. They were having an antipasto salad with the meat on the side and a pizza with mushrooms and olives.

"So." Henry broke the uneasy silence that had fallen between them. "You want to start at the beginning and tell me what happened?" It wasn't a request.

Jason used his straw to stir the ice cubes around in his glass. "Terry said he wasn't going to leave me alone until I talked to him. I agreed to meet him for dinner. I… I had a nice time."

"And you feel guilty about that."

"Shouldn't I?"

"No."

Jason looked up at last. "I do, though. I feel… God. I feel like…." He hesitated, nibbling his lip. He felt like he'd cheated on Henry. Maybe on Terry too. "I feel like shit."

Their salad arrived. Henry waited until the waitress had departed before speaking again. "You and Terry have a history. You wanted to see if the spark was still there—"

"No, Sir. I wanted him to be an asshole like always, so I could tell him we were through. So it would be easy, because… because we do have a history. And Kendra's right, I couldn't just walk out on the last five years as if it had never happened. But I thought… I was so sure he would be a jerk, try to stick his tongue down my throat, try to get me to go down on him in his backseat or something. Only he didn't. He didn't even touch me. I… it was nice.

"I don't have a whole lot of friends," Jason confessed. "When I moved up here, I lost touch with almost everybody, and… and well, I never exactly fit in in fucking Hicksville. I feel like I'm the only gay guy in the whole county. So having Terry as a friend again was… it felt good. We started hanging out. I should have told you. I'd just called you and we were doing… you know. Over the phone. And I liked that too. I like it *so much*," he said plaintively, desperate to have Henry give him back his collar.

But Henry only nodded, so Jason kept talking.

"Last night I got drunk. And I went down on him. Terry. And all I could think about was you." He dropped his gaze to his water glass. The chunks of ice were nearly melted. "But you said I wasn't yours, so when Terry asked me to go into the bedroom, I went. Nothing happened," he repeated. "I got sick and left. But I'm not sure what would have happened if I hadn't."

"I appreciate hearing that."

"What?"

"I appreciate honesty, boy, more than just about anything else, even when it hurts. Which is why I'm not going to try and tell you that it didn't hurt like hell when you said you were out with Terry last night. When you told me you'd *been* going out with him but hadn't told me. No." He held up his hand before Jason could apologize again. "You're right, I told you once that you weren't mine, and despite some pretty wild phone conversations, I haven't... I didn't say some of the things maybe I should have. I didn't tell you... there's probably lots of stuff I should have said but didn't," he admitted. "Truth is, I've been flip-flopping between being the Master I want to be to you and the mentor I think you need without bothering to ask you what *you* want. I haven't been fair to either of us. I'm asking you to forgive me for that."

Jason sat speechless for several long moments. He realized for the first time since Henry's arrival how absolutely bone weary Henry looked. How wrung out he sounded. How genuinely hurt he really was. "Yes, of course I forgive you. I... I don't know what I need, so how can you? Will... can you forgive me?" he pleaded.

"Already done, boy."

The waitress arrived with their pizza; she refilled Jason's water. He hadn't even noticed that he'd drained his glass.

"What now?" Jason asked once they were alone again.

"Now I'm going to ask you if you're willing—able—to let me start over. I'm going to ask if you'd like to talk about a contract."

Jason's breath caught in his throat. God, yes, he wanted a contract! "For how long?"

"Short term. Three months."

His heart sank all over again. "That's awful short. Couldn't we maybe talk about something a little longer? Six months—"

Henry cut him off. "I don't like having to renegotiate terms in the middle of a contract if I can help it. I'd rather have a couple of short-term contracts, then go for six months, and then... then see where it goes from there. Baby steps, okay?"

Jason chewed on the end of his straw. "Yeah, okay. I guess that makes sense. But could we work something out so I get to see you again before January?"

Henry smirked. "I was thinking it might be a good idea for you to come down and visit me for a week or so at the end of the three months. That way we can renegotiate in person. And I can finally get you in my play room."

"I'd like that."

Henry chuckled, some more of the tension draining from his face. "Good. We'll figure out when your semester break is and go from there."

"I think I'm just going to work this summer, not take any classes."

Henry was quiet for a moment. Finally he nodded. "All right. I don't like it, but for right now I'm going to limit my control over your life."

"Sir?"

"Any idiot can see you're not happy, Jason, but there are some decisions you need to come to on your own. Just know that I'll be here to support you when you decide what you want to do with your life."

"Isn't that a little contradictory? I mean if... when you say contract, I assume you mean...." *Slave is the natural counterpart to Master.* And Jason knew Henry was waiting for him to say it aloud. "I assume you mean a slave contract, Sir."

"A Master's job is to take care of his property. Part of that means letting you grow."

Reluctantly, Jason nodded. He knew Henry was right, even if he didn't necessarily like it. It would be so much easier if Henry just told him what to do. "May I... that is... I get some say in this, right? I mean in the terms of the... our... contract?"

"What did you have in mind?"

"I hope I'm not overstepping my bounds or something, but… I don't want… that is… I need to know you're not with anyone else, Sir. Please." He swallowed hard, afraid he was asking for too much.

"I have and I will continue to play with anybody I want to, but I've got news for you, boy: I haven't fucked anybody since I met you. I don't intend to start now."

Jason blinked. He felt guiltier than ever.

Henry went on, "You, on the other hand, will neither play with nor fuck anybody without my permission. You're not allowed to get drunk again, either. Are we clear?"

"Yes, Sir. Crystal clear."

"Good boy. Now I've got a question for you: you got anywhere you need to be tonight or tomorrow morning?"

"No, Sir." He had class, but it was one he could cut without it affecting his grade. He didn't tell Henry that.

"Then I'm getting a room for the night and you're coming with me. We'll talk the rest of this through and get some stuff written down."

"I… I hope you have more than *talking* and writing in mind, Sir," he said coyly.

Henry bit back a snicker and fixed his face in a stern expression. "I think we need to have us a good long talk about what happens to boys who get pushy."

"Yes, Sir." Jason did his best to look contrite; Henry laughed.

DESPITE the easing of the tension and the general levity of the last half an hour, Jason hesitated at the motel doorway. Henry had told him to bring in the duffel bag but grabbed the other case himself. It looked heavy and Jason was almost afraid of what was in it. That wasn't why he hesitated, however.

"Something the matter, boy?" Henry queried over his shoulder.

"I… Sir, I don't deserve this."

Henry paused. Nodded. "Come in and close the door, and we'll talk."

Jason did as he was told. He set the duffel bag down next to the bed while Henry pulled the chair out from behind the desk and put it in the middle of the room. Henry sat. Jason stood in front of him.

"Hands behind your back, boy."

Jason obeyed.

"Higher. Rest them in the small of your back. I want your elbows out."

Silently, he adjusted his position until Henry was satisfied.

"Now, talk to me."

Jason took a breath. Let it out. He tried to gather up his thoughts, but it was like trying to carry a handful of sand. "Sir. Respectfully, Sir, I don't deserve… Sir, I cheated on you. I… I cheated on Terry. I know you want to play tonight, but I don't deserve it. And I guess that makes it worse, because you drove all this way, and if I don't deserve to be… to have your… shit." He sniffled, tears gathering in the corners of his eyes.

"Just say what you want to say and we'll go from there."

"I screwed up. I know that means you should punish me, because even without any kind of contract or anything spelled out, I knew what I was doing was wrong. But if you punish me, you don't get to use me the way I'm sure you'd like to. I'm not sure if you can punish me for having to punish me or how that works, but… but it sucks, and I'm sorry."

Henry sat back and was quiet for a very, very long moment. "All right. I'll concede that you screwed up, and for that you will be punished. Tonight. You cheated on me and you cheated on Terry, and regardless of how I feel about him, you're right, he didn't deserve that. But that does not mean that I won't use your body, boy. It only means that I'm not going to enjoy it as much as I might otherwise. Whether you get to enjoy it has yet to be decided."

Jason swallowed, but the lump in his throat refused to go down. "Yes, Sir."

"Master," Henry corrected him.

"Yes, Master."

"From now on, that's how I expect you to address me when we're alone. Not because I need it, but because it's a word you're still not comfortable with. I expect you to get comfortable with it. And with the word 'slave'."

"Yes, Master."

"All right. Strip. And then go stand in the corner. Do not ask me for how long. When I've decided your time is up, you'll get the crop. Ten strokes for cheating on me. And ten for cheating on Terry. And they will not be light ones."

Jason shuddered. Nodded. "Yes, S-Master."

"I want to make one thing clear, slaveboy: You still have your safewords. I will never, ever take those away from you, but I expect you to use them judiciously. Understand?"

"Yes, Master. Thank you."

Henry nodded, and Jason shed his clothing. He folded it neatly, set it on the desk, and turned toward the corner.

"I want you to come here first," Henry told him.

Jason turned—and his heart started pounding when he saw what Henry held in his hand. It was the gray collar. *His* collar. The one he'd wanted so badly that first day, the one he thought Henry had sold. Henry must have… God, had he really set it aside? *For me?*

"Kneel." Henry instructed.

Jason slid to his knees and put his hands behind his back. "I don't deserve that," he whispered, his voice hoarse, thick with emotion.

"From now on, you let me decide what you do and don't deserve—which isn't to say you don't get input or that I don't want you to voice your opinions. I expect you to tell me what you want. What you don't want. *Respectfully*. But from now on, the final say is mine.

This isn't a gift, boy… or maybe it is. But it comes with a hell of a price tag."

"Sir?"

"The price is me, and I'm no prize."

"May I respectfully disagree?"

"You may. And by the way, that'll be one extra stroke for calling me 'Sir' instead of 'Master'," he said as he fastened the heavy gray leather collar snugly around Jason's neck.

"Yes, Master." Before getting up, Jason leaned in and kissed Henry's feet, but he didn't lay his cheek against them. He hadn't earned that, not yet.

Jason got to his feet, walked to the far corner of the room, and stood there, his hands behind his back, as before.

"While you're standing there, I want you to think about what exactly I'm punishing you for tonight. I want you to dig deep and figure out exactly what you did wrong and why. I want you to understand that you need this, but that after it's over, it will be over. I want you to understand that I'm doing this for you, not for me. I will never raise my hand to you in anger. You don't need to respond to anything I'm saying right now," Henry told him. "I want you to be still. Just think about what it is you're doing in that corner and why I'm going to lay twenty-one stripes on your ass a little later."

Jason closed his eyes. He felt the weight of the collar around his neck. It was so much heavier than the other collar. It felt so right. But the thought of twenty-one strokes with the riding crop scared him shitless. Only he had said he wanted them—or at least that he deserved to be punished.

Was he a masochist?

No. He definitely wasn't getting off on any of this; he wasn't hard. And neither was Henry.

So why were they doing it?

Jason took a breath and let it out. That was the question he needed to be able to answer. He relaxed his shoulders and tried to let his mind be still.…

"Time, boy." Henry's tone was gentle, steady. It sounded like he was right behind him; it might have been ten minutes or an hour later, Jason couldn't tell. "Take half a step back. Brace your hands against the wall, ass out."

Silently, Jason did as his Master instructed.

"I'm going to give you twenty-one strokes. You're going to count them out loud. You don't need to thank me for each one or ask for the next, but you will address me as Master with each stroke. Before we begin, you're going to tell me why I'm doing this."

"Yes, Master. I cheated on you, Master, by going out with Terry and not telling you. You deserved better than that. I cheated on Terry too, and that wasn't fair to him. I let him think there might be a chance for us to get back together when all I really wanted was to belong to you. More than that, I lied. To both of you because a lie of omission is still a lie, Master. I knew that it was wrong and I did it anyway. I… I even lied to Kendra by letting her think I wasn't talking to you."

"Why did you lie, boy?"

"Because it was easier than telling anybody the truth, Master."

"Do you think you deserve additional strokes for taking the easy way out? For lying to your best friend?"

Jason took a breath. Let it out. "I do, Master, but with respect, I'm not sure I can take much more than twenty-one." If Henry said he was going to give him ten more for lying to each of them….

"Four more will make it twenty-five. Think you can handle that?"

He swallowed hard. Licked his lips. Nodded. "Yes, Master."

"One more question. How did you earn the twenty-first stroke?"

"I failed to use the word 'Master' to address you after you'd clearly said that was the word you wanted me to use. You're right, it's not a word I'm comfortable with. But that's no excuse. I need this. I don't like it, I don't want it, but I need it. I need… I need to learn to let go."

"Good boy. Ready?"

"Yes, Master." He tensed—waited. The first blow landed hard across both ass cheeks; he hissed as burning pain spread through the muscle. "One, Master." The second blow landed right below the first. It wasn't any lighter. Nor was the third or the fourth. By five, tears were rolling down his cheeks, and at ten, Henry gave him a few minutes to catch his breath.

"Almost halfway there," he said gently, wiping the moisture from Jason's cheeks. "I'm proud of you, boy."

"Thank you, Master." His whole body felt shaky. Weak. He hoped Henry might decide he'd had enough.

No such luck. Henry told him to resume his stance, to take a breath. To breathe through it as best as he could. Henry reaffirmed why they were doing this and reminded him that they were on eleven. He very carefully struck unblemished skin, continuing to work his way down Jason's buttocks with each stroke, never hitting the same place twice.

By twenty, Jason was squirming, sobbing, his whole ass on fire. When he begged for another minute to catch his breath, Henry gave it to him. He didn't start again until Jason told him he was ready. It was all he could do to stand still, to take the last five blows on the tendermost part of his ass, right where his butt cheeks connected to his thighs, but somehow, he managed it.

Then Henry turned him around and gathered him into his arms. Jason clung onto him and Henry let him sob for as long as he needed. "How do you feel, boy?" Henry asked softly when Jason finally cried himself out.

"Safe, Master. When you hold me, I feel safe. Even when you... while you were using the crop... even then, I felt safe. I knew you weren't mad at me. I knew I just... I needed to get through it. Not for you. For me."

Henry pressed a soft kiss to the top of his head. "Good boy." He handed Jason a tissue and let him blow his nose, then he tugged Jason over to the bed. "I didn't break skin, but I raised a coupla of pretty nasty welts. Think I can get you to lie down so I can have a better look?"

Jason nodded. He let himself be stretched out on his stomach. He hissed in pain when Henry touched his battered skin.

"I'm putting something on that'll help with the pain and bruising."

"I don't mind the bruises, Master."

"I know. But eventually, you're going to want to sit on that ass again." When done dabbing on the ointment, Henry went to the bathroom, got a cool cloth, and washed Jason's face. He gave him a glass of water to drink, then sat down on the bed and gathered Jason into his lap. He undid Jason's ponytail and ran his fingers through Jason's hair.

Jason closed his eyes and snuggled in closer. He felt... good. He'd cheated on both Terry and Henry, he'd lied to them both, to Kendra, but... *but I got punished and it's over.*

"You feeling better?" Henry asked.

Jason nodded. "Yes, Master."

"Good. I'm not going to let you see it tonight, you're in no state, but while you were standing in the corner, I worked up a contract. We'll talk about it tomorrow," he said when Jason started to speak.

"So what now?" Jason wondered.

Henry smiled down at him, his expression so full of... of love? God, Jason hoped so. "Now, we're going to snuggle up in bed and watch a movie. Before we go to sleep, you're going to give me one of those amazing blow jobs of yours. You're not going to get off tonight. You're not going to touch yourself, either. But if I like what you do to me, I'll send you home with a smile on your face tomorrow."

"You've already done that, Master," Jason assured him. "Just being with you, I... I missed you so much."

"I missed you too, boy." Henry leaned in and pressed a warm, welcome kiss to Jason's mouth.

JASON looked over the words on Henry's laptop carefully. His role as a slave was spelled out clearly, if briefly: even though they weren't living together, he would be available for Henry's pleasure, via phone or Internet, at all times of the day or night, unless he was at work or school. He would obey Henry in all things, but if he thought an order would cause a problem with work or school, he was to say so. He would wear a collar—*his* collar, the gray one—at all times unless he had a good reason not to. Jason assured Henry that it was fine for school—he was already considered "the weird kid"—but work would definitely be a problem. There was no way he could hide it under his uniform. However, he didn't give a shit what his father said; he would wear it at home and pretty much everywhere else too. Henry raised an eyebrow but didn't comment.

Jason was to address Henry as Master unless the situation warranted the use of his first name or "Sir." He would phone his Master twice daily—more if Henry directed. He didn't need permission to go out with his friends, but he was restricted from drinking alcohol again. If he wanted a drink, he was going to have to call and ask. Otherwise, he was simply expected to use common sense and conduct himself in a way that would reflect well on both of them.

Jason would keep himself shaved as he'd already been directed, and would follow any other instructions Henry gave him regarding hygiene or general appearance. Henry could not, however, insist on any permanent markings or piercings that Jason didn't consent to. Jason had to get his Master's permission before getting another piercing or a permanent marking on his body.

Jason could only come with his Master's permission and wasn't allowed to touch himself, except for washing up and taking care of Nature's call, without permission either.

Beyond that, there wasn't anything spelled out about play. "We'll talk about hard and soft limits when you come see me," said Henry. "But since we're a little restricted for the next three months anyway, I don't see any reason to clutter things up with agreements and clauses about things we couldn't do over the phone if we tried."

Jason nodded. That made sense.

Henry's role as Master was outlined too, and Jason beamed as he read it. Henry was responsible for his slave's well-being, for treating Jason as the cherished possession that he was. He took it upon himself to help Jason grow and find his strength in his submission—in his whole self—and to mete out punishments as he deemed necessary so Jason could learn and let go. He promised to always put his slave's needs above his own and to do his best to let Jason know not only when he'd screwed up, but also when he'd pleased his Master. "I don't want you just learning from your mistakes, boy. I want you to feel good about your accomplishments."

Henry would never intentionally do, or order Jason to do, anything that would put his well-being, his grades, or his job at risk. He agreed to both respect and push Jason's limits but granted Jason the use of safewords and an outright obligation to tell him when he needed to speak freely about something.

"I thought that by saying 'no', a slave…," Jason floundered, looking for the right words. "I mean, a lot of the stuff I read said that being a slave meant giving up the right to say 'no' or speak freely."

"Every relationship is different, Jason. It's like what I said before: *we* define our roles, not some book. I will expect you to explain yourself if you refuse something," he added firmly, "but saying 'no' doesn't break our contract, it just means we need to talk. Believe me, I would rather have you tell me how you feel than have you get pissed and throw the collar back in my face for something that could have been fixed with a few honest words. As long as you're respectful, I will never punish you for telling me the truth about something. If you can't find the right words, I'll do what I can to help you."

"Thank you for that," Jason told him earnestly. He was sitting in Henry's lap; his ass was sore, not just the skin, but the muscles underneath. Even so, he was happy because it felt good to have Henry's arms around him.

Last night had been amazing in its simplicity. Instead of a movie, Henry found a website where they could watch episodes of *Revolutionary Girl Utena*; they'd cuddled and watched for hours. Occasionally Henry would play with Jason's nipple rings, tugging gently. Mostly he stroked Jason's hair. He held him close. Eventually, Jason went down on him; then they showered and went to bed. This morning, after receiving another blow job, Henry went out to get breakfast. It wasn't much—there wasn't much around—but he'd brought back food Jason could eat: eggs, fruit, coffee. They nibbled while Jason read over their contract; where he'd needed him to, Henry made small amendments, but for the most part, Henry had gotten everything exactly right. Jason knew who he belonged to. He was clear about what Henry wanted from him. Henry was clear about what Jason wanted and was willing to give it to him in writing. Henry would continue to play with anybody he wanted to—he was an active member in the BDSM community and was called on to conduct talks and demonstrations—but he wouldn't be having sex with anyone except for Jason. Jason, of course, wasn't allowed to play with anyone else, but he didn't want to, so that was fine.

"Anything else you need me to add or change, boy?"

Jason looked it over one last time. "No, Master."

"All right." Henry reached around him; he e-mailed a copy of it to his own e-mail address, to Jason, and to two other people. "Just a safeguard. Not that I expect any problems, but it's always a good idea to have 'witnesses'."

Jason nodded even though heat crept up into his cheeks at the thought of anyone else seeing such an intimate document.

"When you come out, you'll meet Lilianna and David. Or rather, Mistress Lilianna and Master David to you, boy," he informed Jason. "Now... I believe I promised to send you home with a smile on your face. I also believe you said something to me about wanting to be tied down and flogged."

Jason blinked. "I... yes... but...."

He flashed a wicked smirk. "Why don't you go to the bathroom, take care of whatever you need to take care of. You're going to be tied up for a while. Don't come out until I call you."

Jason's pulse quickened and his cock stirred. He barely hid his smile. "Yes, Master."

As soon as he stepped into the bathroom, he heard Henry put on some of his favorite string quartet music.

Chapter Fourteen

WHAT Jason saw when he emerged from the bathroom made his heart beat harder. It was a simple construction: a thick three-foot-long board lying on the floor with a crosspiece that was probably only about a foot long on either end. The four eye bolts made it clear that Jason's ankles and wrists would be attached to the ends of the crosspieces, but what made it far more interesting were the two short posts sticking up from the contraption, one at the front and one at the rear. He suspected that his collar would be clipped to one of them, but the second....? Then Jason saw a familiar-looking leather cock ring in Henry's hands.

"Getting a clearer picture, boy?"

He gulped in air. "Yes, Sir. Master. Shit."

Henry chuckled. "It might not be a St. Andrew's cross, but don't think you're going to be doing too much wriggling once your cock's tied to that pole. Hands behind your neck, boy."

Jason obeyed and Henry fastened the thick leather straps around his dick and testicles. Then he caressed Jason's balls, making him shiver. Whimper.

"No fair, Sir, Master," he gasped when Henry ran his thumb over his cock's slit.

Henry merely grinned. He leaned in and kissed Jason until they were both breathless. Somehow, Jason managed to stay still, not to throw his arms around Henry's neck.

"Such a good boy," Henry told him as he stepped back. He picked up a wide leather belt from the bed and showed it to Jason before securing it around his waist. "This is more for protection than anything else," he explained. "I won't touch your ass—except to fuck it—but your back is fair game. This'll keep the lash away from your kidneys."

Jason suspected that it could be used for other things as well— there were D rings on the sides, in the back, and in front. As if to emphasize his point about the importance of protection, however, Henry drew the bearskin flogger out of his case, along with a medium-length double-tail whip. "Since you did so well with the single tail, I thought we might up the ante a little."

Jason grinned. Anticipation made his dick swell within the confines of the leather. "If I say 'thank you, Master', will it get me into trouble?" he asked mischievously.

Henry's grin was every bit as puckish. "Probably, but I think you like being in trouble."

"Oh, no, Master," he said, still grinning.

Henry rolled his eyes. He showed Jason the thick gray leather wrist and ankle cuffs—each one had four D rings identical to the ones on his collar. "I made these special, just for you."

"They're beautiful, Master," Jason told him. He wanted to say he didn't deserve anything like that, but he remembered Henry saying that from now on *he* would decide what Jason did and didn't deserve. Jason stood still while Henry put the cuffs on him; they felt good. Heavy. Solid. He loved the smell of the leather.

"Now, I have something else that's new." Henry leaned over into his duffel back and brought out a large silver metal hook. At the shorter end there was a large metal ball about the size of a very big marble; the other end tapered into a loop through which rope or even chain could be threaded.

Jason gaped at it.

"I take it by your expression you know an anal hook when you see one?" Henry observed.

"Y-yes. I… I'm not sure about that thing, Sir. Master." Fuck.

Henry seemed unflustered by his reaction. He handed the hook to him. "Look at it objectively, boy. Is it any bigger around than I am?"

Jason blinked. Blushed. "No, Master." He ran his hands over it; it wasn't as long as Henry's dick, either, at least not where it counted, the part that would be shoved up his ass. "I guess it looks scarier than it really is. Okay." He handed it back.

"So you're not invoking your safeword?"

"No, Sir. I can handle that."

"Good boy. Down you go."

Jason arranged himself on his hands and knees, and Henry used simple clasps to attach his wrists and ankles to the wooden frame. Another clip was used to attach his collar to the shorter of the two posts and one more to fasten the cock ring to the taller post. The result was that his legs were spread wide, his ass was in the air, and his balls were left very, very exposed.

"How are you feeling, boy?"

"A little vulnerable, Master."

Henry chuckled. "Good." Then he ran his hand lightly over Jason's back. "I won't gag you this time because from this angle I can't see your face enough to tell whether or not you're in distress. Another time, I might, though. All right?"

"Yes, and thank you, Master."

"Don't thank me yet, boy," he said as he slid one lubed finger into Jason's entrance.

Jason groaned and tried to raise his ass higher—and stopped the second he felt pressure on his cock and balls. He relaxed and submitted himself to Henry's ministrations. "Oh God, it feels so much better when you do that than when you have me touch myself. Please, Sir, Master, fuck me?" He couldn't even turn his head to look at Henry as he begged.

"You're not going to get to come," Henry warned.

"I know. But please? Before you put the hook in, let me have your cock. Please, Master. I've missed you so much. I don't need to come, I just need to feel you inside me."

"Give me a minute to get a rubber."

Jason whimpered when Henry withdrew his hand, but a moment later, he felt two fingers pushing past the tight ring of muscles. He relaxed as they entered him. "So good, Master. Everything... everything feels so right. This is right where I want to be, on my hands and knees for you. I always knew... I knew I was different, but... oh fuck!" he cried out when Henry pressed against his prostate. "Oh please!" he begged.

Then he was empty again, but only for a few moments while Henry withdrew his hand and positioned his dick at Jason's entrance. Jason would have pushed against him if he could have, but he couldn't move. He was completely immobile, helpless to do anything but beg and pull against the restraints that held him in place. "Please, yes... please," he whimpered as Henry pressed into him. "Please, more, Sir. More, Master. *Please*. I want all of you! *Please*!"

"When the fuck did you get so chatty, boy?" Henry almost laughed. "Kid I picked up a few months ago couldn't talk to save his life."

Jason smiled too, even though he was in agony of wanting. Of helplessness. "Your fault, Sir, for making me talk so much. Maybe you should have let me keep my mouth shut—or filled it with something more often."

Henry swatted his ass, making Jason flinch—grin. He moaned when the same hand caressed his butt; he tried to arch his back, to entice Henry to take more of him, but he couldn't move.

"Enjoying this?"

"Yes, Master."

Henry continued to caress him as he very slowly pulled out again. "You feel good too, boy. Just right." He plunged back into Jason's body, angling himself so he grazed against his prostate, making him moan some more. Henry continued to fuck him excruciatingly slowly, hitting the sensitive gland with each stroke.

"Cruel, Sir," Jason muttered. His dick was as on fire as his ass had been yesterday, but the thick bands of leather kept him from achieving a full erection, kept him from coming. He whimpered, it hurt so much.

"You asked me to fuck you," Henry reminded him as he grabbed hold of the D rings on the belt and began picking up speed, slamming painfully into Jason's ass, making him cry out in a different kind of pain.

Perhaps it was compassion—or maybe he was just having too good a time—but it was only a few more minutes before Henry came with a loud, satisfied-sounding grunt. He held Jason close for a brief moment, his cheek resting against Jason's back. Then he eased slowly out of him. Jason felt something cool and hard taking his place. "Now hold that there while I clean up," Henry ordered.

Jason quickly realized he had to clench his ass muscles around the hook to keep it from slipping out. He was more than a little grateful when he heard Henry's footsteps coming out of the bathroom. He could only assume what he felt next was Henry threading nylon rope through the eye of the anal hook; the other end of the rope was knotted into one of the D rings of his collar. It was snug enough that if Jason dropped his head, he would feel a pull, but it wasn't enough of a pull to hurt.

"Good?" Henry asked him.

Jason grinned. "I'm not sure 'good' is a word most people would use, Master, but... yeah. Very good."

"Brat." Henry fisted one hand into Jason's hair and used it to pull his head back; it was an awkward angle, but he managed to land a warm kiss on Jason's mouth. "I would say I'm going to beat that attitude out of you, but I'd be lying if I said I didn't enjoy it. You keep me on my toes, boy. That's not something I've said to anyone in a very long time."

Jason smiled. "I'm glad I make you happy, Sir."

Henry scoffed. "Let's see how glad you feel in another hour. Or how much you like it when I send the hook and cock ring home with you. When I tell you to put them on under your clothes and go about your day all trussed up."

Jason stared at him, eyes wide.

"Think I wouldn't?"

"N-no, Sir. Master. No, I'm sure you *would*."

"And you'd do it for me, wouldn't you?"

"Yes, Master." He didn't hesitate to agree.

Henry smiled and kissed him again. For Henry's kisses, Jason would do anything.

Henry stood and picked up the flogger. The thick leather landed against Jason's back with a heavy thump, but it didn't hurt much, at least not at first. Little by little, Henry ramped up the intensity of his blows, until Jason squirmed, desperate to come, to be fucked again. Until he was flying high on endorphins.

He nearly jumped out of his skin when he felt something buzzing against his prostate and realized Henry was holding a vibrator up to the hook. "Jesus, Sir."

Henry snickered. "Not Jesus, just your Master."

Jason smiled. He moaned. He arched his back as far as he was able—and then he whimpered when Henry traced the vibrator along the hook, down toward his entrance, and held it there while Jason tried to buck against his restraints. And *then* Henry touched it to his balls and Jason sucked in air. Henry chuckled as he ghosted the vibrator over Jason's testicles and along his shaft for what seemed like forever. Then he rubbed it gently against his perineum until Jason was pleading to be allowed to come.

"No."

He nearly wept at the denial. "Will you fuck me again?"

"Later."

"Promise?" he begged.

Henry smiled. "I promise, boy." With his free hand, he caressed Jason's ass cheeks, his thighs, his balls until Jason was shaking. "Whose are you, boy?" he asked. "Who does that body belong to?"

"You, Master. Yours. I'm yours. I belong to you."

"Good boy." Henry turned off the vibrator and pressed a soft kiss the middle of Jason's back. "I'm going to switch to the double tail now. I won't be trying to push your limits, but we're still figuring out what those are, so you safeword if you need to. Hear me?"

"Yes, Master."

Jason was too exhausted, too high on endorphins, to be fully cognizant of what was happening as Henry gently unclipped the cock ring from the pole and unscrewed the pole from the wooden frame. He did the same to Jason's collar and removed that pole as well, so Jason could relax a little. When he finally realized he could move his neck, Jason felt dazed. Confused.

"Easy, baby," Henry soothed him, resting a hand on Jason's shoulder. "Just stay still. I'm right here. Do you want some water?"

"I'm okay." His throat felt raw. He wasn't surprised when he felt a cool glass being pressed to his lips despite what he'd said about being okay.

He drank without being told. When Henry took the empty glass away from his mouth, Jason let his chest sink to the floor, but he kept his ass up for his Master's use. Henry released his wrists and Jason used his arms to cradle his head, saying a soft "thank you" to the man his body belonged to. It was a delicious, delirious feeling.

"How're you holding up?" Henry asked him.

"Floaty. It's good."

Henry chuckled. It was an oddly distant sound. Muffled. Then suddenly Jason felt something warm and wet on the tip of his cock.

"Oh God." A tongue? Lips? Henry? Jason lifted his head off his arms and looked to see Henry lying on a pillow, his head under Jason's hips, his tongue playing at the tip of his cock. "Jesus."

"I told you I planned to go down on you. Or... up as the case may be." Henry grinned, tilting his head so they could see each other. "Now how about you drop your hips a little? Let me have more of you." With one hand, he gripped one of the D rings on the belt, guiding Jason into place; with the other, he released the cock ring.

Jason shuddered as his cock sprang fully erect. "Please... say I can come?" he whimpered.

"You can come, boy. But let me enjoy you for a bit first."

Jason groaned in mixed frustration and joy as Henry snaked his tongue leisurely over his shaft, around the head of his dick, and over the slit.

"God, you're good at that... feels... heaven, Sir. Master. Oh please... Oh God, more of that," he rasped as Henry scraped his teeth across his balls, as he ran his hands over Jason's sore ass. Pleasure and pain meshed together, all jumbled up but feeling so good. Henry held him steady, not letting him move his hips, or have any measure of control. He took Jason slowly, teasing, nipping and licking at his balls, nipping at his inner thigh. Sucking him there until Jason cried out, until he was sure Henry had left a dark bruise in his wake.

Jason arched his back when Henry finally returned his attention to Jason's erection, taking it all the way to the back of his throat, sucking like he meant business. "Oh, fuck" was the only warning he was able to give before he emptied himself into his Master's mouth. He was still quivering with aftershocks when he started begging to be kissed.

He wasn't aware of Henry's movements, but a second later he felt warm lips pressing against his. Jason plunged his tongue forcefully into Henry's mouth. Henry seemed too stunned to do anything but yield to the demanding kiss. Jason wrapped one arm around his Master's neck to hold him in place, forcing the kiss to continue until he was completely breathless. Until he had to let go before he fell over.

Henry wiped Jason's bruised lips gently with his thumb. "First you're going to tell me what the hell that was about. Then I'm going to fuck you senseless."

"Already am senseless, Master," Jason murmured. "But I still want you to fuck me."

"And my explanation, boy?" Genuine anger danced in his eyes.

Jason lowered his gaze quickly, respectfully. "I'm sorry, Master, Sir, but I... it was.... Whenever I went down on... on Terry, he wouldn't kiss me after. I never want anybody to feel like he made me feel. Please don't be mad at me. I wasn't thinking straight."

The anger melted from Henry's face at once. He tilted Jason's head up and brushed a soft kiss to his lips. He deepened it slowly, gently forcing Jason to accept rather than demand. He cupped Jason's face in his hands and wiped the tears from Jason's cheeks. "Thank you, boy."

"For what?"

"For being you." He kissed him again, very gently, before letting go and reaching for a condom. "Now. You gonna come again for me?"

"Yes, Master. If… if it pleases you, Sir."

He laughed. "Oh, it pleases me very much, slaveboy."

JASON lay on his side in a haze of pleasure—and a little pain—with his back against Henry's chest. They'd showered; then Henry curled up with him for another couple of episodes of *Utena*. When the second episode ended, Jason rolled over. It was well past checkout time. "Are you staying another night?"

Henry shook his head. "I need to head home and so do you. Besides, if I stuck around, I'm afraid I might never leave."

Jason smiled. "I already never want you to leave."

"Yeah." He ran his thumb over Jason's cheek. His lips. "I'll see you again in a few months," he promised with a soft kiss. "And you'll call me."

"Every day, twice a day," Jason confirmed. He raised his gaze to meet the other man's eyes. "Henry, I—"

"Shhh. Don't, baby."

Jason bit back on the words he'd been about to say: *I love you.* He was sure the look on his face told Henry exactly how hurt he was by Henry's reaction, by his refusal to listen.

"Once something's said, it can't be unsaid, boy. Right now, you're still riding high on an awful lot of emotions. Let yourself settle into 'em a little more before you tell me anything you might wish later you hadn't."

"How do you even know what I'm going to say?"

"Because I'm riding pretty high myself."

Jason opened his mouth. Closed it again. Three months. In three months they'd see each other again. He would say it then. "All right. Can I ask you something?"

"Anything you like."

"What's your favorite flavor of ice cream?"

Henry gave him a strange look, but then he laughed. "Butter pecan. What about you?"

"Pineapple."

"Don't think I've ever seen that flavor at Baskin Robbins," Henry told him.

"When she started having to watch her sugar, Mom started making her own ice cream. Pineapple was both of our favorites."

"I'll have to keep that in mind for when you come visit me."

Jason smiled and snuggled closer. "Do we maybe have time for one more episode before you have to take me home?"

"Yeah, I think so."

They ended up watching two more episodes of *Utena* before finally shutting down the computer and getting dressed. Jason helped Henry take apart the wooden frame and pack up his gear. They went out for a late lunch. And then it was time to go home. Jason didn't tell Henry how much he wished he could run away with him, or how much he didn't want to go back to his own life.

He had school. Work.

He had to call Kendra.

Jason stood at the door until Henry's van vanished around the curve in the road. He felt… empty. Alone. He ran his hand over the thick gray leather of his collar. "I love you, Master," he said aloud. He didn't regret it.

Jason made his way to his room; it was early enough in the day that his father wasn't home from work yet. From the looks of things, he hadn't been home all night. Jason was grateful; he didn't think he could take another dressing down for staying out all night. In his room, he peeled out of his clothes and looked at his ass and back in the full-length mirror on the back of his closet door. Henry hadn't broken skin, but he had left some spectacular welts on Jason's back. They'd gone from angry red to purple in the last few hours. His ass was covered in a series of long black bruises from the crop. It looked awful, but Jason beamed with pleasure. Pride. He slipped gingerly into a pair of loose sweatpants and a soft, comfortable flannel shirt.

Henry had left him with a little BDSM care package: the anal hook, the leather cock harness, and a scary-looking metal chastity device. Henry had shown Jason how to put it on and assured him that it was perfectly safe to wear the metal tube over his cock for extended periods of time. There was a hole, so he would be able to use the bathroom without a problem, and he'd be allowed to remove it to shower—but he was to call first and ask permission to take it off and then call again as soon as it was back on. While the device wasn't exactly uncomfortable, there was no way Jason would be able forget he was wearing it, even for a second. The thought of wearing that thing for a whole week—probably two—was terrifying. He wondered if he could beg his Web design teacher for some kind of extra credit assignment or something, to pull his grade up to a C. There was no way he was going tell his teacher about the chastity device, but maybe he could say he was worried about his grade point average…?

Jason put the chastity device and other things in the shoebox under his bed where he kept his toys: a couple of dildos, butt plugs, and lube.

Gingerly, he sat down on the mattress and picked his phone up from the nightstand where he'd left it yesterday. He had over a dozen messages, and all of them were from Kendra. Bracing himself, he called her back.

"Where the fuck have you been?"

"Hello to you too," Jason answered her scathing greeting.

"Don't even be a smartass. Terry told me you dumped him. What happened?"

"Nothing."

"Don't give me that shit. He said you got trashed, puked your guts out all over his bathroom, and then told him never to call you again."

Anger rose up momentarily. But even if Terry had been plying him with alcohol like Henry thought, Jason hadn't said no. "It sounds like you know what happened, Kendra," he said.

"That's *it*? You got drunk and what…? Decided to throw away the last five years of your life?"

"I'm not throwing away anything. Terry was my first real boyfriend, and that means a lot to me, but we've been over for a long time. I'm sorry I let you—I let both of you—think there was ever any chance of me and Terry working things out, but the truth is that I'm not in love with him anymore."

"So what now?"

"I saw Henry last night."

There was a pause on the other end of the line. "And?" she prompted.

"We're together. Officially."

"Together how, Jason? Are you his boy? His whipping post? His fucking doormat?"

"Don't ask questions you don't want the answers to."

"You need to come up here. You've got to talk to Sue, hear what she has to say."

"I am really sorry that Sue was in some kind of abusive relationship, but her past has nothing to do with me and Henry."

"It has *everything* to do with you and him."

"Was Henry the guy she was dating?" Jason asked.

"No—"

"Then it's got nothing to do with us."

"He *hits* you."

"He doesn't hit me. He doesn't do anything I don't want. Or at least that I don't need."

"Jesus—"

"This isn't a debate. I didn't call to argue with you, I don't need your permission, and I'm not asking for your advice. I just called to check in and let you know I'm all right. I'll talk to you later," he lied. Or maybe he would talk to her later, but things weren't going to be the same between them.

Chapter Fifteen

"YOUR other left, boy." Henry looked like he was trying very hard not to snicker at Jason from the other end of the video chat. About the middle of April, they'd decided to add weekly Skyping to their routine; at the moment, Jason was both grateful for and cursing it. Today's conversation had nothing to do with their usual sessions, however; Jason wasn't fucking himself with a dildo for his Master's pleasure, begging to come, or hungrily watching Henry masturbate, wishing he could be there, touching him. "Undo the whole thing and start over," Henry finally told him.

Jason growled in frustration and pulled the bowtie from around his neck; he nearly threw it to his bedroom floor but stopped himself, knowing that would only make things worse. As it was, his temper had landed him in the chastity device for a week—which meant Henry would probably want multiple video sessions with him this week, just to add to the torment. His only reprieve was that he didn't have to put the much-hated device on until after tonight was over. Henry had a cruel streak the size of the Grand Canyon, but he wasn't without mercy. Dinner with Alicia's family was torture enough without having to wear a stainless steel tube around his dick.

"Take a breath, boy."

Jason did. He let it out again. "With all due respect, Master, I just can't do this!"

"Jason!" his father bellowed from down the hall. "It's almost time to leave."

"Fuck!"

Henry glared. "Make that eight days in the chastity belt."

Jason set his jaw but didn't speak until he was sure he could do so in an even tone. "Yes, Master." Henry had recently decided that he swore too much too.

Henry smirked at his obvious misery. "Now, let's get you tied up."

"I wish."

He laughed. "Come on, straighten it out and start over. Good. Now—"

"*Jason!*" Jason's father was right outside his door.

"Just a minute, Dad," he hollered back, struggling to keep his tone respectful.

"Get off that damned computer and let's go!"

"Temper," Henry warned when Jason balled his hands into fists.

"I'm just getting my tie done," Jason said to his father, his tone still moderate.

"Good boy. Now, left over right... there you go...."

Several agonizing minutes later, he finally had the stupid thing done to Henry's satisfaction. It figured his Master knew how to tie a fucking bowtie and that he was a damned perfectionist about it.

"Thanks, Henry," he said sincerely. As annoyed as he was, he was grateful too.

"Anytime, boy. Call me when you get home."

"Yes, Master." *I love you.*

Henry just smiled.

Jason's father scowled when he came out of the bedroom. "That suit looks like it came from the Salvation Army."

Jason decided not to tell him that that was because it had. "I like vintage clothing."

"It's not vintage, it's just old." He looked Jason over more critically. "Well, at least your shoes are polished. Good job on the tie too."

"Thanks." He followed his dad out to the garage.

The weather had turned warm, finally, and daffodils and tulips were starting to poke their heads up out of the neighbor's flowerbeds. Spring flowers reminded Jason of his mother. He didn't want to think about it, he just made a mental note to add it to the list he was compiling for Henry, because his Master wanted to know everything he liked. Not only sexually, but really *everything*: his favorite foods, his favorite color, his favorite scents.

Of course, Henry also wanted to know the things Jason *didn't* like, like the riding crop, being placed in the corner, the chastity device. Brussels sprouts. He also wanted to know about the things Jason had never tried but that made him curious or nervous or both: tight bondage, sensory deprivation. A bullwhip.

Jason slid into the passenger side of his dad's new car. Dad got a new company car every year or so; this was Jason's first time in the new one. "Nice," he said appreciatively.

Greg gave him half a smile.

"Look, Dad, I know you said not to worry about getting a card or anything, but I feel a little weird." He'd never even met Alicia's parents.

"It's handled."

Jason frowned. "What d'you mean?"

"We got them a family gift."

Jason blinked. "We?"

"Me and Alicia, her girls, Lawrence, and you."

"So what did 'we' get them?"

Greg heaved an irritated sigh. "Don't worry about it. Your name is on the card, that's all that matters."

Not knowing what else to say, Jason thanked his father for including him. It wasn't like he would have had any idea what to get Alicia's parents, anyway. The only thing he knew about them was that they'd been married for fifty years and had two children, Alicia and her brother, Ted.

His dad nodded. "I just didn't want you to look as embarrassed as you did at Amanda's birthday party."

Jason bit back a tart response and focused on the scenery outside the passenger side window instead. Henry was right; if he'd wanted to know what to get Amanda, he should have asked someone.

The next ten or fifteen minutes passed in almost comfortable silence. Finally Jason's father broke it. "I know things haven't always been especially easy for you."

Jason blinked over at him. He bit down another sharp answer; if Henry asked, he'd tell him every last detail of tonight, including how he laughed in his father's face for such a gross understatement of facts. Since he didn't want any more time in the chastity device for unacceptable behavior, he kept his tone neutral. "Life isn't always easy. You take what you can get and make the best of it, right?"

His answer seemed to surprise his father. Jason hid a pleased smile. "I was thinking about summer semester," Dad went on. "If you still want to borrow enough to cover tuition, we can discuss the terms of a loan."

It was Jason's turn to be surprised. "Thanks. But you should know that I've given it a lot of thought, and I'm going into the registrar's office to change my major before the next semester starts."

"Oh?"

"You're right about computers being a better career choice than art, but I'm barely passing a basic Web design class, and that's going to tank my GPA this semester. I talked to my computer teacher just to see if maybe it gets any easier after this class. It doesn't. He doesn't see a career in computers for me any more than I see it for myself."

"What are you going to do?" His father's tone had turned cold.

Jason hesitated. "I think I'm just going to work on getting my required classes out of the way while I figure something out. I've got an appointment to see one of the counselors on Wednesday. Maybe they can help me make some kind of a decision about where to go from here." Hopefully they could help him sort out some kind of financial aid too. He was desperate to get out of community college and into a four-year university.

His father was thoughtful for a long moment. "I suppose I can't fault your logic. I'm still willing to lend you the money for two classes over the summer, but I expect to be paid back *in full*," he stressed. "If you can manage to pay me back before September, I won't charge you any interest. And I might be willing to help you out again if you need it."

He was overwhelmed. "Thank you. And no problem about getting it back to you by September. I've got my car almost squared away." It would mean he'd only be able to go see Henry during the break between semesters, but they could work something out. Henry would understand. "Thanks, Dad," he said again. "I *really* appreciate this. It makes a huge difference."

His father merely nodded.

The dinner for Alicia's parents was being held in Holly, almost two hours away; Jason knew the city because of the Michigan Renaissance Festival, but he'd never been through downtown before.

He glanced uncomfortably around the posh interior of the Holly Hotel, which wasn't actually a hotel anymore, since it only served food. Very expensive food, from the looks of things. He wasn't paying for dinner—Alicia's brother, Ted, was footing the bill—but Jason still felt uncomfortable. Maybe it was because he didn't know anyone. He presumed that the well-dressed older couple sitting at the head of the table, sandwiched between Alicia and Ted, were the guests of honor. In addition, there were several other older couples—friends or siblings, maybe—and a number of people Alicia and Dad's age. Jason assumed that the woman next to Ted was his wife, but nobody introduced them, so he couldn't be sure. Jason's father greeted Alicia with a soft kiss on the cheek before taking his place next to her. The younger members of the family were seated on the other end of the table. Amanda flagged Jason down; she'd saved him a seat next to her.

"You look good tonight," she said quietly as he sat down.

"Thanks, you too," he told Amanda with an affable smile. He wondered if the dress she was wearing was the one Alicia had taken her shopping for; it looked more like Alicia's style than what little he knew of Amanda's tastes. Every time he'd seen her before tonight, Alicia had been wearing silk skirts or oversized sweaters with leggings. Today she was in a suit that looked like something Jackie Kennedy might wear; it was pretty, but it made her almost a carbon copy of her mother and sister. "Thanks for the gift card, by the way," Jason added.

"What'd you get with it?" She kept her voice down but sounded genuinely interested in his answer.

"Music. A friend of mine turned me onto some really cool stuff. I hope you liked... I mean, I didn't know what to get you for your birthday. I hope the gift card was all right."

"Are you kidding, it was perfect! Didn't Mom tell you I was getting my own place and needed, like, *everything* for it?"

"Erm, no." She was joking, right? Alicia didn't tell him anything—or at least nothing useful.

Amanda flashed a bright smile. "Well, lucky guess, then. So... your girlfriend couldn't make it?"

Jason blinked. "Girlfriend?"

"Your dad said you were seeing some girl from work."

He frowned. Who...? Right. "Melissa's just a good friend," he explained. She'd been to the house a few times, so maybe Dad had assumed...? Or maybe he was just more comfortable lying and saying his son had a girlfriend than he was telling anybody that Jason was gay.

"So you *don't* have a girlfriend?" said Amanda.

"No, I...." He hesitated. "My boyfriend lives out of state."

Amanda looked stunned. So did whoever was sitting next to her—one of her cousins, Jason assumed. He looked an awful lot like her uncle Ted. Whoever he was, he was staring wide-eyed at Jason.

"I didn't know you were *gay*," Amanda whispered the word. The wide-eyed cousin next to her turned to Lawrence, who was next to him, and muttered something Jason couldn't hear.

As for Amanda's question, he simply shrugged. He had never made a secret of his sexual orientation, least of all in front of his father.

Dad had even caught him and Terry kissing good night in the driveway a couple of times. He'd seemed more upset by what the neighbors would think than anything else.

"How long have you had a boyfriend?" Amanda asked. She sounded more uncomfortable with the word "boyfriend" than Jason had ever been with words like "slave" and "Master."

"I met Henry in January, but we didn't start going out officially until March."

Lawrence craned his neck around to stare at Jason as if he'd sprouted a second head.

Valerie leaned across the table and said something to him about minding his own business. Jason couldn't make out the rest, but her red-painted lips were pursed.

He decided to try to shift the subject away from him and Henry. "What about you, are you seeing someone?" he asked Amanda.

"I… no. Excuse me." She left the table; Valerie got up and followed.

Before they returned, a waiter came around the corner, carrying a large oval tray on his shoulder. He set it down nearby and began passing out the appetizers. Jason looked at the stuffed mushrooms that were set down front of him. "Excuse me," he said politely to the server. "What's in those?"

From across the table, his father gave him a sharp look. He'd missed the previous conversation, but he had apparently been watching like a hawk when the food came around.

"Shrimp and—"

Jason's expression was enough to silence his waiter. "Thanks. Erm. I don't eat meat. I don't suppose any part of dinner is vegetarian?" Because instead of letting the guests order off the menu, Alicia's brother had preplanned everything, and he apparently neither knew nor cared that one of his guests didn't eat meat.

The waiter looked mortified, as if it was somehow his fault someone wasn't going to be able to eat. "Just the salad, sir." It felt weird to be called *sir*. "But I'm sure the chef can do something for you.

If you can give me a minute to get the rest of this out, I'll let him know that there was some sort of miscommunication about dinner."

Jason gave the young man a sympathetic smile. "Take your time. I wait tables too."

The waiter was visibly relieved that at least one person at the table wasn't going to give him a hard time tonight.

When his father motioned for him to come around to his seat, Jason got up. By then, Amanda and Valerie were back; Valerie was talking to Alicia.

"Jason," his father said in a low, angry tone, "what's wrong with your food?"

"Nothing's wrong with it."

"Then why did you send it back? Shrimp isn't meat."

"Yes it is. Look, it's no big deal. They're going to see if the chef can make something I can eat."

"How is *that* no big deal?"

"It's what restaurants do."

By then his waiter had returned with what looked like a fruit and cheese plate. Jason smiled his thanks to the young man and turned to his father. "See? No problem."

"It would be 'no problem' if you could just eat what was put in front of you instead of inconveniencing everyone around you because of your *whims*."

Jason refrained from reminding his father that he'd been a vegetarian for almost eight years, or that he hadn't wanted to come out to dinner tonight in the first place. "I really don't mean to be difficult." He gave over an apologetic smile to his father, Alicia, and her parents before heading back toward his seat. He was halfway there when Alicia's brother caught him.

"Justin…?"

"Jason."

"Right. Sorry. Is something the matter?"

"No, sir. I'm a vegetarian, that's all. I guess there was some kind of miscommunication." He decided that the waiter had the right tactic.

"Sorry 'bout that, Jason. I'm sure Alicia told me and I just forgot." The apology sounded sincere, even if it didn't seem as if he actually believed the rest of it. "You get it squared away with the kitchen?"

"Yeah. Thanks." Okay, so maybe there were a few real human beings in the family after all. Jason resumed his seat.

AFTER the plates from the salad course were cleared, Jason excused himself. Several of the smokers in the group were stepping outside, which made it seem like a good time to make a call. He needed to hear his Master's voice.

"How's it going, boy?" Henry asked after they'd exchanged hellos.

"Awful," he groaned. Instead of loitering around the building, he strolled down the cobblestone street. The sun had gone down, but the temperature was still moderate enough that he was comfortable in just his suit jacket. "God, these people. Alicia didn't even bother telling her brother that I don't eat meat, and Dad told Amanda that Melissa is my girlfriend."

Henry chuckled in his ear. "Are you making me proud of you in there? Or earning more time in the chastity belt?"

"I'm doing my best to make you proud of me, Sir. And it's not all bad. Unless he gets so pissed at me for sending my shrimp-stuffed mushrooms back that he changes his mind, Dad said he'd lend me the money for summer semester. Which... kind of interferes with our plans."

"We'll work around school, boy. That comes first."

"Thank you, Master." He glanced over his shoulder and noticed that the smokers were starting to head back in. "I'd better get going. I'll call you again if I get a chance, but I... thank you," he repeated, not sure he could put everything he was feeling into words.

"For what?"

"For… for everything. I really…." *I love you.* "I appreciate you so much."

"I miss you too, baby."

Smiling, Jason hung up and pocketed his phone; when he got back into the foyer, he saw his father and Alicia engaged in a tense conversation. He stepped past them quickly, not wanting to overhear.

Amanda looked up when he got back to the table. She gave him a tight-lipped smile. "I didn't mean to make things weird earlier. I just…." She shrugged. "Your father mentioned you had a girlfriend, so I just assumed it was true."

"I think he just wishes I was more like everybody else. Or maybe just less like my mom."

"Was she…?"

"No, she was straight," he clarified quickly. "She was an artist, and that's what I want to be."

"Was she any good?"

"She did a few gallery shows when I was little. Before… before she started going blind."

Amanda blinked. "I had no idea. What happened?"

"She had diabetes, and she didn't take care of herself. The first thing that went was her eyesight."

"Jason, I'm so sorry."

"It was a long time ago."

Amanda opened her mouth to say more, but her mother and Jason's father returned to the table all smiles, asking for everyone's attention because they had a big announcement to make.

"We don't want to upstage anyone else's big day." Alicia smiled apologetically down at her parents, resting one hand on her mother's shoulder and another on her father's.

"Nonsense," her father assured her with a pat of his hand on hers. "We've had lots of big days." He nodded at his wife. "Now what's this news you've got for us?"

Jason's father beamed with obvious pleasure. Then he hesitated. "You know, I forgot something."

Alicia blinked at him. "Greg?" She looked genuinely perplexed.

Greg walked over to her father. "Sir, may I have the honor—and the privilege—to call your daughter my wife?"

Jason and Amanda stared at each other in surprise while Alicia's mother pulled her into a hug and started talking to her about wedding plans.

"I think I need a drink," Jason muttered. He wondered if a text message would suffice for asking his Master's permission for a glass of wine. He doubted Henry would allow him anything stronger.

"JASON."

He turned at the sound of his name—it was his father. Jason had just stepped outside again after the main course but before dessert, trailing along behind the herd of smokers. He smiled at his father. "Hey. Congratulations, Dad." He held out his hand.

His father accepted it. "Thanks. We... I need to talk to you about something."

"Sure." He pocketed his phone. He didn't actually need to check in. He'd had the one glass of wine Henry granted him permission for via text message, and was feeling a little less tense.

"Look, Jason, Alicia and I have been talking about getting married for a while now. It didn't come out of the blue."

"I'm glad you're happy," he said, meaning it. He might not like Alicia, but she obviously made his dad happy.

"I am. The thing is, after we get married, we're going to be moving in together."

"I kinda figured that."

"I just want you to know that this has absolutely *nothing* to do with what you said to Amanda tonight. Alicia has never been comfortable around... well. She's simply not comfortable around people like you."

"Excuse me?"

"It's not as if you're discreet, Jason. Not *everyone* is as liberal as your mother. Some people just... well. The point is that Alicia isn't comfortable living under the same roof as you."

Jason blinked rapidly as a tight fist closed around his gut. "So what you're trying to say is that you're kicking me out?"

"Don't be so melodramatic, I swear you're just like...." He hesitated, but Jason knew what he'd been about to say: *you sound just like your mother*. His father looked him square in the eye. "Alicia and I aren't getting married until the end of June. That's plenty of time for you to figure things out. I said I would lend you the money for summer semester. If you pay me back like we agreed, I might be willing to lend you money for the fall. We'll go from there and see how things work out." He sounded angry, resentful that Jason wasn't more grateful.

"What the... where exactly am I supposed to *live*? I'm your son."

"May I remind you that I didn't even know you *existed* until some lawyer called me five and a half years ago to tell me that not only did I *have* a son, but that his mother, a girl I hadn't even *thought* about since college, had just passed away? I'm sorry if I haven't lived up to your expectations!" He shook his head, running a hand over the top of it as if he still had hair there to run his fingers through. "I'm sorry. This isn't easy on me either, Jason. I never wanted children. When I found out I had one... well, I took you in, didn't I? But you're an adult now. You have a job. You can get an apartment. Amanda just moved out on her own and she's a year younger than you. I've given you more than enough time to sort this out."

Tears stung at Jason's eyes, but he refused to cry. Not in front of his father.

"I think everyone will understand if you'd rather skip dessert. Why don't you take my car and head home? I'm going to Alicia's tonight, anyway." He handed over the keys.

Jason took them. He barely heard himself saying "thank you" before he turned on his heel and fled.

He wasn't sure how long he'd been on the highway before he realized he was in no shape to drive. He pulled off at the first exit he came to and fumbled for his phone, tears streaming down his cheeks. A million questions—fears—ran through his head.

Henry picked up in three rings. Before he could say a word, Jason started bawling. "My dad... he... he's getting married. He's moving in with Alicia. They... she... *he*... doesn't want me there! I get it that he never wanted kids and that even if he had, I'm not the son he would have wanted, but... but two months. I've got two months! I don't have more than three hundred dollars in my bank account, and he fucking well knows it!" To hell with Henry's edict against swearing. He'd wear the goddamned chastity belt for a month. He didn't care anymore.

"They've been talking about getting married since Christmas, and this is how much notice he gives me?" Jason wiped the tears from his cheeks, but it didn't matter. More tears kept falling. "I know Kendra would take me in, but...." Fuck. She lived so far away, and she would make it impossible for him to keep seeing Henry. "I'm sorry, I need to go. I have to figure this out."

"Don't you *dare* hang up!" Henry snapped before Jason could disconnect the call. "You're not going anywhere in the state you're in, boy."

Jason just sobbed. "I have to call someone. I have to do something."

"You did call someone, and you are doing something."

"I don't think sitting by the side of some road I've never heard of, crying, is going to help any."

"How about this, then: when you get yourself under control enough to drive, you go home and pack up your gear and you come here."

"W-what?" Go there? "You mean, to... to your place?" He couldn't possibly be understanding Henry right.

"I'll meet you in Findlay."

"Findlay?"

"You're in no kinda shape to drive all night, and you'd never find your way to my place anyway, believe me. Findlay's pretty close to the middle. Just get on I-75 and keep heading south 'til you get there. I'll find us a hotel and give you a call to let you know where I've settled in. We'll spend the night. Then I'll bring you home."

Home? "Please, Henry, please don't say something like that unless you mean it."

"I mean it. You can stay here."

"For how long?"

"As long as you want."

Jason couldn't stop juddering. "Are... you're really serious?" It sounded way too good to be true. Tears streamed down his cheeks unabated.

"Shhh, baby. I'm serious. This isn't exactly the way I had in mind for things to go, but... but you can stay here as long as you want, okay? Or... baby, if you want to go to Kendra's, that's okay too. I'll come be moral support for you, help you pack, whatever you need—"

"No. Please, no, I don't want to go there. I want *you*."

"Okay, then it's settled. I'll see you in a few hours."

Chapter Sixteen

JASON waited until he stopped shaking to get back on the highway and drive the rest of the way home. His dad's house. He hardly registered anything. He just felt cold.

But as he pulled into the driveway, he started shaking again. Walking up to the front porch, he tripped, almost fell. This couldn't be happening. It couldn't be *real*. His dad wouldn't really kick him out, and Henry…. Jason sat down on the front stoop, unable to move. A month ago, he would have given anything to run away with Henry, but now it was happening, and he was terrified! They barely knew each other.

Bullshit.

Henry's favorite color was red. His favorite flavor of ice cream was butter pecan. He liked mushrooms and olives on his pizza; he preferred round to square, flat to deep dish. Homemade to store-bought. His favorite food was Italian and his favorite dessert was tiramisu. His birthday was November 17. He lived with his half sister, who was eleven years younger than he was and HIV positive. His mother's name was Delilah. She sounded a lot like Jason's mom.

But the most important thing about Henry was that Jason loved him.

Jason pulled himself to his feet and let himself into the house. He made a beeline for his room, grabbed the duffel bag from under his bed, and started stuffing clothes into it. Jeans. T-shirts. Underwear. Socks. His high-tops. A jean jacket. He barely noticed what he was doing, what he packed. He felt... hollow. Disjointed. Too numb to cry anymore.

He slowed down when he got to his photo albums. Pictures of his mother. His grandparents. Him as a baby. God, did he want Henry to see those?

Better that than to leave them with the man who never wanted kids.

He took his mother's ring out of his jewelry box. It wasn't worth much, it was only an emerald, but it was hers. So were the sketchbooks under his bed; they contained some of the last work she'd done, a couple of years before she died. No way was he leaving those behind for his father to find. He gathered up his own sketch pads, his art supplies.

His collar was under his pillow, where he always kept it when he wasn't wearing it. Jason pulled off the stupid bowtie. He ripped off his shirt and jacket. He almost put the collar around his neck. But he wanted Henry to do it, so he packed it into his duffel bag, then pulled a T-shirt on over his head.

God, was Henry *really* serious? Did he honestly want Jason to move in with him? What if he changed his mind? What if...?

Jason pushed the frenzied, panicked thoughts out of his head and padded down the hall to the bathroom, backpack in hand. He threw his toothbrush and razor into it, followed by his brush. Shampoo. Conditioner. Mousse. Hair dryer. Cologne.

Shit, this couldn't be real.

Back in his room, Jason looked around, trying to see what, if anything, he'd forgotten. Nothing jumped out at him.

Jesus, was this *it*? Some clothes and his toiletries? His laptop?

He would need his phone charger too. Headphones. And he had some DVDs that, while not irreplaceable, were expensive enough not to leave behind. He had a couple of autographed CDs. Abney Park. The Clockwork Dolls. Heather Alexander. His mom's autographed Pat Benatar album. God. Vinyl. He'd have to be extra careful with that. He scrounged through his "library" (six milk crates stacked up next to his stereo) and put the few books that were autographed in one crate with his BDSM books, the vinyl album, his DVDs, and his high school yearbook. The one from Troy Athens, *not* the yearbook from Ithaca High School. He left that behind.

Jason surveyed his room again. That was everything. His life boiled down to a duffel bag, a milk crate, a backpack, and his computer case. Feeling more pathetic than ever, he laced up his Dr. Martens, slung his leather jacket over his shoulders, picked up his meager belongings, and walked out of his father's house for what he knew would be the last time. He didn't leave a note. Why bother? The front door key he took off his key ring and placed next to his father's car keys would get the message across: there was nothing he needed to come back for, and he didn't care where his father thought he'd gone.

Loading up his car felt... surreal. It was like he was watching a movie or reading a book, because real life couldn't possibly get this fucked up this fast. Any second now he was going to wake up. He was going to laugh and call Henry, tell him about the psycho dream he'd just had.

Henry.

Jesus. Henry really wanted.... Jason checked his phone, but there were no messages. It was probably too soon for Henry to have checked into a hotel. By the time Jason was to the end of the street, he was crying again. He almost called Henry just to have someone to talk to, but he wasn't sure he could drive and talk in the state he was in. And anyway, wasn't Henry doing enough for him, offering to let him move in? Was it fair to ask Henry to hold his hand over the phone too?

Jason hit the McDonald's drive-through and got the biggest cup of coffee they had on the menu. He didn't just need the caffeine, he needed the warmth. He put on the radio because he needed something to think about other than what was happening. He didn't start to worry about Henry not calling him back until his coffee cup was empty and he started seeing signs for Ann Arbor. The Ohio border was only forty-five minutes away. Once he hit that, he was only an hour from Findlay.

Henry wouldn't change his mind. He *couldn't*. Jason chewed his lower lip until it bled.

It was late. He was exhausted. The caffeine was wearing off. He was terrified. What if Henry wasn't all of the things Jason had built him up to be in his head? What if he couldn't find a job? What if Henry's friends hated him or thought he was too young or immature? What if Henry's sister hated him? Where would he go if—when—Henry threw him out?

And what about school? Jason wasn't sure if he could withdraw so late in the semester. Even if he could, he wouldn't get any of his tuition back. He hadn't thought about that before he left. He just... ran away. He hadn't thought about work or Melissa or anything.

Tears began to fall all over again. According to the sign up ahead, he was seven miles from Bowling Green, thirty miles from Findlay. What if Henry wasn't waiting for him like he'd promised? If his own father could chuck him out....

Suddenly his phone rang. Jason grabbed it off the passenger seat. "Hello?"

"It's me," said Henry.

Jason drew in a ragged breath. "I... I was starting to worry."

"Shhh. I'm right here, right like I said I'd be. Tell me where you are."

"Coming up on Bowling Green."

"You're almost here, baby. I just checked into the Drury Inn. You'll be able to see it from the highway. Take the Trenton Street exit and follow it around."

"Trenton Street," he repeated. "Yeah. Okay." He knew he should hang up, but he was afraid that if he did.... God, he was being irrational. Henry wasn't going to vanish into thin air if he hung up his phone!

"You hungry?" Henry asked, thankfully oblivious to Jason's stupid paranoia.

"I don't know. Maybe. I had coffee."

"Well, if you decide you want to eat, I got us some dinner. If you just want to sleep, that's okay too. It'll keep 'til morning."

"Why are you doing this?"

"What?"

"Why are you… Jesus, Henry. You met me four months ago! My father's known me for the last five years!"

"I agreed to take care of you, remember?"

Jason bit back a sob. He needed this to be about more than a fucking slave contract.

"Just get here, baby. We'll sort out the details tomorrow. Right now, all I want is to know that you're safe."

Safe. "Yeah, okay. Thank you," he added weakly. "Thank you" didn't seem adequate.

"You're welcome. I'll see you soon."

Unable to think of anything else to say, Jason hung up. He concentrated on driving, on staying in his own lane. On obeying the speed limit, even though all he wanted to do was press the gas pedal all the way to the floor and make the last thirty miles go past as fast as possible.

The last time—the only other time—Jason had felt so lost, so completely drained, the last time he'd cried this much, was after his mom died and he was told he had to go live with some man he'd never met. His father. And maybe it wasn't easy on his dad either. "But at least he's still got a fucking *home*." Jason wiped the angry tears from his face. He'd cried so much and so hard that his whole face felt swollen and achy. Did his father seriously think that lending him the money to pay for school made up for kicking him out?

At last he spotted the bright-red letters of the Drury Inn's neon sign. Then he saw the sign for Trenton Street and eased off the highway. Jason followed the brightly lit road around to the lot, found a parking spot, got out, and grabbed his duffel bag. Then he realized that Henry hadn't told him the room number. Well, it wasn't like he couldn't ask at the front desk. But when Jason got into the lobby, he saw Henry standing there, waiting for him. He swept Jason up into his arms and held on tight. They both did.

"Thank you," Jason murmured when he finally trusted his voice to work. "Thank you so much." He was crying again.

"Shhh, I'm here. I've got you." Henry cupped Jason's face and pressed a fierce kiss to his lips. He kissed his cheeks. His forehead. Then he leaned in close. "Somebody's not wearing his collar."

Heat flooded Jason's cheeks. "N-no, Sir, I... suit and tie...," he stammered, biting his lip.

Henry's chuckle was gentle. He wasn't angry. "You have it in your bag?"

"Yes, Sir." Jason wiped the last remnants of the tears away, hoping that was really the last of them.

"Good boy. Come on, let's get you upstairs." He slid his arm around Jason's shoulders and guided him toward the elevator.

Jason leaned into him, letting Henry take all of his weight. He felt so heavy. So tired. He closed his eyes as the car began to rise.

"If you're hungry, I've got some spinach pie and hummus with pita," Henry offered.

Jason shook his head. "I can't eat. Maybe later?"

"Whatever you need."

When the doors dinged open, Jason opened his eyes but didn't pay much attention as they walked down the hall. Henry opened the door of their room and pulled Jason inside. "Why don't you take a shower?" he suggested. "Hot water'll do you good."

"Yeah. Okay, a shower sounds good. Thank you." Again, the words weren't adequate.

But Henry didn't seem to mind. "You're welcome. By the way, I expect you to come out of there naked, boy," he informed Jason.

He smiled. "Yes, Master."

Henry pulled him into another quick kiss before letting go.

JASON stood under the hot spray with his eyes closed. He stayed there until his fingers had turned into prunes, until his stomach settled. Until his thoughts were less jumbled. Until he was barely thinking at all. Until he felt warm all over.

As soon as he turned off the water, he heard harp music playing in the other room but it wasn't classical. Jason recognized Bon Jovi's "It's My Life" almost at once. Well, there was a certain appropriateness to that. He smiled and pulled his hair back into a knot at the base of his neck. Jason emerged from the bathroom to find Henry sitting on the bed, wearing a pair of plaid flannel pajama bottoms. They gray collar was sitting on the nightstand next to him.

"Probably not my best look," Henry admitted with an almost sheepish grin.

"I think you look adorable."

Henry quirked an eyebrow at him. "Adorable, huh?" He seemed to be having a hard time looking stern. "Get over here, boy."

Grinning, Jason knelt in front of him, and Henry fastened the collar around his neck. He made no apology for going through Jason's bag to find it.

Since Henry's feet were tucked up under him on the bed, Jason made do with leaning his head against his Master's knee. His pajama bottoms were as soft as he'd thought, but Henry's gentle caress was softer.

"We're gonna have to take a look at our contract tomorrow," Henry told him gently. "And make a few changes."

"Sir?" He wasn't ready for more change in his life.

"It was written with us living four hundred miles apart, boy. Lotsa stuff's going to be different now… well, for as long as you're living with me, at least."

Jason closed his eyes, desperately hoping Henry hadn't changed his mind about him staying. Or…. "Was… was your sister okay with having me stay with you?"

"She's fine with it. Believe me, I told her what happened and… well. Yeah. She's more than okay with you moving in."

"What about the other stuff?"

"Other stuff?" Henry queried.

"You know. The, ah… the terms…?"

"She knows I'm a kinky son of a prick, if that's what you're trying to ask."

"So, erm, what… what kinds of changes did you have in mind? For our contract, I mean."

"I don't want you to worry about it right now, I just want you to think about it. Why don't you come on up and stretch out? Backside up."

Jason nodded. Obeyed. He wanted… but what he wanted didn't matter. That was what being a "slave" meant, right? He would have to get used to doing what he was told, putting his own needs on hold, even when he was so wrung out emotionally that all he wanted to do was cuddle. Sleep. "Where would you like my arms, Master?"

"Just get comfortable."

Jason pillowed his arms under his head and closed his eyes. He felt Henry get up, heard him moving around. A moment later, the bed sagged again as Henry sat back down—and then a pair of oil-slick hands kneaded into his shoulders. Jason let out a moan. "Oh, God."

Henry chuckled. "I keep telling you I don't need that much responsibility, boy," he said as he continued to work out the knots in Jason's shoulders. It was heaven. A little bit of hell. Henry seemed to know just where the knots were and what to do to get rid of them; it would hurt momentarily, but then it was pure bliss.

At length Jason turned his head and glanced up at him. "Will you teach me how to do this?"

"What, massage?"

"Yes, Sir."

"Why do you want to learn?" he asked, sounding genuinely perplexed.

"Because it feels good and I figure you must get awful sore too."

Henry's expression was impossible to read, and for a moment, Jason wondered if he'd miscalculated somehow. But all he wanted was to be able to make Henry feel as good as the other man made him feel. How could that be wrong?

"Henry?"

"I'll teach you anything you want to know, boy. All you ever have to do is ask," he promised softly. "But right now, how about you just let me pamper you a little?"

Jason nodded and turned his head back to the mattress.

"Can you move your arms to your sides? Good. Now, just relax," he said as he took Jason's left arm and bent it at the elbow, settling his wrist against his lower back.

"And here I thought tonight wasn't going to end up being kinky— oh, God," he groaned when Henry pressed skilled fingers up underneath his shoulder blade. "Fuck. That hurts."

"Good hurt or bad hurt?"

"Like I should know the difference." He smirked over his shoulder.

"*Boy.*"

"Good hurt, I think, Master," he said demurely. Henry dug in a little deeper, and Jason moaned. "*Fuck.* No, it's still good... Jesus. How'd you know... ohhh... shit...right there. God, right there." Henry had somehow zeroed in on the most painful part of his back.

"You think you're the first waiter I've ever worked on?"

"I... oohhh... I didn't think waiters could afford massage therapists. And I thought you weren't doing it anymore. *Shit.* Hurts!"

"Breathe through it... there...." He eased up on the pressure and rubbed more gently. "Just relax and breathe. And I do still work on a few people, mostly for trade."

Jason glared up at him.

"Jealousy isn't a pretty emotion, Jason. It's not one I'm going to put up with, either. Sebastian is a friend of mine. And yes, he is a submissive, and yes, we have played together," he added. Then he eased Jason's hand back to his side. "Tell me where the tension went?"

"Straight to my shoulder. And I'm not jealous."

"Lying will only get you into trouble. I haven't forgotten those eight days in a chastity device you owe me. Care to make it nine?"

He swallowed hard and lowered his gaze. "No, Master. If it pleases you, I would rather not make it nine. Maybe I'm a little jealous." It was hard not to be. He didn't know who this Sebastian was, if he was cute. If he wanted Henry.

"You're a lot jealous. I suggest you stop it. Rest your head on your arms so I can get your neck."

As much as he wanted to tell Henry being jealous wasn't something he could just turn off at will, he wasn't up for arguing with anyone who was making him feel so good. He also wasn't going to tempt Henry into giving him any more time in the chastity device. "Have you ever slept with him?" he asked in as neutral a tone as he could muster, because that was the one thing he needed to know.

"Yes."

It wasn't the answer Jason wanted to hear, but there wasn't much he could do about it, either. He closed his eyes and tried to just relax.

"You are my most cherished possession, Jason," Henry told him. "But you're not the only person in my life. I'm not the only person in yours, either."

"Right now, it feels like it." He sounded pathetic.

"I know. I also know it'll all work out. I know people say that all time, and it bugs the shit out of me too. Which is why I wouldn't say it if I didn't believe it. You're going to be okay."

"Thank you."

After Henry worked out the worst of the knots in his neck and shoulders, he made Jason drink a big glass of water. He made him eat. Then he tucked him into bed and curled protectively around him. Jason was asleep almost before his head touched the pillow.

HE WOKE disoriented, alone in a strange bed. The sheets were white. They smelled lightly of bleach and fabric softener. There was a shower running. He rolled over—the curtains were drawn. No light seeped in. A hotel room.

Henry. Yesterday, Jason's whole world had come crashing down, and Henry had been there to pull him out of the rubble. Jason smiled as his hand rose to his throat and the leather collar. He was really going home with Henry.

In the bathroom, the shower shut off. A moment later, Henry emerged, his hair dripping, his face free of stubble, and wearing only a white towel wrapped around his waist. "How long've you been awake?"

"Just a few minutes. Sorry if… if you wanted me to come join you or…."

Henry shook his head. "I'm glad you got a little extra sleep. You had a rough day yesterday." He sat down on the bed and coaxed Jason into his lap. "A lot of things happened awful fast yesterday, for both of us."

Jason worried at his lower lip and snuggled in closer, grateful when Henry's arms closed tighter around him.

"I don't know where I'd be if you hadn't… if I weren't here, Sir." *Please don't be having second thoughts.*

"If you weren't here, you'd be at your dad's house, trying to figure out which of your friends had a sofa you could crash on." His tone was matter-of-fact but otherwise impossible to interpret. "You'd be going to work. You probably oughta call in, let your boss know what's going on."

"I-I guess."

"Having second thoughts, boy?"

Jason blinked up at him, startled. "No." Was Henry really afraid of the same things he was?

Henry smiled. He ran his thumb over Jason's cheek. "Jason, you are capable of making it on your own. You don't need me. I just… it was kinda like that very first day at the hotel, when I invited you back to my room, even though I would've smacked anybody else for being so stupid. When you told me your old man chucked you out, I didn't think, I just reacted. I needed to know you'd be safe."

Jason snuggled a little tighter into his chest.

Henry took his chin in hand and tilted it up so that Jason had no choice but to look him in the eye. "I want you to listen to me here, okay?"

"Yes, Sir."

"This isn't... I had this plan." He almost laughed. "My friends tell me I plan way too much, and they're probably right, but I had it all figured out. You were gonna come visit me in June. I'd cook for you. Pamper you. Fuck you senseless. Leave you with some marks to remember me by. I was gonna invite you to Dragon*Con with me, maybe see if you could swing a few extra days so I could show you the city some. Then I wanted you to come visit me again a few times so we could work our way through this. So we didn't make any mistakes."

"Everybody makes mistakes."

"I know. But I don't want you waking up one day resenting me for... for anything. Everything."

"*Resent* you? I love you." The words were out before he could stop them. Jason searched Henry's face hoping, wanting... but he didn't say anything. "Sir... I... Henry... I didn't mean—"

Henry pressed a finger to his lips. "Shhhh. Why don't you go take care of whatever you need to in the bathroom and let me get dressed."

"I... yes, Sir." Defeated, Jason slipped out of Henry's lap, out of the bed, and padded into the bathroom, wondering if he'd just changed things somehow. Or *how* he'd changed them, because saying "I love you" changed everything. Why did he have to be so stupid all the time? Why couldn't he learn to keep his big mouth *shut*? Why couldn't he just enjoy it when something good happened?

Fighting back tears, he took care of business. He washed his hands and splashed cold water on his face. It was said. It couldn't be unsaid. He would just have to deal with the consequences.

Jason was about to go get his toothbrush and razor when Henry appeared in the bathroom doorway dressed in jeans and a T-shirt. He didn't say anything. Jason didn't say anything, either.

Finally, Henry came and stood behind him exactly like he had that first day—only his expression was different today. It wasn't full of heat, lust. Jason couldn't interpret the look on his face, except that he seemed... distant. Quiet. Jason leaned back anyway, and Henry wrapped his arms around his shoulders. He ran his left hand over Jason's chest in a soft caress that made goose bumps rise on his skin.

It took several moments for Jason to realize that Henry's right hand was closed around something. When he looked down, Henry opened his hand to reveal a small heavy-looking antique lock. It was beautiful, etched with scrollwork. Henry flipped it over so Jason could see that the back was engraved with Henry's initials.

"This was mine," he said. "Back when... when I first started out and I spent a year in service to another man. Not quite a slave, but close."

Jason balked at the idea of his Master kneeling at somebody else's feet.

Henry smiled. "Hard to imagine? I was new, almost as new as you were when I met you. David made sure I didn't fall in with the wrong crowd and get myself hurt. He gave me an earful when I told him 'bout you too. He also told me.... Well, he told me lotsa stuff. Point I'm really trying to make is that nobody's ever worn this but me." As he spoke, he tugged Jason's collar around his neck so the clasp was in front. "Being somebody's slave is about more than being able to do what you're told, Jason. Anybody can follow orders, even me. Belonging to another man's about... it's about giving him every part of you. It's about trusting me, knowing I'd never intentionally do wrong by you, but like you said, everybody makes mistakes. That's why you've gotta talk to me when you think there's a problem. *If* this is really what you want."

Jason met his gaze in the mirror. He held it a long moment. Then he dropped his chin and lowered his eyes. "Master" was all he said.

Henry slipped the lock through the clasp on Jason's collar. "You don't get the key to this," he warned. When Jason didn't protest, he snapped it shut. Then he pressed a soft kiss to the back of Jason's neck. "Come on, boy. It's time to go home."

H.B. PATTSKYN remembers writing her first short story in the second grade—it wasn't very good, but it was a good start! Growing up as an only child being raised by her grandmother, she preferred to spend time alone in her bedroom reading, writing, drawing rather than playing sports or hanging out, like most kids her age.

She started writing fan fiction in her early twenties, in response to the dreaded "it didn't really happen" third season of television's *Beauty and the Beast,* and has been writing it ever since. It was only a few years ago that she entered the world of M/M slash—and she hasn't looked back since. As one of her readers put it, "boys kissing is hot."

In addition to being a writer, Helen is an artist and tarot reader. She shares her life with a wonderful man, an occasionally wonderful teenager, two cats who graciously allow her to live in their house, and a spoiled rotten xolo dog. She can be found hanging out at science fiction conventions in her home state of Michigan.

Visit H.B.'s website: http://helenpattskyn.com. You can also e-mail her at thylacine.yawn@gmail.com.

Also from H.B. PATTSKYN

http://www.dreamspinnerpress.com

Romance from DREAMSPINNER PRESS

http://www.dreamspinnerpress.com